John S. C. Abbott

The life of Christopher Columbus

John S. C. Abbott

The life of Christopher Columbus

ISBN/EAN: 9783337954468

Printed in Europe, USA, Canada, Australia, Japan

Cover: Foto ©Raphael Reischuk / pixelio.de

More available books at **www.hansebooks.com**

THE LOSS OF ROLDAN'S SHIP.

THE LIFE

OF

CHRISTOPHER COLUMBUS.

BY

JOHN S. C. ABBOTT.

ILLUSTRATED.

NEW YORK:

DODD & MEAD, PUBLISHERS,

PREFACE.

A SERIES of volumes, upon the Pioneers and Patriots of America, would certainly be defective if they did not contain an account of the adventures of Christopher Columbus, the most illustrious of all the pioneers of the New World. Columbus had his enemies. He has been vehemently assailed. The writer has endeavored to give a perfectly correct account of his character and career, and has been careful to present to the reader his authority for every important statement. Many may think that the assaults upon his character do not deserve so much attention as is allotted to them in these pages. But when the reader has seen all that the most determined enmity can bring against him, a more correct judgment can probably be formed of his true merits and defects.

JOHN S. C. ABBOTT.

CONTENTS.

CHAPTER IV.

A Tour among the Islands.

CHAPTER V.

Romantic Adventures.

CHAPTER VI.

The Return Voyage.

CHAPTER VII.

The Second Voyage.

CHAPTER VIII.

Life at Hispaniola.

CHAPTER IX.

The Coast of Cuba Explored.

CHAPTER X.

The Return to Spain, and the Third Voyage.

CHAPTER XI.

The Return to Spain, and the Fourth Voyage.

CHAPTER XII.

The Shipwreck at Jamaica.

CHAPTER XIII.

The Closing Scenes of Life.

CHRISTOPHER COLUMBUS.

CHAPTER I.

Struggles of his Early Life.

Parentage and early life—State of the times—Adventures of the
Sailor Boy—His studies—Personal appearance—Visit to Lisbon—Result of his studies—Rumors of other lands—His high
ambition—Application to the Court of Naples—Royal Perfidy—
His marriage—Departs for Spain—Scene at Palos—Visits the
Military Court of Ferdinand and Isabella—Weariness of hope
deferred—Conference of the philosophers—The astonishing
decision.

IN the magnificent maritime city called Genoa the
Superb, there was born, about the year 1435,* a child

* The date of his birth is a *vexata quæstio.* Washington Irving,
rleying upon the evidence given by Bernaldez, in the " Cura de los Palacios," states it to be about 1435 or 1436. This inference he draws from
the remark of Bernaldez that he died " in the year one thousand five
hundred and six, at the age of seventy, a little more or less." Juan Bautista Munoz, in his " Histoire del Nuevo Mundo," concludes that he was
born in 1446. Don Ferdinand, the Admiral's son, relates, that in a
letter addressed by his father to the King and Queen, and dated 1501,
he states, that he had then been forty years at sea ; and in another letter
that he was fourteen years old when he went to sea ; so that, allowing
a year either way for probable inattention to minuteness in these statements, we get the date of his birth, fixed by his own hand, at about 1447.

1*

now known throughout the whole civilized world as Christopher Columbus. Even the precise year of his birth is not known. He was the child of humble parents; and his father, a very worthy and industrious man, who followed the employment of a wool comber, labored hard for the support of his household.

The harbor of Genoa was filled with shipping from all the commercial ports of the then known world. The wharves were crowded with sailors, speaking diverse languages and dressed in every variety of costume. The boy had received from nature a reflective mind, a poetic imagination, and a strong love for adventure. As he strolled the streets, and gazed upon the majestic ships, his childish spirit was roused to visit distant lands.

There were four children in the family, three sons and a daughter. The father must have been a worthy and intelligent man, for he seems to have given each of his children a good common school education. Christopher was well instructed in writing, grammar, and arithmetic. He also made some proficiency in the Latin tongue, and in the arts of drawing and design. He even entered the University of Pavia, where he prosecuted, with great success, the studies of geometry, geography, astronomy, and navigation.

When but fourteen years of age, the father of Christopher intrusted him to the care of a relative,

by the name of Colombo, to make his first voyage.
This veteran seaman had already acquired much distinction for his nautical skill.   He had attained the
rank of Admiral, in the Genoese navy, and had commanded a squadron.

The seas were then so infested with pirates that
every merchant vessel was compelled to go well
armed, ever ready for battle. We know not the incidents of this voyage. But the first voyage of
Columbus, of which we have any account, was a
naval expedition.   Colombo, in command of a squadron, sailed from Genoa to aid King René in an
attempt to recover his kingdom.   This was in the
year 1459.   The conflict lasted for four years.   The
squadron of Colombo gained much renown for its
intrepidity.

Christopher Columbus subsequently, in a letter to
Ferdinand and Isabella, gave a brief account of an
expedition upon which he was detached to cut out a
galley from the harbor of Tunis. His crew chanced to
learn that the galley was protected by two other ships ;
they were so much alarmed as to refuse to proceed
on the expedition.   Columbus apparently assented
to their wishes, and led them to think that he had
decided to go back to obtain the reinforcement of
another vessel.   He altered the point of the compass
and spread all sail.   Night soon came on.   In the

morning the ship was entering the harbor where the galley lay.

We are not informed of the result. But the incident strikingly reminds us of the still more important stratagem to which he subsequently resorted to induce his disheartened crew to press forward over the wild sea toward the New World. The Atlantic Ocean was, at that time, quite unexplored. A few enterprising seamen had coasted along the shores of northern Europe, and had cautiously sailed down the western coast of Africa. But the commerce of the world was mainly confined to the Mediterranean. These were days of violence, lawlessness and crime.*

Every merchantman was compelled to go armed. Pirates, often sailing in fleets, infested all seas. A mariner was of necessity a soldier, ever ready to grasp his arms to repel an assailing foe. It was through this tutelage Columbus was reared. We have no record of his early voyages. It is simply known that he traversed much of the then known world. He vis-

* There is one story told of Columbus to which I ought to allude, though the most reliable authorities discard it. Ferdinand, his son, first relates the incident. He says that he was engaged in a desperate sea fight. The two vessels were lashed together by iron grapplings. Hand grenades were thrown, and both were wrapped in flames. Columbus leaped into the sea and was buoyed up by an oar to the shore, a distance of six miles. See *Letters of Columbus*. Translated by H. H. Major, Esq. of the British Museum. Introduction, p. 39.

ited England.   His adventurous keel ploughed the
waters of the North Sea till he reached the arctic
shores of Iceland.   It is not improbable that he
might there have heard vague tales of the expeditions, centuries before, of the Northmen to the ice-
bound coasts of Labrador and Greenland, and of the
limitless shores reaching thence down south, no one
could imagine how far.   Subsequently, in one of his
letters, he writes:

" I have been seeking out the secrets of nature
for forty years.   And wherever ship has sailed there
have I voyaged."

In the course of his wanderings he at length
found himself at Lisbon, the capital of Portugal, then
one of the most renowned seaports in the world.   He
had attained the age of thirty-five years.   No particular description of his personal appearance has descended to us.   We simply know that he was a tall
man, of sedate and dignified demeanor, and with no
convivial tastes.   He was thoughtful, studious, pen-
sive ; of a deeply religious nature ; ever pondering the
mystery of this our sublime earthly being, emerging
from nothing, and, after a short voyage over life's
stormy sea, disappearing into the deep unknown.

He was a man of great simplicity of character,
with the organ of veneration strongly developed.   He
was modest, sensitive, and magnanimous.   He was a

natural gentleman, exceedingly courteous in his bearing and without a shade of vanity.   Intellectually, he
certainly stood in the highest rank, being quite in
advance of the philosophy of his times.

In the biography of Columbus, given by his son,
we are informed that he was an earnest student.   He
read the works of Aristotle, Seneca, Strabo.   Many
midnight hours were spent in reading the accounts
of the explorations of Marco Polo, and of Sir John
Maundeville.   He deeply pondered the questions
which these discoveries suggested.   But the volume
which interested him most and which most thoroughly aroused his mind, was the " Cosmographia "
of Cardinal Aliaco.   It was a strange medley of folly
and wisdom, of true science and absurd fable.

Columbus found at Lisbon many mariners—
intelligent, observing men—who had explored all
known seas.   From them he heard of drift-wood
which had been found, different from any vegetable
growth known in Europe.   Rude carvings had been
picked from the waves, evidently cut by some savage
implements.   And, most strange of all, two corpses
had been washed upon the Azores, presenting an
appearance very unlike any of the known races of
Europe or Africa.

Gradually the idea seems to have dawned and
expanded in the mind of Columbus, that there must

he other and vast realms on this globe, not yet discovered by Europeans.   But a small portion of our
globe had then been visited by civilized men.   The
mind of Columbus became greatly excited, as alone in
his room he examined the meagre maps of those days.
With pencil in hand he sketched the familiar shores
of the Mediterranean, and the less known coast of
Africa, from Cape Blanco to Cape Verde.   He then,
in imagination, pushed out boldly into the Atlantic
Ocean, as for as the Azores.   Here he had to stop.
All beyond was unknown and unexplored.

With flushed cheek he pondered the wonderful
theme, as thoughtful men now often find their souls
agitated, in contemplating the sublime and awful
mystery of infinite space.   What is there, he asked,
in that vast ocean, extending, limitless, to the west?
Is the earth a plain?   If so, where is the end, and
what is there beyond?   Is it a globe?   If so, how
large is it?   In the boundless ocean are there other
lands?   Would it be possible for a bold adventurer
to sail around it?   It now seems marvellous that this
globe could have existed so many thousand years,
inhabited by thoughtful men, while questions of
such infinite moment as these should have slumbered in the mind.

The following interesting and apparently well-
authenticated statements are given by Hon. William

Willis, in his very valuable Documentary History of the State of Maine.

In the year 1477 Christopher Columbus went out to explore and reconnoitre the old northern route, by the way of Iceland, toward the west. It is probable that he had heard of the discoveries of the Northmen in that direction, and of the short distance which was supposed to exist between the extreme north of Europe and the shores of Asia.

He made several trips, preparatory to his grand undertaking. On the south he visited Madeira, the Canary Islands, and the coast of Guinea. He carefully studied all the routes of the Portuguese navigators, and also made himself familiar with the remotest of their discoveries toward the Azores, or Western Islands. Humboldt thinks it probable that he made an excursion to the extreme western outport of Portuguese discovery.*

He also tried the northern route, sailing toward Iceland, and some distance beyond it. It is probable that he had read the Northmen's account of Greenland, Markland, and Vineland. The last ship had returned from Greenland to Iceland, only about one hundred years before the visit of Columbus to that island. Malte Brun supposes that Columbus, when

* Humboldt, "Kritische Untersuchungen," vol. I, p. 231 Berlin, 1852.

in Italy, had heard of the exploits of these bold adventurers beyond Iceland ; for Rome was then the
centre of the world, and all important intelligence
immediately flowed there.*

A Danish author suggests that Columbus, who
eagerly sought out all books and manuscripts containing an account of voyages and discoveries, had
met with the writings of the well-known historian
Adam of Bremen, who very emphatically announces
the discovery of Vineland.† These suggestions probably induced him to make his trip to Iceland ; and,
according to the account of Fernando Colombo, his
son, he not only spent some time in Iceland, but sailed
three hundred miles beyond, which must have brought
him nearly within sight of Greenland.‡

The renowned Danish historian, Finn Magnusen,
remarks : " If Columbus had been informed of the
most important discoveries of the Northmen, it is
much easier to understand his firm belief in the pos-
sibility of the rediscovery of a western country, and
his great zeal in carrying it out. And we may conceive his subsequent discovery of America, partly as
a continuation and consequence of the transactions
and achievements of the old Scandinavians." *

* Malte Brun, " Histoire de la Géographie, 2, pp. 395, 499.
† Finn Magnusen, l. c. p. 165, note 1.
‡ Vita dell' amiraglio Christophoro Colombo, ch. 4.   Venetia, 1571.
‡ Om de Engelskes Handel pua Island in Nordisk Tidsskrift
for Oldkyndighed.   2 Bind. p. 116.

Columbus, a self-taught philosopher, ascertained just how long it took the sun to traverse the two thousand miles' length of the Mediterranean Sea. From that, he inferred the distance of space over which it would pass in twenty-four hours. This was true Baconian philosophy. Such problems not only expanded his mind, but disciplined his reasoning powers, and removed him from the baleful influence of visionary dreams.

The exciting study absorbed his whole intellectual being. Pleasure was unthought of. The ordinary pursuits of ambition were forgotten. He was ever conversing upon the subject with all his friends and acquaintances. This drew many mariners to his studio, with narratives of what they had seen or imagined.

Gradually Columbus came to the conclusion that the world must be a globe; and that, by sailing directly west, the shores of Asia would eventually be reached. By his measurement of the sun's apparent speed, he had formed a pretty accurate estimate of the size of the globe. It was not his supposition that there was any land between Europe and Asia on the west, but he expected that one would reach the coast of Asia about where he subsequently found the shores of the New World.

Vague reports of the great island of Japan, sit-

ated just off the eastern coast of the Asiatic continent, had reached Europe. Columbus thought that
he should find it about where he afterward discovered
the island of Cuba. He was eminently a religious
man. Notwithstanding the fanaticism of those days
of darkness, it cannot be doubted that there were
many souls inspired with the most exalted principles
of religious enthusiasm.

"These vast realms," said Columbus, "are peo-
pled with immortal beings, for whose redemption
Christ, the Son of God, has made an atoning sacrifice.
It is the mission which God has assigned to me to
search them out, and to carry to them the Gospel of
Salvation. The wealth of the Indies is proverbial. I
shall find boundless riches there. With these treasures, we can raise armies. With these armies, we
can rescue the sepulchre of the Saviour of the world
from the hands of infidels who dishonor it."

Columbus was poor. It was entirely out of his
power to fit out an expedition for so momentous a
tour of discovery. Most people deemed him a half-
crazed visionary. His plan was considered as absurd
as a proposition would now be regarded to visit the
moon. It was in vain to apply to wealthy individuals. Still he found some men of intelligence who
examined his plans and pronounced them worthy of
serious consideration.

His hope was that, by the aid of such testimonials, he could secure the coöperation of some one
of the courts of Europe. A sovereign state could
easily supply the means, and could confer upon him
that dignity and that authority which he deemed
essential to the accomplishment of his plans. The
court, in return, would acquire great wealth and
power, with renown, which would cause it to be
envied by all Europe.*

He applied first to the Portuguese Government.
King John II. gave him a respectful audience, and
listened attentively and apparently with much interest to his plans. Columbus by no means considered himself a humble suppliant at the foot of royalty. He considered himself a man to whom God
had communicated thoughts which would aggrandize
the riches and fame of the loftiest monarch, and which

* It is worthy of observation that while Mr. Goodrich, after a very
careful examination of the life of Columbus pronounces him to be
mean, selfish, perfidious, and cruel. Mr. Helps, after an equally close
scrutiny of his career, writes :

"There was great simplicity about him, and much loyalty and veneration. He was as magnanimous as it was possible for so sensitive
and impassioned a person to be. He was humane, self-denying, and
courteous. He had an intellect of that largely inquiring kind which
may remind us of our great English philosopher, Bacon. He was
singularly resolute and enduring. He was rapt in his designs, having
ever a ringing in his ears of great projects, making him deaf to much
that prudence might have heeded ; one to be loved by those near him,
and likely to inspire favor and respect."—*Life of Columbus*, by Arthur
Helps, p. 54.

would cause a new era to dawn upon the world.   He
demanded, in requital of all his services, that he
should be appointed Viceroy of the realms he might
discover, and that he should receive one-tenth of the
profits which might accrue.

   While residing at Lisbon, he attended religious
service at the chapel of the Convent of All Saints.
Here he became acquainted with an Italian lady, by
the name of Dona Felipa, who was residing with her
widowed mother.   She was of high birth, but impoverished in fortune.   Their marriage ere long ensued
It seems to have been a very happy union until
death separated them.   They had one son, Diego.

   The king considered these demands as extravagant.   Columbus was a poor and obscure sea-captain,
without rank or money or friends.   And yet the
strange, earnest man, with his wild enthusiasm, was
expecting to leap, at once, into the rank of kings.
The monarch politely bowed the dismissal of the
ambitious sea-captain from his audience room.

   But the dignified and solemn demeanor of the
man, and the entire confidence he manifested in the
correctness of his views, deeply impressed the mind
of the king.   He could not shut out the thoughts
which had been presented to him.   After revolving
the matter, for some time, he summoned a council
of the most scientific men in Lisbon, and presented

the subject to them. They met in careful deliberation. Some of the most eminent men of the council pronounced in favor of the views of Columbus.
But the decision of the majority was decidedly
against them. They reported to the king, that his
plans were so visionary as to be unworthy of further
consideration.

Still the king was not satisfied. The impression
made upon his mind was too strong to be thus easily
laid aside. And the fact that some of the most
eminent philosophers accepted the suggestions of
Columbus, contributed to diminish the influence of
the report. The king then stooped to an exceedingly dishonorable measure. He fitted out a secret
expedition, ostensibly to the Cape Verde Islands.
Availing himself of all the information he had obtained from Columbus, he gave the captain private
instructions to push boldly on, in the track which
Columbus had marked out: hoping thus to *steal* the
discovery. The captain obeyed these directions.
But his sailors became alarmed. They were lost in
unknown seas, and were going they knew not where.
A terrible Atlantic tempest arose. This capped the
climax of their fears. With united clamor they
refused any longer to brave such perils. The captain was compelled to yield and to return.

Columbus was informed of this treachery. His

indignation was greatly aroused. With his anger
there were blended emotions of disappointment and
sadness, that the royal-court, to which he had been
accustomed to look with such reverence, could treat
him so perfidiously.

He was then a widower, with an only child,
Diego. Devoting his time to study and to the furtherance of his plans of exploration, he had no
leisure to attend to his own pecuniary interests. A
humble support was gained by making and selling
charts. Taking his child with him, he set out for
Genoa, the home of his boyhood. Here he was
doomed to experience the truth of the adage, that
" A prophet is not without honor save in his own
country and in his own house."

He applied to the Genoese Government to aid
him in an undertaking, which not only the general
voice of the community had pronounced to be fanatical, but which the assembled philosophers of Lisbon had denounced as unworthy of notice.

"And who is this Christopher Columbus?" it
was asked. "Why, he is a sailor of this city," was
the reply; "the son of Dominico Colombo, a wool-
comber. He has two brothers and a sister, residing
here in humble circumstances."

This settled the question in the proud court of
Genoa. The application of Columbus was contempt

uously rejected. He could not even obtain a respectful hearing. He was now in deep poverty. Hope and his inborn energies alone were left to sustain him. After revolving many plans in his mind, he finally decided to try his fortune in the court of Spain.

Taking his son Diego with him, he embarked in a coasting vessel at Genoa, and after a short cruise landed at Palos, a small Spanish sea-port at the mouth of the River Tinto. Ferdinand and Isabella were then engaged in a very desperate warfare against the Moors. They were both at that time with their army, near Cordova, at the distance of nearly one hundred miles north-east of Palos. All-absorbed as their energies were in the conduct of the war, it was an unpropitious moment in which to attempt to enlist them in an expensive and doubtful enterprise.

Columbus, with a light purse and a heavy heart, set out on foot to traverse the weary leagues which separated him from the royal camp. He was pale, thin, and care-worn in aspect. His garments were thread-bare. He had no luggage to encumber him, but a small package at his side. Little Diego walked, holding his father's hand.

They had advanced but about a mile and a half from the village of Palos, when they came to a massive stone convent. Columbus was a devout man, cordially accepting Christianity as developed in the rituals and ceremonials of that age. The monks were regarded by him with great reverence.

Diego was hungry and thirsty. His father knocked at the door of the convent, and asked for a cup of water and slice of bread for his child.

It so chanced that the prior of the convent at that moment came to the door. The polite address, the dignified demeanor, and the intellectual features of the stranger deeply impressed him. He invited Columbus to walk in, entered into conversation with him, and became not only intensely interested in the novel views which he advanced, but, by the cogency of his reasoning was quite convinced that they must be true. He detained Columbus for several days, entertained him with all the hospitality the convent could furnish, and invited, to meet him, a neighboring physician, who was eminent for his scientific attainments.

In the quiet cloisters of the convent of La Rabida, Columbus, the prior, and the physician, spent many hours in discussing the question whether this world was a globe or a flat expanse; and whether by sailing west it were possible to reach the shore of the Asiatic continent, which was far away in the east.

The prior of the convent was a man of learning, and, as was frequently the case in those days, was of

2

high rank, and of influence at court. He became so deeply interested in Columbus and his enterprise, that he persuaded him to leave his son Diego at the convent, to be educated, and gave him letters of introduction to the confessor, or, as we should say, the chaplain of Queen Isabella.

Cheered by this visit, and by the ample provision which had been made for his child, Columbus, with much more buoyant spirits, resumed his journey to Cordova.

It may be proper here to mention, that Mr. Irving, in the later editions of the Life of Columbus, accepts the statement of Navarrete, that Columbus, upon his arrival in Spain first visited the Duke of Medina Sidonia. The splendor of the enterprise which Columbus proposed, for a time charmed the duke. But upon more sober reflection he rejected the scheme as the dream of an enthusiast.

Columbus then, it is said, repaired to the Duke of Medina Celi. Here also his first reception was favorable. The duke was on the point of equipping three or four vessels for the expedition, when it occurred to him that the Spanish sovereigns might be displeased at his undertaking so regal an enterprise on his own account. He therefore dismissed Columbus, but he furnished him with a letter to Queen Isabella, strongly recommending his plans to her attention. The queen returned a favorable reply, and requested that Columbus should be sent to her. He went, bearing a letter from the duke.

If this statement be accepted, the visit to the convent of La Rabida must have taken place some time afterward.

Wonderful was the military display which met the eye of Columbus at the camp at Cordova. The splendors of the courts of both Castile and Aragon were there assembled. All the chivalry of Spain were congregated on that extended field, magnificently mounted, with gleaming armor and gorgeous retinue. The tents, as of an immense city, were spread around. Glittering banners and waving plumes were everywhere to be seen, and the music of martial bands filled the air.

But all this pomp was nothing to Columbus, compared with the themes which engrossed his mind. He presented his letter to Isabella's chaplain, whose name was Fernando Talavera. He was a haughty prelate, cold and reserved. He received Columbus scarcely with civility, listened with evident reluctance to a recital of the plan he had to propose, and dismissed him, saying:

" I should deem it a great intrusion to present so chimerical a project to her majesty, when oppressed by all the cares of this campaign."

The appearance of Columbus was anything but imposing. He was poor, shabbily dressed, and downcast with disappointment. But the rumor of his plans had filled the camp. The courtiers pointed derisively to the thread-bare adventurer, as one who had realms boundless in extent, and inhabited by millions, which he wished to present to the sovereigns of Spain.*

Columbus knew not what to do or where to go. He lingered at Cordova while the Spanish army advanced to attack the last foot-hold of the Moors in the province of Granada. He felt assured that victory would crown the royal banners, and that then perhaps there might be an opportunity for his appeal. In the autumn Ferdinand and Isabella returned in triumph. They soon established their court, for the winter, at Salamanca, nearly three hundred miles distant. In the meantime Columbus, unable to obtain an audience with the queen, earned a frugal support by designing maps, charts, and plans.

The scenes which were transpiring at Cordova and its vicinity had drawn to that point the most

---

* The only probable way of accounting for the extent of these demands, and his perseverance in making them, even to the risk of total failure, is that the discovery of the Indies was but a step, in his mind, to the greater undertakings, as they seemed to him, which he had in view, of going to Jerusalem with an army and making another crusade." —Helps' *Columbus*, p. 72.

illustrious men, from all parts of Spain. This gave
Columbus the opportunity to approach the most
philosophic minds. Thinking men were deeply impressed with the dignity of his bearing, the pro-
foundness of his convictions, and the varied information and conversational eloquence with which he advocated his views. Occasionally he met with one
who cheered him with approval.

A gentleman of intelligence and wealth became
so much interested in Columbus that he invited
him to his house as his guest. This gentleman
introduced him to the pope's nuncio, Antonio Geral-
dini, and to other gentlemen of much distinction in
court and state. Mr. Irving writes:

"While thus lingering in idle suspense in Cordova, he became attached to a lady of the city,
Beatrix Enriquez by name, of a noble family, though
in reduced circumstances. Their connection was
not sanctioned by marriage, yet he cherished sentiments of respect and tenderness for her to his dying
day. She was the mother of his second son, Fernando, born in the following year, 1487, whom he
always treated on terms of perfect equality with his
legitimate son Diego, and who, after his death,
became his historian."

Columbus followed the court to Salamanca.
Here he was introduced to the Archbishop of Toledo,

grand cardinal of Spain. This illustrious prelate had such influence with the king and queen that he was called the third king. Gradually, he was so impressed by the force of the arguments with which Columbus urged his views, that he consented to introduce him to the royal presence.

The first audience was probably with Ferdinand. The splendors of royalty could not overawe Columbus. He deemed himself the heaven-appointed instrument to unfold a new era to the human race. With great eloquence he urged his cause. The king was a shrewd, sagacious man, who was not at all likely to be influenced by romantic dreams. He listened, with philosophic coolness, to the enthusiastic advocate.

The ambition of the king was strongly excited by the idea of the grandeur which would redound to Spain, if successful in making discoveries and acquisitions so magnificent. The achievement would give Spain the pre-eminence over all other nations. But Ferdinand was a very cautious man, of slow deliberation. He summoned a council of the most learned scholars of Spain, to hold an interview with Columbus, carefully examine his plans, and report to him their opinion.

The conference was held in the Dominican convent of St. Stephen, at Salamanca. The assembly summoned by the call of royalty, was imposing in numbers and dignity. It was composed of profes- sors in the universities, the highest dignitaries of the church and statesmen of prominent rank. Before such an array, of the most learned astronomers and cosmographers of the kingdom, any ordinary man would shrink to appear. Columbus rejoiced in the opportunity. He was so fully convinced of the cor- rectness of his views, that he could cherish no doubt that such intelligent men would give them their approval.

But he soon found, greatly to his chagrin, that even in the minds of the most learned men, prejudice and bigotry could triumph over all the powers of reason. The philosophers and the clergy alike as- sailed him with arguments which now provoke the derision even of the most common minds. The fol- lowing passage, from Lactantius, was quoted as a triumphant refutation of the statement of Colum- bus, that the world was round.

" Is there any one so foolish as to believe that there are antipodes, with their feet opposite to ours ; people who walk with their heels upward and their heads hanging down? That there is a part of the world in which all things are topsy-turvy ; where the trees grow with their branches downward, and where it rains, hails, and snows upward? The idea of the roundness of the earth was the cause of the inventing this fable of the antipodes, with their heels in the air; for these philosophers, having once erred, go on in their absurdities, defending one with another."

The views of Columbus were denounced, not only as unphilosophical but also as unscriptural. It was said that to maintain that there were inhabitants on the other side of the globe, would impeach the veracity of the Scriptures. The Bible stated that all the inhabitants of the world were descended from Adam. But it was impossible that any of his descendants could have wandered so far.

Again it was argued that, admitting the world to be round, should a ship ever succeed in getting to the other side, it could never return; since no conceivable force of wind could drive the ship back over the immense rotundity of the globe.*

To these theological and philosophical arguments, Columbus returned the answers with which the most unintelligent are familiar at the present day. Though the convention reported against him, there were many individual members who were deeply

* "One learned man of the number, Diego de Deza, afterward bishop of Seville, appreciated the eloquent and lucid reasonings of the adventurer, and, aiding him with his own powers of language and erudition, not only gained for him a hearing, but won upon the judgments of the most learned men of the council."—*Introduction of Letters of Columbus*, by R. H. Major, p. 51.

impressed by his reasoning. Among others was
Diego de Deza, afterward Archbishop of Seville.
With all his powers, he supported the cause of
Columbus, but in vain. The majority reported that
it was both false and heretical to assume that land
could be found by sailing west from Europe. And
this was made by one of the most learned bodies
in the world, only about four hundred years ago.

2*

CHAPTER II.

First Voyage.

Columbus at Cordova—Power of the Feudal Nobility—New Rejec-
tions—Return to La Rabida—Hopes revived—Journey of the
Prior—Persistent Demands of Columbus—Interview with Isa-
bella—The Dismissal—The Recall—The Hour of Triumph
—Exultant return to Palos—Fitting out the Expedition—Its
Character—Departure of the Fleet.

. COLUMBUS was bitterly disappointed at the result
of the convention at Salamanca. But the conference
had made his scheme known, and had caused it to
be talked about throughout all Spain. Though the
wits assailed the unsuccessful adventurer with all
sorts of jests, there were many individuals, of high
intelligence, who were convinced that his suggestions ought not to be dismissed with a sneer.

While this important question was under discus-
sion, Columbus was regarded as an attaché to the
court. It was a period of great political agitation.
All minds were engrossed by the fierce war with the
Moors, which still continued to rage. During the
summer of 1487, the king and queen were with the
army conducting the memorable siege of Malaga.

The tall form of Columbus could be seen, thoughtfully, despondingly, passing from tent to tent, urging his claim wherever he could find a listening ear. There was something very touching in the aspect of this plain man, in his simple attire, but with his strikingly dignified demeanor, moving silently about, amidst the pomp and pageantry of these military movements.

In September, Malaga having surrendered, the court returned to Cordova. Then for eighteen months it was constantly on the move, still engaged in the great conflict. Columbus accompanied the court, in all its changes of place, still clinging to the hope, in which he was encouraged by a few devoted friends, that he might again obtain access to the royal ear. In the spring of 1489, through the influence of these friends, he succeeded in obtaining an order from Ferdinand, for the assembling of another conference of philosophers and ecclesiastics, at Seville. Again, he was doomed to disappointment. The dreadful war received a new impulse. Terrible battles, with tumult, and carnage, and woe, ensued. All energies were engrossed. Not a thought could be given to Columbus and his wild, doubtful schemes.

A weary year passed away. During these sad months Columbus lingered at Cordova. He was, however, supported at the expense of the court.

With the opening spring, Ferdinand and Isabella,
were engaged in preparations for one of the grandest
enterprises of the war—the siege of Granada.
Columbus made a desperate effort to gain a hearing,
before the court advanced upon this all-important
movement ; but he received the disheartening reply,
that the sovereigns could pay no more attention to
him until the conclusion of the campaign. The
blow fell heavily upon Columbus. But it did not
prostrate him. His indomitable spirit was not thus
to be plunged into despair. He sat down calmly,
and inquired of himself what was to be his next
resource.

These were the days of feudal wealth and power.
The eminences of Spain were dotted with the massive castles of dukes and barons. According to some
accounts, and as it seems to the writer the most
probable account, it was at this time that Columbus
appealed to the Duke of Medina Sidonia. This
powerful lord, whose castle was an almost impregnable fortress, of stone and iron, was one of the most
illustrious of the nobles of Europe. He rivalled kings
in the splendor of his court and equipage. He had,
from his own means, furnished the monarchs with
quite an army of cavaliers, with a hundred vessels of
war, and with a large sum of money. We have
already given an account of the result of the visit of

Columbus to the castle of the duke, and of his subsequent appeal to the almost equally powerful noble,
the Duke of Medina Celi.

Thus baffled, Columbus decided to try his fortune
at the court of France. He had by this time gained
a number of influential and wealthy friends, who
undoubtedly opened their purses to his moderate
wants. Before crossing the Pyrenees, on his long
journey to the French capital, he set out to visit his
son Diego, at the convent of La Rabida, near Palos.
It would seem that he took this journey on foot, or
on the mule's back. Whatever small sums of gold
may have been given him by his friends, it is certain
that he found it necessary to practise the most rigid
economy. He had a long and expensive journey
before him, and 'it was very uncertain what reception he might meet with in the proud court of the
French king.

Columbus stood at the door of the convent, in
very humble garb, and covered with the dust of
travel. But neither thread-bare clothing nor dust
could conceal the native majesty of the man. He
was one of nature's noblemen, who did not require,
in vindication of his claims, the tinsel of costly dress.
Seven years of incessant toil and disappointment had
passed away since he first stood at the door of that
convent to ask for a cup of water for his thirsty child.

These anxieties and toils had bent his frame and
whitened his locks. His cheeks were ploughed with
those furrows which intense and disappointing
thoughts are so prone to give.

The worthy prior of the convent received the
way-worn adventurer with truly fraternal kindness.
He had become fully convinced that the views of
Columbus were rational, and that they merited the
immediate and earnest attention of the Spanish
court. When he ascertained that Columbus contemplated a visit to France, to offer his magnificent plans
to the French court, his spirit of patriotism was
aroused and intense solicitude excited, lest Spain
should lose the renown of the great discovery. He
immediately summoned to the convent the learned
physician to whom we have before alluded, and communicated to him his fears. Many other influential
friends were invited in, to confer with Columbus upon
the all-important question, which the prior deemed so
vital to the glory of Spain.

There was residing in the neighborhood a gentleman, illustrious for his family, his wealth, and for
his own renown in maritime adventures. This man,
Martin Alonzo Pinzon, was capable, from his own
experience, of appreciating the force of the arguments presented by Columbus. Warmly he espoused
his cause, and pledged to him not only his pecuniary

support, but also his influence in again bringing the
question before their majesties Ferdinand and Isabella.   The prior of the convent had, in former years,
been chaplain of the queen.   He wrote to her in
very urgent terms; pleading that Spain might not
lose so glorious an opportunity of rising to pre-
eminence among all the nations.

These were not the days of stage-coaches and
postal facilities.   An old worn-out sailor was intrusted with the letter, and mounted upon a mule,
was sent to Santa Fé, where the court then resided,
while conducting the siege of Granada.   The distance
was about one hundred and fifty miles.   The courier
safely accomplished the journey, and presented the
letter to the queen.   Isabella, notwithstanding all
the cares which then engrossed her mind, was deeply
impressed by its contents.   She returned an encouraging answer, and urged her esteemed friend, the
prior, immediately to come and see her.

When this answer was brought back, it revived
new hopes in the heart of Columbus, and created
intense joy throughout the little coterie at La Rabida.   It was mid-winter, and chilling breezes swept
the bleak mountains and treeless plains, even of
southern Spain.   But the worthy prior at once
mounted his mule, and jogged along the lonely
road toward the court of his sovereign.

The queen received her former chaplain even affectionately. Though reserved and undemonstrative in her manners, there slumbered, beneath this cold exterior, warm affections. She listened sympathizingly to the arguments of the prior. He was a learned man, and from his intimacy with Columbus, was fully. prepared to present his views in the strongest light. The queen had never before paid much attention to the subject ; for though it had been presented to the king, and to the convention of scholars, the appeal had not been directed to her personally.

It will be remembered that Ferdinand was the King of Aragon only. Isabella was the sovereign queen of Castile, with her own revenue, her own army, and her own court. She promptly decided to take Columbus under her protection, and sent for him immediately to repair to Sante Fé. As he was thus called upon to act in obedience to the order of the queen, she forwarded to him a sufficient sum of money to enable him to purchase a mule, to provide himself with suitable clothing for his appearance at court, and to pay the expense of the journey

When the prior returned to La Rabida, with these joyful tidings, great was the rejoicing there ; and new hopes were infused into the world-weary heart of Columbus. A fine mule was bought, the traveller was neatly clad, and almost with renewed youth,

buoyed up by sanguine hopes, he was soon trotting
over the hills, and through sheltered valleys, of beautiful Andalusia.   He arrived at Granada just in time
to see the Moorish banners torn down from the
walls of the Alhambra, and the united flags of Ferdinand and Isabella unfurled in their stead.   It was
the proudest hour in the reign of these two illustrious sovereigns, and was deemed the most glorious
to the arms of Spain.

It was in the midst of these national rejoicings,
that Columbus presented himself before Queen Isabella.   He did not assume the attitude of a humble
suppliant, but that of a heaven-sent ambassador,
who had immense gifts to confer, in requital for
trifling favors received, to aid him in the accomplishment of his plans.   In respectful words, he said to
the queen :

" I wish only for a few ships and a few sailors, to
traverse between two and three thousand miles of
the ocean to the west.   I will thus point out to your
majesty a new and short route to India, and will re-
veal hitherto unknown nations, majestic in wealth
and power.   In return I ask only that I may be
appointed Viceroy over the realms I may discover,
and that I shall receive one-tenth of the profits which
may accrue."

The courtiers of the queen were astonished at

what they deemed the extravagance and audacity of
the demands of Columbus. In their view he was
but an obscure sea-captain, penniless and friendless,
seeking the assistance of the queen to enable him
to enter upon a maritime expedition. And yet he
was demanding, in recompense, wealth and honors
which would place him next in rank to the crown.
Influenced by these representations of influential
members of her court, the queen summoned Columbus again before her, and offered him more moderate
terms. But he was inflexible. He would make no
abatement of the requirements he had put forth.
His proud spirit revolted from the idea of embarking
on his glorious expedition as a mere hireling employé
of a prince. Isabella, perhaps a little annoyed by
his refusal, dismissed Columbus and his claims.*

.This was the darkest hour in the career of the
great discoverer. No day star appeared in his horizon, the harbinger of a possible dawn. Sadly he
placed his saddle upon the back of his mule, and
slowly, despondingly, commenced his journey back
to his friends at La Rabida. He was revolving in

* It is said by some that Columbus, discouraged by his repulse at
the court of Ferdinand and Isabella, sent his brother Bartholomew to
England, to present his plans to Henry VII. Bartholomew was captured by pirates, and it was some time before he obtained his release.
He then presented his plans. The king eagerly accepted them. But
it was too late. Columbus had already engaged in the service of
Isabella.—*History of Columbus*, by Aaron Goodrich, p. 186.

his mind whether it were worth his while to go to France, and offer his often rejected services there.

But as he left the cabinet of the queen, she was greatly troubled. The character of the man, and the grandeur of his views, had produced a profound impression upon her mind. She could not shut out the thoughts he had introduced. As she contemplated the loss to Spain, should any other court accept his services, and his views prove a reality, she was exceedingly troubled. It so chanced that just at that moment, Ferdinand entered her cabinet. She expressed to him her solicitude. He replied:

" The royal finances are absolutely drained by this war." Isabella was silent for a moment pondering the question. She then seemed inspired by a sudden and unalterable resolve. With enthusiasm she exclaimed:

" I will undertake the enterprise for my own crown of Castile, by the pledge of my own private jewels, to raise the needed funds.*

---

* Mr. Goodrich scouts the idea advanced by the biographers of Columbus, that the queen was so poor that she had to pawn her jewels to fit out two small vessels for such an enterprise. He says :

" This story is as absurd as many others coined by Ferdinand to embellish the history of his father. The coffers of Spain were then well filled. The treasury of the queen had received an extraordinary increase from her perfidious conduct toward the Moors of Malaga, from whom she had obtained millions."—*History of Columbus*, by Aaron Goodrich. p. 190.

The day star had arisen upon Columbus; though, looking down, not up, he had not seen it. At that moment he was toiling along through the sands, having advanced but a few miles on his journey. As he was entering a gloomy defile among the mountains, he heard a voice calling behind him. Turning his head, he saw a courier approaching in hot haste. The messenger requested him, in the name of the queen, to return.

For a moment Columbus hesitated whether to obey the summons. For weary years he had encountered nothing but discouragement, and he was led entirely to distrust the Spanish court. It seemed to him that both the sovereigns, while unwilling to aid him in his enterprise, were still more unwilling that he should enter into the service of any other monarch, thus rendering it possible that some other crown might gain the glory which Spain had rejected. Assured, however, by the courier, that the queen was entirely in earnest to see him again, he turned his mule and spurred back to hold another interview with Isabella.*

* "And now, finally, Columbus determined to go to France, and indeed had actually set off one day in January of the year 1492, when Luis de Santangel, receiver of the ecclesiastical revenues of the crown of Aragon, a person much devoted to the plans of Columbus, addressed the queen with all the energy which a man throws into his words when he is aware that it is his last time for speaking in favor of a thing which he has much at heart. He concluded by saying

The queen, having once come to a decision, was prompt in action. She immediately informed Columbus that she cordially assented to all his demands, and would immediately aid in fitting out a suitable expedition. He was appointed Admiral and Viceroy of whatever realms he might discover, and was promised one-tenth of the profits which might accrue from the voyage. Arrangements were however made, at the request of Pinzon, that he should be allowed to contribute one-eighth of the expenses, and receive one eighth of the gains. The momentous question was thus finally settled. Columbus set out on his return to Palos, probably the happiest man in the world. Little did he then imagine the tempestuous career of disappointments, indignities, and woes, which eventually brought down his gray hairs in sorrow to the grave.*

A royal decree was immediately issued, for the town of Palos to furnish two small vessels, suitably

---

' that all the aid Columbus wanted to set the expedition afloat was but a million of maravedi, equivalent to about £308 English money of the period.'

" These well-addressed arguments, falling in as they did with those of Quintanilla, the treasurer, who had great influence with the queen, prevailed."—Helps' *Life of Columbus*, p. 74.

* There is considerable diversity in the statement of the amount of money required. Mr. Helps writes:

" From an entry in an account book belonging to the Bishopric of Palencia, it appears that one million one hundred and forty thousand maravedi were advanced by Santangel, in May 1492, being the sum he

victualled and manned, for the voyage. Columbus
himself furnished another, through his friend Pinzon,
so that he had three, with which to commence his
enterprise. Two of these vessels were light barks,
such as in those days were called caravels. They
were built with cabins for the officers, and forecastles
for the crew, but without a general deck. The third
vessel was called the *Santa Maria*. This was the
Admiral's ship, and was decked throughout. Sixteen
persons composed the ship's company. The *Pinta*
was commanded by Martin Alonzo Pinzon, with a
crew of thirty men. The *Nina* was manned by
twenty-four sailors, with Vincent Yanez Pinzon as
commander. The vessels were all of small size,
probably of not more than one hundred tons burden; therefore not larger than the American yachts,
whose ocean-race from New York to Cowes was
regarded as an example of immense hardihood, even

lent for paying the caravels which their highnesses ordered to go as the
armada to the Indies, and for paying Christopher Columbus, who goes
in said armada." Helps' *Life of Columbus*, p. 80.

It is said that Isabella offered, if needful, to pledge her jewels, but
not that she actually did pledge them. Captain Galardi, secretary of
the Duke of Veraguas, writing to the duke in the year 1666, upon the
personal history of Columbus, says:

"As the conquest of Grenada had exhausted the finances of Ferdinand and Isabella, Luis de Santangel, secretary of Ferdinand, lent, for
the expedition, sixteen thousand ducats."

A ducat was worth about five dollars. Thus the sum furnished
amounted to about sixty-four thousand dollars. Surely, this was a
very trifling sum to exhaust the treasury of the sovereigns of Spain.

in the year 1867. But Columbus considered them very suitable for the undertaking. The whole company entering upon this expedition amounted to one hundred and twenty persons.*

In popular estimation, the enterprise was perilous in the extreme, and almost sacrilegious, tempting Providence. It was deemed far more foolhardy than the attempt to cross the ocean in a balloon would now be considered. Consequently, it was exceedingly difficult to engage a crew. At length the government was compelled to resort to force, and to impress seamen for the cruise.†

It was early in the morning of the 3d of August, 1492, just as the sun was rising over the billows of the ocean, when the little fleet spread its sails for the most adventurous and momentous voyage ever recorded in the history of this world. In the mind of Columbus, the religious element largely prevailed in the conception of the enterprise. A sermon was preached in the cathedral. Anthems of supplication and praise were sung. Earnest prayers were offered ;

* Helps' "Columbus," p. 81.

† "A proclamation of immunity from civil and criminal process, to persons taking service in the expedition, was issued at the same time. The ship of Columbus was therefore a refuge for criminals and runaway debtors ; a Cave. of Adullam for the discontented and the desperate. To have to deal with such a community was not one of the least of Columbus's difficulties."—*Life of Columbus*, by Arthur Helps, p. 80.

and the whole population of the little place gathered in the sanctuary, and gazed solemnly upon the spectacle, as the officers and the crew, upon their knees, received the sacrament of the Lord's Supper.

Emotions were excited too deep for mirth. There was no revelry : no voice uttered a huzza; the robed priests accompanied the seamen to their boats. As the sails were unfurled, and the frail vessels with a favoring breeze sought the distant horizon, tears, lamentations, and sad forebodings oppressed the hearts of all who were left behind.*

* It may be well to listen to the views of Mr. Goodrich on this occasion. He writes, in his angry assailment of the discoverer "Columbus, on arriving at Palos with his orders, did not meet with an enthusiastic reception from the inhabitants. They were unwilling to follow an unknown adventurer on a long voyage. Two of the ships were secretly scuttled. The delay and difficulty increased, and threatened seriously to impede the undertaking, when the Pinzons, those brave brothers, seeing how matters stood, and having part of their fortunes embarked in the enterprise, came forward, and offered each to take command of a caravel. The men of Palos, by whom the Pinzons were held in great esteem, now came forward willingly. Two small caravels, the *Pinta* and the *Nina*, were commanded respectively by Martin Alonzo and Vincent Yanez Pinzon. The *St. Mary*, a somewhat larger vessel, equipped at the expense of the Pinzons, was under the command of the henceforth ' Admiral Don Christopher Columbus ' ; like all new-born nobility, his right to which title neither he nor his son will ever forget. This prospective enjoyment of a ponderous title, is amusing, in view of the ultimate grandeur of his command : three small vessels, ordinary fishing-smacks of from thirty to sixty tons burden, two of them without decks ; and for the best of these he is indebted to the man whom he will afterward gratefully term, ' one Pinzon.' "—*History of the Character and Achievements of the so-called Christopher Columbus.* By Aaron Goodrich, p. 90.

The first portion of the track which Columbus pursued was familiar to him. He directed his course toward the Canary Islands. The wind was fresh and fair ; and very propitiously the little fleet ploughed the waves. The crews of the three vessels were composed of ignorant and superstitious men, and, as we have mentioned, many of them were forced into the service. As they beheld the mountains of their native land disappearing behind them, their hearts failed through fear. It would seem as though Columbus stood almost alone in his enthusiasm, aided only by doubting and reluctant followers.

Very early in the voyage, indications of discontent, and almost of mutiny, were manifested. On the third day out, the rudder of one of the vessels was unshipped. Columbus had reason strongly to suspect that it was intentionally done by some of the disaffected seamen. The nautical skill of the commander soon caused the injury in some degree to be repaired. But still the vessel was so far crippled that it could only keep up with the others by their shortening sail. A voyage of seven days brought them within sight of the Canary Islands They had thus accomplished about a thousand miles from the port of Palos. Here Columbus was detained three weeks. The crippled vessel was condemned as unseaworthy. But they found it impossible to obtain another ves-

3

sel, and they therefore made a new rudder for the
Pinta, and endeavored to strengthen her for the
voyage.

Again, after a detention of three weeks, on the
6th of September Columbus unfurled the sails.
He now entered upon unknown seas. The Canary
Islands were at the outermost limits of the then
known world. They had hardly left sight of the
islands, when a dead calm ensued. For three days
the vessel rolled, without progress, upon the massive
yet glassy undulations of the ocean. Again the seamen were terrified.

On the 9th, a fresh breeze arose, filling the sails,
and they pressed on their way. It was the morning
of the Sabbath, a cloudless sky overarched them,
and the apparently boundless ocean, in all its sublime
glories, was spread around. But there was no joy on
board those vessels. Discontented looks alone were
seen, and murmuring words alone were heard.
Columbus did everything in his power to remove the
despondency of the mariners, and to inspire them
with a portion of his own enthusiasm. Perceiving
that every league they sailed increased their fears that
they should never be able to return home, he resorted
to the artifice of keeping two records of their daily
progress. One of these was for his own instruction.
The other was to be exhibited to the mariners, to

give them the impression that the distance they had passed was much less than in reality it was.* Days of great anxiety and constant watchfulness passed slowly away, while Columbus pressed onward with all possible speed toward the goal, which he felt so confident he should ere long find.

It is a little singular that he did not expect to find land within the distance of about three thousand miles. Still he was on an expanse of water which had never before been seen by mortal eyes. No one could tell what objects might at any point open up upon them.

Columbus was on deck, carefully watching everything, until the last rays of the evening twilight had disappeared. And again, with the earliest dawn of the morning he was at the bows of his ship, on the

---

* Mr. Goodrich makes the remarkable assertion, that it was not the crew, but Columbus, who wished to return. He writes :

" Here also explodes another popular error founded on the untruthfulness of Columbus and those who have sung his praises. It is said that the men mutinied, and that the rest of the expedition desired to return to Spain, but were led on and encouraged by Columbus.

" Now, as we have stated above, the *St. Mary* was always in the rear, the others having frequently to lay by for her. It is scarcely probable that the *Pinta* and *Nina* would have continued thus in advance, had their commanders wished to have turned back. Besides according to the testimony of several witnesses in the celebrated law suit of Don Diego, " Columbus against the Crown," Columbus himself, after sailing some hundred leagues without finding land, wished to return, but was persuaded by the Pinzons to continue the voyage."— *Life of Columbus*, by Aaron Goodrich, p. 131.

watch. The changing color of the sky, the hue of the water, the form of the clouds, and the variations of the wind, were examined with the closest scrutiny. On the night of the 14th of September, a very brilliant meteor flamed through the sky, and fell into the ocean, at a distance of but a few miles from the ships This greatly increased the alarm of the superstitous mariners.

They struck the trade winds. Day after day they were swept along from east to west. Again the seamen were terrified. They thought they should never be able to return. They had reached a tropical climate of marvellous salubrity. It was a luxury to breathe the softened air. Columbus was exceeding y encouraged in meeting masses of floating sea-weed, which he knew must have been torn from shores in the west. On one of these patches they caught a live crab. Day after day the steady, gentle breeze filled their sails, while the sea, as Columbus remarked, "was as calm as the Guadalquiver at Seville."

Indications of approaching land revived the hopes of the crew. A rich reward had been promised to the one who should first discover the land. On the evening of the 18th of September, a large flock of land birds was seen, winging their flight toward the north-west. Clouds were observed in that direction, such as usually hang over the land. Columbus sounded, but could find no bottom.

Again the crew began to be alarmed, in view of the immense expanse of ocean they were leaving between them and their homes. It required all the tact and authority of Columbus to quiet their fears. Still, indications of approaching land rapidly increased. Several land birds lighted upon the ship, and some so small that it was evident that they could not venture far in their flight. Still no bottom could be found by the sounding line. Another dead calm ensued. The ocean was as smooth and polished as a mirror, and the meridian sun poured down upon them with rays which blistered the decks. On the 25th, without any rising of the wind, there came on a heavy swell of the sea. It was probably the effect of the undulations caused by some distant gale.

The mutinous condition of the crew varied with all the changes they encountered. Still Columbus maintained a serene and self-confident air. Some of the disaffected he soothed with gentle words. Some he overawed with menaces, and upon some he inflicted signal punishment. Again a gentle breeze and fair sprang up, which filled the sails, though it scarcely rippled the surface of the sea. The ships kept so near each other that Columbus could easily converse with his companion officers. While thus engaged, a shout was heard from the *Pinta*. A man upon the stern pointed to the south-west, and cried out, " Land, land. I claim the reward." All eyes were immediately turned in that direction, where there was, apparently at about the distance of sixty miles, a ridge of cloud-capped mountains. Columbus fell upon his knees in a prayer of thanksgiving, and then with his whole crew, repeated the " Gloria in Excelsis," or Glory to God in the highest.*

Indescribable enthusiasm inspired the hearts of all the crews. They ran up the shrouds, climbed up the mast-heads, and all eyes were strained in that direction. It was late in the afternoon. The sun soon sank behind the mountainous clouds. The short twilight of the tropics vanished, and the gloom of midnight overspread the ocean. Through the night, the ships steered toward the expected land. With the earliest dawn, all were upon the deck. To their bitter disappointment, an unobstructed horizon was spread out before them. Not a vestige even of a cloud appeared. Still the breeze was propitious, the sea smooth, and the climate delightful. Dolphins sported at their bows, flying-fish leaped upon

---

* This fact is stated by Navarette in his "First Voyage of Columbus," vol. i.

the deck, and the sailors amused themselves, it is said, in swimming around the vessels.

According to the private reckoning of Columbus, he had sailed from the Canary Islands, a distance of two thousand and twenty-two miles. But according to the reckoning exhibited to the crew, he had passed over but one thousand seven hundred and forty miles.* A few days more passed away of slow progress, when the spirit of discontent and insubordination again began to manifest itself. It was, however, soon quelled, by the appearance of large flocks of birds, and other indications that they were approaching land.

The eager seamen were frequently giving false alarms, mistaking distant clouds for mountain peaks.

---

* Such is the statement made by Navarette, vol. I, p. 16. But it must be admitted that there is much force in the following statement, made by Aaron Goodrich.

" Both the Pinzons were skilful navigators, each of them commanded a caravel, and they were generally ahead. They naturally made frequent observations ; the pilots also could not have been so easily deceived. Should we, therefore, give credence to this story, we must make the Pinzons, the pilots, and officers, parties to the fraud, an imputation for which there is no basis, save the statement of Columbus. Besides, if the latter had thus deceived his crew, it would have rendered another of his statements futile. On leaving the Canaries, he declared that when they had sailed seven hundred and fifty leagues west, they should reach land. The false reckoning and its diminished distances, in leading the men to believe that they were farther from their destination than the really were, and that the voyage would be prolonged beyond their expectations, would therefore have defeated his avowed object."—*History of Columbus*, p. 196.

To prevent this, Columbus issued an order that should any one cry out Land! and land not be discovered for three days afterward, he should forfeit all claim to the reward. It is said about this time Columbus entered into an agreement with his crew, that he would abandon the enterprise if land were not discovered within three days. But there is no satisfactory foundation for this statement. It rests upon the authority of Oviedo. Fernando, the son of Columbus, in his minute history of his father, has not mentioned it. It is not alluded to by Bishop Las Casas, who was intrusted with the examination of the papers of the admiral. Neither Peter Martyr nor the Curate of Los Palacios, who were contemporary historians, have mentioned it

"Fortunately," writes Mr. Irving, "the journal of Columbus, written from day to day with guileless simplicity, and all the air of truth, disproves this fable, and shows that on the very day previous to his discovery he expressed a peremptory determination to persevere in defiance of all dangers and difficulties." *

* Irving's "Columbus," vol. i. p. 159.

CHAPTER III.

Land Discovered.

The Mutinous Crew—The gleam of the torch—The account criti-
cised—Landing at San Salvador—Doubts as to the identity of
the island—Enchanting scene—Two days on the island—Story
of the Dead Pilot—Traffic with the Natives—Their Innocence
and Friendliness—Exploring the island—Uncertainty of the
language of signs.

JUST as the mutinous crew were becoming desperate, they met with indisputable evidence that
they must be in the vicinity of land. Fresh weeds
were found, such as are torn from the banks of rocks
and rivers. The branch of a thorn tree was picked
up, with green leaves and berries upon it. They also
found, most encouraging of all, a piece of plank and
a staff curiously carved.

The Admiral invariably had religious service on
board his ship, where the Vesper Hymn to the Virgin was sung. This evening he seemed to be impressed with even unusual solemnity. Always grave,
sedate, and thoughtful, his spirit seemed to be overawed by the consciousness that he was on the eve
of accomplishing his life long desires. In earnest

3*

tones he addressed the crew, reminding them of the
protection they had received from God, and assuring
them that, in his judgment, without any doubt, they
were approaching the land very near the point at
which he had expected to find it. Indeed he asserted that he thought they would make the land
that very night. He ordered a vigilant watch to be
kept on the forecastle, and offered, in addition to the
rewards promised by the sovereigns, the gift of a
velvet doublet to the man who should first descry
the coast.

With the night, the breeze increased, and very
rapidly the little fleet ploughed the waves. The
Pinta was the best sailor of the three, and kept
a little head. Sixty-seven days had now passed
since the highlands of Spain had vanished beneath
the eastern horizon. It was the 11th of October,
1492. The tropical night was cloudless and, brilliant with stars. A gentle and refreshing breeze
swept the almost unrippled waters. Intense excitement pervaded the hearts of all on board the three
ships. Scarcely an eye was closed, Columbus took
his stand on the bows of his vessel, and with anxious
glance surveyed the horizon.

About ten o'clock, he was startled by the faint
gleam of a torch, far away in the west. For a moment it burned with a very distinct flame, and then

suddenly and entirely disappeared. His heart
throbbed with emotion. Was it a meteor? Was
it an optical illusion, or was it a light from the land?
As he stood trembling in his excitement, the light
again beamed forth, distinct and indisputable. He
immediately called to his side Pedro Gutierrez, one
of the most distinguished gentlemen of his companions. He also saw the light. They then called a
third, Rodrigo Sanchez, who had been sent on the
expedition as the representative and reporter of
their Majesties. But the light had again disappeared. Soon, however, it was again manifest, and
Sanchez also saw it. Still it might be a meteor.
They could not declare it to be a torch on the land.
In the journal it is stated that,

"It appeared like a candle that went up and
down; and Don Christopher did not doubt that it
was true light, and that it was on land. And so it
proved, as it came from people passing with lights
from one cottage to another."

These gleams were so transient that not much
importance was attached to them by the ship's company, though Columbus seemed to be sanguine in
the conviction that it was light from the shore.
The little fleet pressed on for four hours, when at
two o'clock in the morning the land was first seen
from the *Pinta* by a seaman, by the name of Rod-

rigo de Triana. A gun from the *Pinta* announced the joyful news that land was discovered. Very soon the outline of the land, dark, but clearly defined, was visible from all the ships. The promised pension of ten thousand maravedis, to the man who should first see land, was adjudged to Columbus, though many thought it justly belonged to Rodrigo de Triana. Navarette does not seem disposed to admit that the land was discovered by Columbus. He writes :

" The Admiral says that this island, Guanahani or San Salvador, is very flat, without any mountain. How then can he pretend to have seen a torch at ten o'clock at night, at the distance of fourteen leagues, which rose and fell on a flat shore, destitute of elevations. Calculating by the table of tangents of the horizon, according to the altitude from which they advanced, and supposing the vision of the observer to be elevated twelve feet above the level of the sea, which is as much as can be supposed when the smallness of the caravels is borne in mind, the result is that the land must have had an elevation of twenty-two hundred and fifty-four feet above the level of the sea, for its summit or highest point to have been visible at fourteen leagues' distance.

" How is it that the men of the *Pinta*, which was

in the advance, did not see the light, since they discovered land at two o'clock in the morning? Why
did not Columbus shorten sail, and lie to, when at
ten o'clock at night, he was certain he was near
land, and as was done when the *Pinta* sighted it, and
as prudence and reason would have required, when
we consider the swift sailing of the ships?

"Why does he say that at first he saw the light
so confusedly that he did not affirm it to be the
land, as it would appear but to a few to be an indication thereof; and that he nevertheless afterward
held it for certain, and yet took none of the precau-
tions which such certainty of opinion would have
required? Might not this have been the binnacle
or some other light, of the *Pinta*, which was ahead,
or of the *Nina*, which would have been visible at
another point of the compass, for he does not inform
us in which direction he saw the light? It might
very well have been alternately visible and invisible, according as the ship rose and fell. Those who
think that the light seen by Columbus was Wat-
ling's Island, in the neighborhood of which he must
have passed at ten o'clock at night, have not considered or traced his route, and seen that, according to
this supposition, the rate of sailing, and the situation
of that island, he had, at the hour indicated, crossed

its meridian, leaving it south-east, when he was navigating west.*

The remaining hours of the night passed swiftly away. The morning dawned bright and beautiful, and revealed to the entranced eye of Columbus a spectacle which Paradise could hardly outrival. There was spread out before him a low island, in the richest of tropical luxuriance and bloom. Nature's orchards, lawns, and parks extended in all directions. Multitudes of the natives were seen emerging from the woods, and running along the shore, in a state of intense excitement. They were all perfectly naked. Weary as the voyagers were of gazing for so many weeks upon the wild waste of waters, the scene opened before them like the enchantments of fairy-land. It is not strange that they should have imagined that they had reached blest realms, whose inhabitants were dwelling in primeval simplicity and innocence.

The boats were lowered and manned from each of the caravels. Columbus took the lead, very richly dressed in scarlet robes, and with Castilian plumes. It is said "distance lends enchantment to the view."

* Navarette, vol. iii. p. 612. This train of reasoning leads Nava-rette to conclude that it was the sailor Rodrigo de Triana, or as some call him Juan Rodriguez Bermejo, on board the *Pinta*, who first sighted the land; and that he was justly entitled to the reward which, through favoritism, was conferred upon Columbus.

But as they drew nearer the shore, the scene grew more picturesque and beautiful. The dwellings of the natives were scattered throughout the extended groves. The gentle eminences and the valleys were filled with trees of new aspect, and with every variety of foliage. There was an abundant display of flowers of gorgeous hue, and such as the adventurers had never seen before. Fruits, of great variety of form, and color, hung from the trees. Columbus speaks particularly of the songs of the birds, which filled the air; of the pure and balmy atmosphere, and of the crystal transparency of the water.

As soon as Columbus stepped upon the shore, he fell upon his knees and gave thanks to God. The sailors gathered around their illustrious leader, with sympathy and penitence for their mutinous conduct. Many wept, kissed his hands, and implored forgiveness. Those who had been the most mutinous were now the most cringing and sycophantic, for they hoped to receive favors which would enrich and ennoble them all.

With imposing religious ceremonies, Columbus planted upon the shore the banner of Spain. In devout recognition of the goodness of God which had guided him thus far, he named the island San Salvador. He then exacted from the companies of the three ships, the oath of allegiance to him, as

Admiral and Viceroy of all the realms upon which he was now entering.

The natives gathered timidly around, and gazed awe-struck upon these movements. It is said that when they first beheld the ships, moving apparently without effort, and shifting their enormous wings, they supposed they must be monsters of the deep, or birds who had come on gigantic wing from their aerial homes. When the sailors landed upon the beach, with their glittering coats of mail, their strange attire, and their weapons of war, they fled in terror to the woods. But seeing that they were not pur sued, and that no hostile movements were manifested, they slowly began to return. The commanding stature of Columbus, his lofty bearing, his costume of scarlet, and the deference which was paid him by all his companions, led the natives to regard him with the highest degree of veneration.

It is the invariable testimony that the natives generally thought the Spaniards had descended from the skies. One of the chiefs subsequently inquired how they came down, whether by flying or by descending on the clouds.*

As the two parties gazed upon each other, the amazement was mutual. The spectacle presented to the Spaniards was fully as extraordinary as that which was opened to the view of the natives. The land-

* Herrera, "Hist. Ind.," lib. iv. cap. 5.

scape, in all its varied aspects, was as novel as if the strangers had been transported to another planet. The trees, the fruits, the flowers, were all different from any which they had before seen. The climate, in its genial yet not sultry warmth, without a chill, and without the sensation of excessive heat, seemed to be perfect. The Eden-like innocence, modesty, and simplicity of the natives excited their wonder and admiration. Their clear golden complexion is represented as beautiful. Their limbs were rounded into forms of symmetry and grace which would have rivalled the far-famed statues of Venus and Apollo.

These scenes probably impressed the Spaniards more deeply than the natives were moved, in their superstitious minds, by the spectacle, as they supposed, of beings descending from the skies, or rising from the deep.

Columbus supposed that he had landed upon an island at the extremity of India. He therefore called the natives Indians. This name has gradually extended to all the native inhabitants of the New World. Notwithstanding the almost universally received opinion that the island now called San Salvador was the one upon which Columbus first landed, there are those who dispute that statement, and who certainly bring forward some pretty strong arguments in support of their views.

The learned and impartial Navarette, whose in-telligence and integrity no one will doubt, after a careful examination of the diary of Columbus, comes to the conclusion that the island upon which he first landed must have been the Great Turk Island ; the largest of the group called by that name. This island is nearly two hundred leagues south-east of San Salvador. He writes :

" From a careful examination of the diary of Co-lumbus, in his first voyage, its courses, descriptions of lands, of islands, coast, and harbors, it appears that this, the first island discovered and occupied by Columbus, and named by him San Salvador, must be the one situated most to the north of those called the Turk Islands, and itself called the Great Turk. Its latitude is twenty-one degrees, thirty minutes." *

Some years ago, Mr. Gibbs, who had resided for many years on Turk's Island, presented a paper to the New York Historical Society, in confirmation of the views of Navarette. The following is a con-densation of his arguments.

Columbus states in his journal that there were several islands in sight of Guanahani. When Mr Gibbs visited the island now called San Salvador, he

* See " Introduction to the Letters of Christopher Columbus," by R. H. Major, Esq., of the British Museum, published by the London Hakluyt Society, 1847.

sent sailors to the mast-head to look for land. But no other island could be seen. He went ashore, and ascended the highest eminence. But the ocean in all directions extended in an unbroken line to the horizon. Columbus speaks of soundings, a little to the eastward of Guanahani. No such soundings can now be found eastward of San Salvador. The Spaniards sailed around the island of Guanahani in one day. This would be impossible at San Salvador. All the marks wanting at San Salvador are found at Turk's Island. Columbus describes Guanahani as well-wooded, and with a great abundance of water. He says there was a large lake in the centre and two considerable streams flowing into the sea. This is not a correct description of San Salvador, but is minutely correct in reference to Turk's Island One-third of its surface is covered with lakes of salt and fresh water. Some of these are still connected with the sea, except when their outlets are temporarily closed by storms choking them with sand. Though the island is now treeless, in former ages it was well-wooded. The remains of ancient forests were plainly seen half a century ago.*

Mr. Irving, notwithstanding these statements, after carefully examining the subject, and giving his reasons, in his illustrations of the Life of Columbus,

* See " London Athenæum," for 1846.

comes to the conclusion that San Salvador was the place of the first landing of Columbus. In this opinion nearly all modern historians coincide. And here it may be proper to state that Mr. Aaron Goodrich emphatically denies that Columbus is entitled to the credit of being the first to discover the islands of the West Indies. His account of the matter, which he affirms to be sustained by several ancient documents, is in brief, as follows :

About the year 1484, eight years before the voyage of Columbus, a Spanish sea-captain, or pilot, as he was called, was sailing from Spain to the Canary Islands. His ship was struck by so fierce a tempest from the north-east, that he was compelled to run before it, in a westerly direction, for twenty-eight days. During all that time clouds so intercepted the sun that it was impossible to take an observation.

At length they caught sight of an island, cast anchor, went on shore, and with their instruments accurately ascertained the meridian altitude of the sun. All this the pilot carefully wrote in his log-book. The island was twenty-eight days' sail west of the Canaries. This fact, together with a description of the land, led subsequently to the surmise that the island thus discovered was the one now called Hayti or St. Domingo. The pilot, having made this accidental discovery, took a fresh supply of wood and water and commenced his return to Madeira, where Columbus at that time happened to be residing. The crew, consisting of seventeen, fell sick, and twelve died. The five survivors reached Madeira, but in a very forlorn condition. They were all suffering from the sickness which had carried off their companions. Columbus received them at his house, and carefully nursed them as one after another they died. He listened eagerly to the communications which they made of the new lands they had discovered, and added them to the testimony he had collected, in reference to lands in the west." *

He sustains it by the authority of Gomara's History of the Indies, and by the narrative of Garcillasso de la Vega. But, on the other side, Spotorno writes :

"As to the idle tale, which was current in Spain, that Columbus had taken the idea of a New World from a pilot of whom a number of tales were told, I shall not stop to refute it."†

We can hardly assent to the statement of Mr. Irving, that if this story can be proved to be true, it would destroy all the merit of Columbus as an original discoverer.‡ We are much more ready to assent

---

* "History of Columbus," by Aaron Goodrich, page 164.
† Spotorno's "Historia Memoria," p. 29.
‡ Irving's "Columbus." Appendix No. 11.

to the statement of De Ovalle, of Chili, in his rela-
tion of the kingdom of Chili, that, even if the views
of Columbus were confirmed by the statements of
these mariners, to whom none others paid heed, it
would not detract from the glory of the achievement
of the great discoverer.*

Neither is it easy to understand why Columbus
should have spent so many weary years in the vain
endeavor to prove that lands could be found in the
west, without giving prominence, or even alluding to
the fact, that these realms had been actually visited,
and their position ascertained.

It is safe to say, that the most reliable historians
of Columbus dismiss the story as without foundation.

Ferdinand Columbus, one of the earliest of the
annalists of his father's career, states that Christopher Columbus formed his views upon the basis of
three pretty distinct lines of argument. The first
was drawn from his own philosophical investiga-
tions. The second, from evidence which he found in
the written or published narratives of voyages and
travels. The third was from such testimony as he
could obtain from the wild and often absurd stories
of wandering sailors.

The natives, receiving no harm from their strange
visitors, became more and more confiding and affec-

* See " Churchill's Voyages," vol. iii. p. 88.

tionate. They lavished upon the Spaniards the highest testimonials of their hospitality. The sailors
fearlessly wandered through the groves, devouring
the fruit, untasted before, which hung from so many
boughs. The testimony seems unequivocal that
Columbus was, by nature, a kind-hearted man ;
though, influenced by the darkness of that dark age,
he was subsequently guilty of many cruel acts.
He completely won the hearts of the natives by the
gift of a few glittering beads or tinkling hawk's bells.
These articles were regarded by them as of inestimable value.

The beautiful maidens, apparently perfectly modest
in their demeanor, would hang these bells around their
waists, and dance with delight as they listened to the
tinkling music. In the description which Columbus
gives of them, he says that they had not the crisped
hair of the African, but that it was long, very black,
and that it frequently hung down upon their shoulders. Only in front were the locks cut off, to prevent their disturbing the vision. Their features
were agreeable in expression, with high foreheads
and very fine eyes. Their complexion is represented
of a bright copper color ; at times it was compared
with the golden hue of the coin just issued from the
mint. One fact struck the strangers as remarkable :
that nearly all the natives they saw were under

thirty years of age. There seemed to be no old
people among them. What could this signify?

But another fact excited the attention of the
thoughtful, as indicative that they had not entered
a country resembling paradise before the fall. They
had war clubs, and sharp-pointed javelins, armed
with the lacerating teeth of the shark. When Columbus spoke of these, by signs, they described to
him that they were used in war, to make assaults or
to repel attacks. And some of them pointed to
wounds which they had received in battle.

In the evening all the Spaniards returned to
their ships. The night passed quietly away, though
the excitement was too great for much sleep to be
enjoyed. With the earliest light, an immense concourse of the natives had gathered upon the shore
from all parts of the island, to gaze upon the astonishing spectacle. Their confidence in the strangers was
such, that many of them plunged into the sea and
and swam to the vessel. The water seemed to be
their native element. They had many canoes.
They were composed of trunks of trees, ingeniously
hollowed, and with great labor. Some of them were
so small and fragile that they would float but a single man. Others were so large that they would
accommodate a party of forty armed warriors.

These canoes, having no keels, were easily over·

turned : but this was considered by the natives a mere trifle. They swam about like ducks, righted the canoe, bailed out the water with calabashes, and were in again, with but a few moments' delay.

It was a bitter disappointment to Columbus, to find that these people were poor in the extreme. Though they had a delightful climate, comfortable little huts, fruit in abundance, and needed no clothing, yet they had 'nothing with which Columbus could freight his ships, to enrich himself and his companions, and to reward the cupidity of the Spanish monarch. The poor natives had nothing to offer the Spaniards but gorgeous parrots, which they were fond of domesticating, and balls of cotton yarn. These balls were frequently twenty-five pounds in weight, and were of some value—we know not how much—in the markets of Spain. They had also a sort of native bread, made of a root called *yuca*, which was palatable food on the islands, but not an important article of export.

As Columbus landed the next day, amidst a throng of natives, he saw several of the girls with trinkets of gold suspended from the nose, instead of the ears. The glittering metal quickly caught his eye. Eagerly the Indian belles exchanged their plain yellow trinkets for gorgeously colored beads of the most insignificant value. Columbus inquired

4

earnestly of the natives where this gold was procured.

It is exceedingly difficult to obtain information
where the language of signs alone can be used; and
this difficulty is greatly increased when such signs
as are used by savages are received in exchange for
the signs of the civilized man. Columbus was undoubtedly greatly deceived by the intelligence which
he thought he had gained from the natives. He
understood them to say, that at some distance to
the south, there was a powerful chief who had great
abundance of gold, that he was served upon dishes
of that precious metal. He also received the impression that there were nations at the north who
often went in warlike bands to attack the southern
nations, and returned with immense plunder of gold.
In his ardent imagination, he fancied that they told
him of a magnificent city, with gorgeous palaces, at
not a great distance from them, and that he had
landed in the rural districts of one of the most
magnificent of earthly empires.

Thus the 13th of October passed away. It was
a memorable day with voyagers; a day full of excitement and delight. The next morning, Columbus manned his boats to reconnoitre the island. An
expedition of more intense interest, in the bright
morning of a tropical day, amid scenes of marvellous

novelty and beauty, can scarcely be imagined. Columbus represented the island as surrounded by a
reef of coral rock, with but a narrow entrance.
Within the reef, waters still and deep would afford
safe anchorage for all the ships in the world. It was
upon this placid expanse that the boats commenced
their exploring tour. They directed their course
toward the north-east. The water, it was said, was
as still as in a pool.

The island he described as well wooded throughout, as we have before mentioned, with several
streams of water and a large lake in the centre. As
the boats glided along, within a few rods of the
shore, they passed many picturesque villages em-
bowered in groves of great luxuriance. The inhabitants—men, women, and children—ran to the shore,
and in great excitement followed the progress of the
boats. Individuals occasionally prostrated themselves, performing ceremonies, which the Spaniards understood to be either thanking heaven for
their arrival, or worshipping them as celestial beings.

By signs which could not be misunderstood, the
natives invited them to land, offering them cool
water and rich fruit. As the boats continued their
course, several of the natives threw themselves into
the sea and swam out to them, being apparently
as much at home in the water as on the land.

Others followed in canoes. The kind-hearted Admiral received them all with smiles, and made them very happy by the present of a few insignificant trinkets, which they received as celestial gifts. Columbus often repeats the declaration that the natives regarded them as angelic beings.

This, however, must be somewhat doubtful. The idea was not easily communicated by signs. And it may be questioned whether the natives had even a dim conception of worlds, such as Christianity has revealed, where angel spirits dwell. Thus the boats continued, propelled by oars, till they reached quite an important headland, where there were six Indian dwellings, surrounded by groves and gardens which Columbus declared to be as beautiful as any which could be found in Castile. Here they landed for rest and refreshment; and then prepared to return to the ships, taking with them seven of the natives, whom they wished to teach the Spanish language, that they might serve as interpreters. That same evening they spread their sails, and directed their course toward the south.

CHAPTER IV.

A Tour among the Islands.

Number of islands—The Wrong and the Reparation—Kindness
of Columbus—His description of the natives—The Discovery
of Concepcion ; of Fernandina—Beauty of the scenery—Landing
at Exumata—Disappointment of Columbus—Cuba discovered—
Exploration of the islands—Manners and customs of the inhabitants.

IT is not easy to determine, from the narrative
of Columbus, whether islands were actually visible
from San Salvador. It is probable that he may
have relied upon such testimony as he supposed he
had received from the natives. According to the
statement of Marco Polo, the Indians on board the
Admiral's ship informed him that the i lands in these
seas were innumerable,'and that the natives were
generally at war with one another.* They even
mentioned the names of over a hundred of these
islands. Soon, they caught sight of a very large
island on the south-west, at apparently the distance
of about fifteen miles. The Indians represented the
natives there as much richer than those of San

* Marco Polo, b. iii. ch. 4. Translated by W. Marsden.

Salvador, and said that they wore bracelets and other large ornaments of massive gold.

As night was approaching, and the ships were in unknown seas, Columbus ordered them to lie to until morning. With the rising sun, the sails were again spread, but their progress was so impeded by counter currents and baffling winds, that the sun was disappearing before they cast anchor at the island. The next morning the boats were manned, and they went ashore. Here, there was a repetition of essentially the same scenes which had been witnessed at San Salvador. The climate was the same; the foliage, flowers, and fruits were the same; the natives were the same—unclothed, gentle, affectionate people, equally destitute of gold. Columbus looked eagerly, but in vain, for the golden bracelets and anklets. Whether their existence anywhere was a fiction of the Indians, or the credulous idea of his own excited imagination, cannot he ascertained. He, however, took possession of the island, with religious ceremonies, upon which the natives gazed with childish wonder. He gave it the name of Santa Maria de la Concepcion ; and again spread his sails for the continuance of his voyage.

Just as they were weighing anchor an event took place which painfully indicates that some, at least, of the natives on board the Admiral's ships were

captives, not voluntary interpreters.* One of these
Indians, of San Salvador, on board the *Nina*, of
which Vincent Yanez Pinzon was captain, seeing a
large canoe filled with natives, at not a great distance, plunged into the sea, and with almost the
rapidity of a fish, swam for his escape, and was
received by his countrymen. A boat was immediately put off in pursuit, but the natives vigorously
plying their paddles reached the shore before
they were overtaken, and with the agility of deer
disappeared in the woods.

The sailors seized their canoe and carried it back
to the ship as their prize. It was a gross act of
injustice, which even the most ignorant of barbarians
would condemn. But soon another still more atrocious outrage was attempted by the sailors. An
Indian, who had heard that the Spaniards would
purchase balls of cotton, came alone, in his fragile
canoe, to the Admiral's ship. As he approached the
bows he held up his cotton to the sailors. They
lured him near, and then two or three of them, who

* "I took some Indians, by force, from the first island I came to,
that they might learn our language and tell what they knew of their
country. The plan succeeded excellently. Soon, by word or signs,
we could understand each other. Though they have been with us now
a long time they continue to think that we descended from heaven.
When we arrive at any new place they cry, with a loud voice, to the
other Indians, 'Come and look upon beings of a celestial race.'"
—*Letter of Columbus to Don Raphael Sanchez.*

were good swimmers, leaped into the sea, seized his
canoe, and dragged the trembling man on board as
their prisoner.

Columbus, who was stationed on the high poop at
the stern of the vessel, witnessed the transaction.
He ordered the captive to be brought before him.
The poor Indian came forward trembling like an
aspen leaf, and held up the ball as a gift to obtain
the mercy of his captor. The Admiral received him
with the utmost kindness, put a gayly colored cap
upon his head, a bracelet of gorgeous beads upon
each arm, hung one or two hawk's bells upon each
ear, and then ordered him to be replaced in the
canoe with his ball of cotton. These gifts were to
the poor Indian as joy-exciting as the legacy of
thousands of dollars would be to a poor man in civilized life. With delight he paddled to the shore.
Columbus was much interested in seeing the groups
gather around him, examining his treasures and
listening to the story of his kind treatment.

As Columbus sailed from Concepcion, he saw, at
the distance of several leagues to the west, another
large island, to which he directed the ship's course
When half-way between the two islands, his vessel
overtook a single Indian in an exceedingly frail
canoe. He was paddling from one island to the
other, apparently with the intention of communicat-

ing the news of the arrival of the Spaniards. He had
a string of beads, which he had obtained at San
Salvador. Columbus admired the intrepidity of the
man who dared to make such a voyage in so slight a
canoe. Both the Indian and his canoe were taken
on board. The guest was treated with great kindness, and regaled with wine, bread, and honey. A
very gentle breeze swept the glassy sea, and it was
not until the evening twilight had faded away that
they cast their anchors.

The Indian's canoe was launched overboard, and
the happy man was sent on shore, laden with gifts to
propitiate the natives and lead them to welcome the
arrival of the Spaniards. The tidings were so rapidly spread throughout the island that, with the rising of the sun, an immense concourse of the natives
was seen upon the beach, while the water seemed
swarming with their canoes. They crowded to the
ships, bringing fruits, roots, and pure water. Columbus gave all some trifling presents, and feasted them
with sugar and honey.

Soon, parties from the three ships rowed to the
shore. Here they witnessed the same scene of
apparent peace and happiness which had before
greeted their eyes. They spent a few hours upon
the island, charmed with the simplicity and affec-
tionateness of the natives. Their dwellings were

4*

pavilions of reeds and palm leaves, very graceful in structure, and neat and orderly in interior arrangements. The following extract from the journal of Columbus reveals the impression which the natives made upon him.

"Because they had much friendship for us, and because I knew they were people that would deliver themselves better to the Christian faith, and be converted more through love than by force, I gave to some of them some colored caps and some strings of glass beads for their necks, and many other things of little value, with which they were delighted, and were so entirely ours that it was a marvel to see. The same afterward came swimming to the ship's boats, where we were, and brought us parrots, cotton thread in balls, darts, and many other things, and bartered them with us for things which we gave them, such as bells and small glass beads. In fine, they took and gave all of whatever they had with good-will; but it appeared to me that they were a people very poor in everything. They went totally naked, as naked as their mothers brought them into the world."*

To this island Columbus gave the name of Fernandina, in honor of King Ferdinand. It has since been called Exhuma. Columbus endeavored to cir-

* "Journal of Columbus," as quoted by Helps, p. 100.

cumnavigate the island. In sailing toward the north-
west he found a very fine harbor, where a hundred
ships could ride in safety. Running into this harbor,
he landed with a party of men for water. While the
sailors were filling the casks, Columbus wandered to
a little distance from them, and threw himself upon
a grassy mound, in admiration of the scene which
surrounded him.

"The country," he exclaims in his journal, "is
more beautiful than any I have ever before seen."
It was as fresh and green as is Andalusia in the
month of May. The trees, the fruit, the herbs, the
flowers, were entirely different from those of Spain.
The natives were exceedingly obliging. They conducted the Spaniards to the sweetest springs of pure
water; assisted them in filling their casks, and aided
in rolling them to their boats.

Though Columbus saw much to charm his imagination, he was bitterly disappointed in not finding
more gold. As it was apparent that he could not.
expect to obtain any quantity of the precious metal
upon the island he was then exploring, he spread his
sails, on the 19th, for another island, which the
natives called Saometa. He had inferred, from the
signs of the natives, that mines of gold were there;
that it was the residence of the sovereign chief, or
king, of all the surrounding islands, and that the

monarch was richly clad "in garments embroidered with jewels and gold."

They had landed upon the island, but neither monarch nor mine of gold was there. The natives were numerous, the island was delightful, and the subordinate chief was decked with trivial ornaments. To the excited imagination of Columbus, almost every island appeared more beautiful than those previously visited. Indeed there was much variety in the scenery which was presented. This island was covered with trees and flowering shrubs of exquisite beauty. The interior was rounded into eminences of considerable height. The air seemed to him peculiarly balmy, and the fine sand of the beach, which girdled the island, was laved by billows of almost crystal transparency. In the interior he found several fine lakes of fresh water. To the island he gave the name of Isabella, in honor of the queen whose memory he cherished with such loyalty of devotion. Of this island, which is now called Exumeta, he wrote:

"Here are large lakes, and the groves about them are marvellous. And here, and in all the islands, everything is green. The singing of the birds is such that it seems as if one would never desire to depart hence. There are flocks of parrots that obscure the sun, and other birds, large and small, of so many kinds all different from ours, that it is wonderful

And besides there are trees of a thousand species, each having its particular fruit, and all of marvellous flavor, so that I am in the greatest trouble in the world not to know them ; for I am very certain that they are of great value. I shall bring home some of them as specimens ; also some of the herbs.

"As I arrived at this cape there came thence a fragrance so good and soft, of the flowers and trees of the land, that it was the sweetest thing in the world. I believe there are here many herbs and trees which would be of great price in Spain for tinctures, medicines, and spices ; but I know nothing of them, which gives me great concern." *

Not only the birds, which flitted from bough to bough, were of gorgeous plumage, but the fishes, with which those crystal waters abounded, flashed upon the eye all the gorgeous hues of the rainbow. They rivalled the birds in the brilliancy of their coloring. The dolphins, especially, which were easily taken, charmed the beholders with the wonderful changes of colors they exhibited. It is quite remarkable that there should not have been found any four-footed animals excepting of a small size. There was one resembling a dog, but which never barked. There were also rabbits, and numerous lizards; which latter the Spaniards at first regarded

* " Primer Viage de Colon," ch. i.

with loathing and dread, as if they were venomous reptiles. They afterward ascertained that they were perfectly harmless, and that their flesh was esteemed a great delicacy.

But gold was the object of search of these discoverers. Employing the very obscure language of signs, Columbus was continually inquiring of every chief whom he met, where gold could be found. Either the natives intentionally deceived him, or Columbus, in his eagerness, misinterpreted their language. They continually pointed to the south, and described, with expressive gestures, a very large island full of people, and abounding with gold, and which they seemed fond of designating by the beautiful term of Cuba, Cuba, Cuba.

All on board the ships became familiar with the name which the events of subsequent centuries have rendered so conspicuous. All were eager to reach the island of Cuba. It was understood that there were large cities upon the island, and that in the harbors there were large ships.

It was the latter part of the month of October. The rainy season of the tropics was setting in, accompanied with dead calms and baffling winds. At midnight of the 24th of October, Columbus again spread his sails and directed his course in search of the island of Cuba. The canvas, however, flapped idly against the cordage until about noon of the next day, when a delightful and favoring breeze sprang up. Sailing in a south-westerly direction, he came in sight of many small islands, where he did not think it worth his while to tarry. He, however, touched at one group, which he called the Isles of Arene, and which was probably that now known as the Mucaras group.

On the morning of the 28th of October, the magnificent mountains of the Queen of the Antilles hove in sight. Never can the writer forget the emotions he himself experienced, when in the bright rays of one of the most brilliant of tropical mornings, the mountains, the vales, the wondrous foliage and verdure, and the apparent boundless expanse of this grandest of earthly isles, opened before him. It was probably not far from the spot upon which Columbus stood when the entrancing view first caught his eye.

In the most glowing language he describes the grandeur of the mountains, reaching to the clouds, the luxuriance and the bloom of the extended valleys, the bold, forest-crowned promontories, jutting into the sea, the headlands fading away in the far distance toward the north-west and the south-west. A beautiful river, on the northern coast of the island, invited the entrance of his ships. Here he cast anchor. The water was of such transparency that fishes and the pebbles could be seen at the depth of several fathoms. Smooth white sand paved the bottom of the stream, while the banks were covered with the richest foliage.

Columbus landed. As usual, he took possession of the island in the name of the Spanish monarchs, and called it Juan, in honor of Prince Juan, the son of Isabella.* The river he called San Salvador. The inhabitants observed the approach of the ships, and fled in terror from the appalling phenomenon. Two deserted cabins were found upon the shore. They contained a few fishing implements, such as nets ingeniously woven from fibres of the palm tree, with fish-hooks and harpoons made of bone. One of the little dogs which never bark was running around. The inmates of these huts were rich, according to the savage estimate of wealth. Their palm-thatched cabins protected them from wind and rain. Silken grasses supplied them with a soft and even luxurious couch. They needed no clothing. They had but to put forth their hand to pluck the richest fruits from the overhanging boughs. The river supplied them with any amount, and a large variety, of fish.

But when we contemplate these people in the light of civilized life, their poverty was extreme.

* "First Voyage of Columbus," as given by the Hakluyt Society, p. 4.

The hut they dwelt in, and all its furniture, was worth scarcely the smallest coin of Spanish currency. Columbus ordered that not an article in or around the huts should be taken away. With a boat's crew he commenced ascending the serpentine and placid river. Exclamations of delight were continually bursting from his lips.

" Cuba!" he wrote in his journal; " it is the most beautiful island eyes ever beheld. One would live there forever."

As the boat, propelled by the oars of the seamen, ascended the river, vistas of ever-increasing loveliness were opening before them. The banks were covered with the gigantic trees of the tropics, while flowering shrubs, scattered profusely here and there, gave an Eden-like bloom to nature's fairy garden. There were several villages upon the banks of the river, but the inhabitants, upon the approach of the boat, fled to the mountains. Columbus writes that the houses were more substantial than those which he had before seen. The villages were not laid out in regular streets, but the houses were scattered picturesquely through the groves, like the tents in a military camp. They were neatly built of palm leaves, and were remarkably clean and orderly in the interior.

Returning to his ship, the sails were again spread,

and the voyage was resumed along the coast toward the west. Columbus was still deceived by the thought that he was on the shores of India, and that he was not far from the main land of that vast continent, then so renowned for its opulence and for its vast population. As cape extended beyond cape, and headland beyond headland, far away in the distance, Columbus was continually straining his eyes, in search of the domes and pinnacles of some oriental city. He supposed that Cuba was the far-famed island of Japan. But as he coasted along the shore for three days, and found no termination to the island, he came to the conclusion that he must have already reached the main land of India.

They arrived at length at a very imposing headland, densely covered with palm trees, to which Columbus gave the name of the Cape of Palms. It is supposed that this is the headland which forms the eastern entrance to what is now called the Laguna de Moron.

Columbus now invited the two Pinzons into his cabin, to confer respecting their future course. The three concurred in the opinion that Cuba was not an island, but the main land, extending indefinitely far away to the north. This led Columbus to the opinion that, being upon the main land of Asia, he could not be very far from the renowned realm of Cathay. From the language of the natives, he inferred that there was a great capital on a vast river, not very many leagues to the north. He strug- gled along for a few days against contrary winds, when, finding that the interminable coast was still extend- ing before him, and the weather threatening a storm, he turned back, and cast anchor in the mouth of a little river, which he called Rio de los Maries.

It was now the 1st of November. There was a small cluster of houses on the bank, beneath a grove of cocoa and palms. With the sunrise a boat was sent on shore. The inhabitants fled in terror. Again, in the afternoon, Columbus made an attempt to open communication with the group of trembling natives gathered upon the beach. There were three Indians on board the *St. Mary*, from San Salvador. Columbus sent one of them, in a boat, to assure the natives of his peaceable intentions.

As soon as the Indian arrived within hailing dis- tance of the group, he shouted out to them words of friendship. It would seem that they understood his language. He plunged into the sea and swam ashore, thus placing himself, utterly helpless, in their power. They received him kindly, listened to his words, and he succeeded so effectually in allaying their fears that before nightfall sixteen canoes, filled with the natives, were clustered around the ships.

They brought cotton yarn to sell ; but Columbus looked in vain for gold. Not even the smallest golden trinket was to be seen. One man had a small piece of wrought silver, hung as an ornament from his nose.

Columbus understood these Indians to say that the metropolis of their sovereign was in the interior, at the distance of about four days' journey. He therefore decided to send an expedition, escorting two ambassadors to the royal court. Of these men, whose names were Rodrigo de Jerez and Luis de Torres, the latter was a converted Jew, who was somewhat familiar with the Hebrew, Chaldaic, and Arabic languages. Columbus thought it not improbable that the Oriental prince might be familiar with one at least of these tongues.

Two Indians were sent with this delegation, as guides. One of these was from San Salvador; the other was from the little hamlet on the banks of Rio de Los Maries. The ambassadors were well supplied with trinkets, to defray their expenses by the way, and with more valuable articles, as gifts for the sovereign. They were also furnished with a letter, expressive of the desire of the King and Queen of Spain to enter into friendly relations with the governments of the East. The ambassadors were instructed to gain all the information in their power, respecting the country through which they were to pass, and its inhabitants. Six days were allowed for the journey.

While waiting for the return of the embassy, Columbus was busily employed in repairing his ships, and sending out exploring parties into the region around. He himself took a boat, and was rowed up the river about six miles. Here he landed, and climbed a bluff which gave him quite a commanding view of the prospect around. Nothing, however, was to be seen, as far as the eye could extend, but a dense mass of the most wild and luxuriant foliage. He sought in vain for those spices and drugs which were deemed of great value in the marts of Europe. Occasionally he met with the natives, and exhibiting to them pearls and gold, inquired where such could be found. But the replies he received, by words and signs, were only bewildering. The natives seemed to describe nations, whose people had but one eye, others who had the heads of dogs, others who were cannibals, cutting the throats of their victims, and sucking their blood.*

Great as was the disappointment of Co'umbus in failing to obtain gold, he could not refrain from constant exclamations of delight in view of the charming scenery which surrounded him. It is said that,

* "First Voyage of Columbus," as given by Navarette.

during this short tour up one of the most beautiful rivers of Cuba, he saw the natives one day baking in the ashes a small bulbous root about the size of an apple. They used it as food. It was mealy, and very palatable, and was called by them, *batatas*. This bulb has since become an indispensable article of food throughout the whole civilized world. The discovery of the potato, of which Columbus thought nothing, has proved of more value to the human family, than if he had discovered a mountain of solid gold.

On the 6th of November, the ambassadors returned. All crowded eagerly around them, to listen to the story of their adventures. The narrative was not very encouraging. After travelling about thirty miles, through a forest path, they came to a little hamlet, of about fifty huts, similar to those they had already seen, but a little larger. They probably greatly overestimated the population of the village, in judging it to amount to a thousand souls, which would be twenty for each hut. The natives received them kindly, seated them upon blocks of wood fantastically carved, and regaled them with fruits and vegetables.

The learned Jew tried all his languages upon them, but in vain. Their Indian interpreter attempted a speech. How far it was understood cannot be known; but at its close, the natives gathered around the white men, with renewed manifestations of astonishment and almost adoration.   They examined their clothes, passed their hands over their skin, and seemed to regard them in all respects as superior beings.   All the natives they had met with before, were apparently upon an equality.   Here, for the first time, they saw indications of a diversity of rank. There was one among them, who was recognized as a chieftain of some authority.   But there was no gold here; there were even no rich spices to be found. The envoys decided that it was in vain to push their explorations any further.   They therefore returned to the ships.

According to their representation the whole population of the village wished to accompany them. This honor they declined, but took with them one of the principal men and his son.

"On their way back," Mr. Irving writes, "they, for the first time, witnessed the use of a weed, which the ingenious caprice of man has since converted into a universal luxury, in defiance of the opposition of the senses.   They beheld several of the natives going about with fire-brands in their hands, and certain dried herbs which they rolled up in a leaf, and lighting one end, put the other in their mouths and continued inhaling and puffing out the smoke.   A roll of this kind they called ' a tobacco,' a name since transferred to the plant of which the rolls were made. The Spaniards, though prepared to meet with wonders, were struck with astonishment at this singular and apparently nauseous indulgence." *

The envoys gave a glowing account of the beauty and fertility of the region they had traversed, and of the friendliness of the people. The inhabitants were very social, and seemed to be harmonious and happy in their intercourse with each other. Their villages consisted of a few houses clustered together, each with a well-cultivated garden of Indian corn, potatoes, and other vegetables. There were also considerable fields of cotton. This they twisted into cord, of which they made nets and very tasteful hammocks.

The luxuriant groves were filled with birds, many of brilliant plumage; and water-fowl, in great variety, floated upon the lakelets. But no tidings could be gained of any inland city, or of any precious metals. Columbus was greatly disappointed, though he seemed to be travelling through an enchanted region, full of fairy beauty and novelty.

It cannot be denied that Columbus was a visionary man; and his enthusiasm led him to believe, upon very feeble evidence, whatever he wished to believe.

* Irving's " Columbus," vol. i. p. 195.

He understood the Indians, with whom he was tarrying, during the absence of the envoys, to inform him that, far away to the eastward, there was a very populous island, a district where the people found, by torch-light, gold on the river banks, and that with hammers they wrought it into bars. The tropical summer was rapidly passing, and the winter season, with often chilly nights, was approaching. In southern Spain, Columbus was accustomed to seasons almost as mild as those of Cuba. Thus far he had found no place which suited his views of establishing a colony. He had no thought of founding merely an agricultural settlement, but wished to find some populous and opulent region, where he could establish lucrative commercial relations, and freight his ships with oriental merchandise, which would enrich himself and his patrons, and which would astonish his countrymen.

But thus far, he had met with but naked savages, living in frail huts of the most primitive simplicity, and, with the exception of here and there a small bit of gold as an ornament, the most valuable commodity he had found, to take back to Spain, was a limited quantity of coarse cotton yarn.

Columbus gave the name of Mares to the river where he had cast anchor. From that place he took with him several natives, choice specimens of beauty

5

and intellectual brightness, to convey to Spain, that he might teach them the Spanish language, and that they might serve as interpreters in future voyages. We know not whether they consented to this, or were kidnapped. He selected young men of fine proportions, and beautiful girls. The amiability and docility of the natives led Columbus to believe that they could easily be converted to the Christian faith.

Peter Martyr gives the following account of the manners and customs of the inhabitants of Cuba.

" It is certain the land, among these people, is as common a possession as the sunlight and the water. The words ' mine and thine,' the seeds of all misery, have no place with them. They are content with so little that, in so large a country, they have rather superfluity than scarceness; so that they seem to live in a golden world, without toil. Their gardens are open, not intrenched with dikes, divided with hedges, or defended with walls. They deal fairly one with another, without laws, without books, and without judges." *

It is manifest that this description must be received with some grains of allowance. The inhabitants of the new world were found with murderous weapons of war in their hands. Many of them bore marks of severe wounds, received on the battle-field.

* Peter Martyr, decade 1, book 3.

And they gave vivid accounts of marauding bands, desolating islands with robbery and death. We do nowhere find angelic society among the fallen sons of men.*

* " There are some apparent contradictions in the scenes which Columbus describes. These diverse statements are sometimes doubtless to be referred to the different localities visited. But this does not fully explain the discrepancy. In one case he says that, ' They neither carried arms nor understood such things. Their darts were without iron, but some were pointed with a fish's tooth.' It is true that these darts might have been used simply for hunting or fishing."—*Life of Columbus*, by Arthur Helps, p. 100.

CHAPTER V.

Romantic Adventures.

SO far as it was possible to ascertain the religious
views of the natives, it seems that they had a vague
belief in the immortality of the soul. They imagined
that, after death, the spirit of man went to the dense
forests and craggy mountains, and that, immured in
caves, it was supernaturally fed. The echoes, often
heard from the mountain cliffs, they supposed to be
the answering voices of departed souls.

On the 12th of November, 1492, Columbus turned
his course to the south-east, retracing his passage
along the coast of the island. It is supposed that
Columbus had sailed a distance of nearly two-thirds
the length of Cuba. A few more days' sail would

have brought him to the western extremity, and would thus have disabused him of the idea that he had reached the continent.

For two or three days he skirted the coast, without making any delay to explore the interior. A gale of wind rendered it necessary for him to run into a harbor, to which he gave the name of Puerto del Principe. Here, as usual, he erected a cross, and took formal possession of the country in the name of his sovereigns. There were many small and very beautiful islands in the vicinity, which he explored in his boats, and which subsequently became known by the poetical name of El Jardin del Roy, or the Garden of the King. To the gulf or bay, which these islands adorned, he gave the name of Nuestra Senora. Dense forests covered these picturesque mounds, emerging from the ocean. The intricate channels and solitary coves of this lovely region in after years became infested with pirates, who inflicted woes upon humanity which demons might blush to perpetrate.

On the 19th of November, Columbus again spread his sails, designing to reach an island about sixty miles to the eastward, to which the natives gave the name of Babique. In his frail little vessel he struggled for twenty-four hours against adverse winds and a rough sea. It would seem as though, through some evil destiny, man is doomed ever, in whatever enterprise, to contend with difficulties, disappoint-ments, and innumerable adverse influences.

Martin Alonzo Pinzon, commander of the *Pinta*, was a man of wealth, and an experienced seaman. He had furnished large funds for the enterprise, and was not disposed to look upon Columbus as, in any respect, his superior. The admiral was a man of kingly bearing and assumption. It is probable that, for some time, antagonistic views had been rising between them. Columbus put about ship, to return to the harbor, and signalled to the other vessels to do the same. Pinzon paid no heed to the signal. Abandoning the two other ships, he apparently de-cided to enter upon a cruise on his own account. When the morning of the 21st dawned, the *Pinta* was nowhere to be seen.*

Columbus was greatly disgusted. He feared that it was Pinzon's intention to hasten back to Spain, with the tidings of the great discovery, and to enjoy

* In reference to this desertion, Mr. Goodrich, who loses no op-portunity to assail Columbus, writes, " Many authors can hardly find sufficient vent for their indignation at what they term this desertion on the part of Pinzon. But the latter, who had been one of the chief pro-moters of the scheme, can hardly have been expected to take no other part in the exploration save that of following Columbus, to whom he certainly owed nothing, but who may be said to have owed him everything, in the accomplishment of his enterprise."—*Life of Co-lumbus*, by Aaron Goodrich, p. 203,

the triumph which the announcement of so glorious
an event would surely give him. To pursue the
fugitive was useless. Agitated and, desponding the
admiral returned to Cuba. On the 24th of November he ran into a fine harbor, which he called St.
Catherine. It was near the mouth of a river, whose
banks were fringed with green meadows of surpass-
ing loveliness, interspersed with groves of pines and
oaks of majestic growth.

He then continued cruising along the coast of
Cuba, to the eastward, with scenes of beauty opening before him, which elicited continued exclamations of rapture. The serene skies, the salubrious
atmosphere in mid-winter, the rivers of crystal purity,
the harbors as rich in landscape beauty as they were
valuable in the security they offered, the luxuriant
foliage, the fruit, the flowers, the bird songs, the
amiability of the men, the loveliness of the women,
elicited rapturous expressions of delight from his
pen. In one of the harbors, which he called Puerto
Santo, he wrote, in a letter to the Sovereigns.

" The beauty of this river, and the crystal clear-
ness of the water, through which the sand at the
bottom may be seen ; the multitude of palm-trees of
various forms, the highest and most beautiful that I
have met with, and an infinity of other great and
green trees; the birds, in rich plumage, and the ver-

dure of the fields, render this country, most serene princes, of such marvellous beauty, that it surpasses all others in charms and graces, as the day doth the night in lustre. For which reason I often say to my people that, much as I endeavor to give a complete account of it to your majesties, my tongue cannot express the whole truth, nor my pen describe it. And I have been so overwhelmed at the sight of so much beauty, that I have not known how to relate it."

Some of these trees were of such enormous magnitude that the natives would dig out, from a single tree, a canoe of sufficient size to carry one hundred men. Sailing slowly along, Columbus reached the extreme eastern end of the island on the 5th of December. As he regarded this as the most easterly cape of the continent of Asia, and consequently the first point of the main land to be reached in coming from Europe, he named the cape Alpha and Omega, the beginning and the end.

Columbus was in much perplexity as to the course he should pursue. The Indians gave marvellous accounts of Barbique, and, guided by their directions, he sailed from the end of Cuba toward the east, when he discovered, in a south-easterly direction, high mountains towering above the horizon. But when the Indians on board his ship saw him sailing toward it, they thought it the island of the Caribs, and were terrified They implored him not to go, assuring him that the inhabitants were ferocious and cruel in the extreme ; that they killed and devoured all their prisoners. This proves conclusively that these islanders partook of the common characteristics of fallen humanity, and that sin, with woe as the consequence of sin, had reached their shores.*

The atmosphere of the tropics is so wonderfully pure, that objects at a great distance can be seen with wonderful distinctness. Columbus was approaching the beautiful and magnificent island of Hayti. God has created this island one of the most lovely spots of our planet. Man has converted it into as gloomy a theatre of crime and woe as can be found anywhere on the surface of our globe. The towering eminences pierced the clouds. Their sides were covered with luxuriant forests. From the base of the mountains verdant plains and valleys, with groves of fruit trees and parterres of flowers, swept down to the ocean. Columns of smoke,

* The island inhabited by the renowned Caribs was the one now known as Porto Rico. Columbus writes : "A people dwell there, who are considered, by the neighboring islanders, as most ferocious. They feed on human flesh. They have many kinds of canoes, in which they cross to all the surrounding islands, and rob and plunder wherever they can. They use bows and javelins of cane ; with sharp-ened spear-points on the thickest end. By the other Indians they are regarded with unbounded fear."—*Select Letters of Christopher Colum-bus*, p. 14.

5*

ascending through the foliage, gave evidence that
the region was crowded with inhabitants. It was
subsequently ascertained that the island was about
four hundred miles in length, and, at its centre, one
hundred and fifty miles in breadth. It contained
nearly thirty thousand square miles, being about the
size of the State of Maine. Nearly the whole of this
imperial island was recently offered our country as a
free gift. But Congress rejected the offer.

In the evening of December 6th, Columbus
entered a harbor, near the western end of the island,
to which he gave the name of St. Nicholas. It is so
called still. The region was of Eden-like beauty.
There were majestic groves, and trees loaded with
fruit. On one side a green and luxuriant plain
extended into the interior, through which a river of
pure water meandered, flowing down from the mountains. There were many canoes upon the shore,
and picturesque villages were discerned on the smooth
sward beneath the shade of the trees. But the
natives, as if conscious that the greatest foe they had
to dread on earth was their fellow-man, had all fled.

Leaving this harbor, without gaining access to
the people, they slowly coasted along the shore
toward the east, gazing with delight upon the mountains and the sweeping plains. One of the deep and
broad valleys which opened before them, appeared

to be in a high state of cultivation. They entered
a fine harbor, which Columbus named Port Concepcion, but which is now known by the name of the
Bay of Moustique. Here another beautiful river
meandered through the garden-like region. The
waters of the bay and of the river were swarming
with fish of great variety. They took large numbers
with their nets. Some were found almost precisely
like those in Spain. There was one bird whose
warbling, strongly resembling that of the nightingale,
reminded them of the groves of their native Andalusia. These incidents led Columbus to call the island
Hispaniola, or Little Spain. The French subsequently called it St. Domingo.*

A detachment of six men, well armed, accompanied by Indian interpreters, was sent into the interior
to open, if possible, some communication with the
natives. They found houses, villages, and gardens;
but not an Indian could be seen. The affrighted

* Columbus, in his letter to the court, says: "Hispaniola is greater than all Spain, from Catalonia to Fontarabia. One of its four sides
I coasted, in a direct line from west to east, 540 miles. There is one
large town, of which I took possession, in a remarkably favorable spot.
I ordered a fortress to be built there, in which I left as many men as
I thought necessary; and engaged the favor of the king in their behalf,
to a degree which would hardly be thought credible. The people are
so amiable and friendly, that even the king took a pride in calling me
his brother."—See *Select Letters of Columbus*, issued by the Hakluyt Society, p. 13, slightly abridged.

natives had fled to the inaccessible cliffs of the mountains.

On the 12th of December Columbus erected a cross, and took possession of the island with as imposing religious rites as the occasion could afford.

During the tarry in this harbor, some of the sailors, who were rambling about, fell in with a small party of islanders, who fled like deer. The sailors pursued. Seeing a beautiful young girl, of about eighteen years and graceful as a fawn, but who was unable to keep pace with the more athletic runners, they united in the chase, and succeeded in capturing her. With great exultation they brought their fascinating prize to the ships.

Columbus received the maiden with parental kindness. He loaded her with presents, and decorated her person with the little tinkling hawk's bells, which had for the natives an indescribable charm. There were several native women on board the admiral's ship. They soon, with their assurances, restored peace to the mind of the young captive. In an hour she appeared to be entirely at home, and was so well pleased with her reception that she was quite indisposed to return to the shore.

The only ornament which this beautiful Indian girl wore, when taken, was a ring of pure gold, suspended from the nose. Columbus was quite excited

by the sight of the precious metal. It was strong
evidence that gold could be found upon the island.
The admiral clothed the maiden with some of the
robes of civilization, and sent her on shore, with
friendly messages to her countrymen. Several of
the crew accompanied her, and three Indian interpreters. Her village was far inland. The sailors, not
deeming it safe to wander among savages, who were
reputed to be ferocious and hostile in the extreme,
returned to the ship. The happy girl was left to
repair to her friends alone.

The admiral, confident that her report would
awaken only a friendly feeling among the natives,
sent, the next morning, a well-armed party of nine
men, with a Cuban interpreter, to follow the trail,
through the luxuriant tropical wilderness, to the
native village. At the distance of about twelve
miles they found quite a large cluster of huts, picturesquely situated on the banks of a beautiful river.
Navarette says that this village was subsequently
called Gros Morne, and that it was situated on the
banks of a stream which the French called Trois
Rivières, and which empties itself near the Port
de Paix.

The envoys counted a thousand houses. But
not a solitary villager could be found. They had
evidently regarded the maiden as a decoy, which

wily and wicked men had used, to lure the natives into their power. The Cuban interpreter followed after the fugitives. When they saw him approaching alone, they advanced to meet him. It would appear that, on all the islands, essentially the same language was spoken. The Cuban gave the terrified natives such an account of the strangers, that some of the more courageous of them, about two thousand in number, slowly ventured back. They advanced, however, with trembling and·hesitating steps. Las Casas says that they were exceedingly graceful in form, and of fairer complexion, and more delicately moulded features, than any of the natives they had thus far seen.

Confidence was gradually established. Still the natives, it is said, regarded the strangers as celestial beings, invested with supernatural powers. They were, in their view, armed with thunder and light-ning. Thus the whole multitude of two thousand trembled in the presence of nine celestial visitants. Frequently they would bow low to the ground, pla-cing their hands upon their heads in token of rev-erence and submission.

While enjoying this friendly interview, another group of Indians appeared approaching. They brought, upon their shoulders, the beautiful captive, decorated with European robes, and with the glitter·

ing trinkets she had received, more dazzling, in their
eyes, than the most precious pearls and gems which
ever adorned the brow of a duchess.   The Indians
conducted the strangers into their houses, and feasted
them with their choicest viands.   Freely they offered
their guests, as presents, everything they possessed;
tame parrots, fruits, flowers, and richly woven mats
and hammocks.

The Spaniards returned to their ships, enchanted
with the beauty of the country they had traversed,
and with the hospitality of the inhabitants.   But
alas! there was no gold.   It is evident that Columbus and his followers were, at that time, in a mood
of mind which led them not to see any dark side to
the picture.   One may truthfully describe a lovely
June morning, and forget that November glooms
and chills may succeed, when storms may howl,
which shall wreck both earth and sky.   Columbus, in
a letter addressed to Louis de St. Angel, writes:

"True it is that after they felt confidence and
lost their fear of us, they were so liberal with what
they possessed that it would not be believed by
those who had not seen it.   If anything was asked
of them, they never said No; but rather gave it cheerfully, and showed as much amity as if they gave their
very hearts.   And whether the thing were of great
value or of little price, they were content with what-

ever was given in return. In all these islands it
appears that the men are contented with one wife;
but they give twenty to their chieftain or king.
The women seem to work more than the men, and
I have not been able to learn whether they possess
individual property; but I rather think that whatever one has, all the rest share."

The work to be done must have been exceedingly small. There were no clothes to be made or
washed; no carpets to be swept or dusted; no china
to be cared for; no fires to be built, save for very
simple cooking; the fruit hanging, upon every bough,
furnished ample food.

Peter Martyr gives an account of the primitive
simplicity of these people, which he says he obtained
from conversation with Columbus himself. The
description he presents of the scenes witnessed in
Hayti are hardly surpassed by that which the
Apostle John gives as he beheld, in vision, the realms
of the blessed. As Columbus continued his explora
tions, he discovered the island of Tortugas, which, in
subsequent years, obtained unenviable notoriety as
the head-quarters of the buccaneers, who for so long
a time infested those seas. He landed and made
a short excursion into the country.

Here again the natives fled the approach of their
brother man, as they would that of the most raven-

ous beasts of prey. Their alarm fires were seen at night, blazing along the heights, to announce to those at a distance the approach of danger. To one lovely plain, which opened before the eye of Columbus, he gave the name of the Vale of Paradise. On the 16th of December, at midnight, Columbus left Tortugas to return to Hispaniola. He met, far out at sea, an exceedingly frail canoe, navigated by a single Indian. The wind was high, and the sea rough. It seemed impossible that the boat could be kept above water. Columbus took the man and his canoe on board. Upon reaching Hispaniola, he anchored in the Port de Paix. He then sent the man ashore, having feasted him and loaded him with presents.

As was invariably the case, this kindness won kindness in return. The report he carried to the Indians dispelled their fears, and soon friendly intercourse took place. One of the most illustrious chieftains, with his retinue, visited the ship. He was a courteous man, of dignified demeanor. Some of his retinue had small ornaments of gold. They did not seem to attach any special value to the metal, but readily exchanged it for the merest trifle.

The more Columbus explored this island, the more was he charmed with its beauty. Its lovely and luxuriant valleys were well watered, and many of the most lofty eminences could be ploughed, with oxen, to their summits. One day a young chief from the interior visited him, with quite an imposing display. He was borne upon the shoulders of four stout men, in a highly decorated palanquin. A cortege of two · hundred natives composed his train. The young man, entirely unembarrassed, and perfectly familiar with the etiquette of his court, entered the tent where the admiral was dining, and took his seat by his side. Two venerable men accompanied him, and seated themselves at his feet. His two attendants seemed to regard him with religious devotion.

They watched every movement. They seized every word, as uttered from his lips, and eagerly endeavored to convey the meaning to the admiral. The prince ate very sparingly, but was careful to see that his attendants were all provided for. After dinner he presented Columbus with a beautiful belt, very curiously wrought, and two pieces of gold. In return he received a piece of cloth, some brilliant beads, and a few other trinkets. Columbus also dazzled his eyes with an exhibition of gold coin, containing the effigies of Ferdinand and Isabella; with silken banners embroidered in gold, and also with the Standard of the Cross. He very earnestly endeavored to convey some idea of the great atoning sacrifice, when God, manifest in the flesh, suffered on the cross for the sins of man. A salute was fired from the ships, in honor of the cacique, and he took his leave, departing in the same state in which he had come.

Though the natives readily gave away whatever gold they had about their persons, but little was obtained. Again, on the 19th of December, Columbus spread his sails, and running along the coast for about thirty-six hours, entered a fine harbor, which he called St. Thomas, but which is supposed to have been that which is now known as the Bay of Acul. The region was thickly populated. The inhabitants had probably heard of the arrival of the strangers, and of their friendly disposition. They manifested no fear, but came off to the two ships in crowds, some in canoes and some swimming. They brought fruits, rich in fragrance and flavor, which they gave away with great generosity. They also readily gave away their golden ornaments, seeming to have no idea of traffic, which constitutes so important a part of civilized life.

Columbus refused to take advantage of this wonderful liberality, and issued strict orders that, in every case, some equivalent should be paid in return. They anchored in this harbor on the evening of the 20th. As the sun was rising on the morning of the

22d, an imperial canoe was seen in the distance,
rapidly driven by the oars over the tranquil sea. It
was of immense capacity, and contained the ambassador of a sovereign chief, with a large retinue. It
was a beautiful spectacle, as the canoe, with its lofty
crest and waving plumes, glided over the placid
waters of the bay.

The name of this chief was Guacanagari. He
was the acknowledged sovereign of all that part of
the island. One of the most distinguished members
of his court was sent on this mission to Columbus,
bearing a present to the admiral, consisting of a belt
of ingenious workmanship, embroidered with beads
and ivory, and also a neatly sculptured head, with
the eyes, nose, and tongue of solid gold. The ambassador delivered a message from his prince, inviting the admiral to visit his residence, with the ships.

Contrary winds prevented the immediate accept-
ance of this invitation. Columbus therefore sent a
boat's crew, with one of his officers, to announce his
intended arrival. The king resided in a pleasant
town, on the banks of a river which flowed through
an exceedingly fertile valley. It was the largest and
best built town they had yet seen. The buildings
surrounded a public square, which had been swept
and decorated, in their best style, for the important
occasion. From all the region around, the popula-

tion was crowding toward the royal village. The hospitality with which the officer and the sailors were entertained, surpassed everything ever known in civilized lands. All were received as honored guests, and were literally offered everything the natives possessed, without money and without price. Whatever was given to the natives, they accepted with gratitude, and treasured up as a sacred relic. The Spaniards called the river Punta Santa. It has since been known as Grande Rivière.

In the evening of this eventful day, the boat returned to the ships. The wind proved favorable on the morning of the 24th, and before sunrise the sails were again spread. Toward evening the wind died away into a perfect calm. Columbus, who was one of the most watchful and careful of navigators, often spending the whole night upon deck, feeling perfectly secure, retired to rest. The man at the helm, unfaithfully followed his example, and, placing the helm in the hands of a mere boy, fell asleep. The rest of the sailors were also soon slumbering.*

* Columbus, in the. following terms, alludes to this shipwreck: "On the 24th of December, while lying off the coast of Hispaniola, it pleased the Lord, seeing me gone to bed, and we being in a dead calm, and the sea as still as water in a dish, that all the men went to bed, leaving the helm with a boy. Thus it came to pass that the current easily carried away the ship upon one of those shoals which, though it was night, made such a roaring noise that it might be heard a league off."—*Letter of Columbus.*

A strong current, which had not been perceived, swept the vessel upon a sand-bank. The boy probably fell asleep also; for, though the breakers struck the bank with a noise which could be heard at a great distance, he gave no alarm until the keel grated upon the sand. Columbus, who ever slept, as it is said, with one eye open, was the first upon deck. A scene of great confusion ensued. To lose the ship in those distant seas would be an irreparable disaster. The sailors lost all self-possession. Every effort to save the vessel was in vain. Had the sea been rough, probably all would have perished. As it was, the breakers opened the seams, the vessel soon filled, and Columbus, with his crew, was compelled to take refuge on board the caravel, *Nina*, which was the smallest vessel of the three.*

A delegation was sent on shore to inform the friendly chief Guacanagari of the disaster. The village of the chief was about a mile and a half from the scene of the shipwreck. The sympathy of this kind-hearted man was such, that he even wept over their

* Mr. Goodrich comments upon the shipwreck in the following terms: "The sheer carelessness and incapacity of Columbus, in thus losing his vessel in a dead calm, are fully demonstrated. We do not wonder he had need of the skill and superior knowledge of Martin Alonzo Pinzon. We are first told that the current carried the ship to the shoal; then, that the sea was ebbing so that the ship could not move. Thus did the elements combine and change, at his will, that he might appear blameless in the disaster."—*Life of Columbus*, p. 207.

misfortune. He sent all his people, with every canoe which could be mustered, large and small, to aid in unloading the vessel. The cacique himself, and his brother, worked diligently, both on the sea and on the land. So valuable was this assistance, that nearly all the contents of the vessel were saved. Neither the chief nor any of his men asked anything for their labors. Instead of this, the chief invited all to his village that he might feed and shelter them. A large number of canoes came from a distance, bearing crowds of natives, with subordinate chiefs. A wonderful scene of fraternal kindness was presented. Though treasures of inestimable value to the natives were accumulated on the shore, not an article was pilfered or lost.* The countenances and gestures of the people indicated heart-felt sorrow for the calamity which had befallen the strangers. Columbus, in his journal, writes to Ferdinand and Isabella:

"So loving, so tractable, so peaceful are this people, that I declare to your majesties there is not, in the world, a better nation nor a better land. They love their neighbors as themselves. And their dis-

* "Guacanagari was very careful that nothing should be lost. He himself stood guard over the things which were taken out of the ship. He put all the effects under shelter, and placed guards around them. The wrecker's trade might flourish in Cornwall; but, like other crimes of civilization, it was unknown in St. Domingo."—*Life of Columbus*, by Arthur Helps, p. 108.

course is ever sweet and gentle. And though it is true that they are naked, yet their manners are decorous and praiseworthy."

Columbus and all his remaining men were now assembled on board the single caravel, *Nina*. Guacanagari had given three houses, as a temporary shelter for the rescued goods and for such of the Spaniards as remained on shore. Seeing the eagerness with which the strangers sought ornaments of gold, he exerted himself to have all presented to them which could be obtained. The natives were exceedingly fond of dancing. Their childish delight was almost inexpressible, when, having attached the glittering and tinkling hawk's bells to their persons, they listened to the musical tones which responded to their movements. Very considerable quantities of gold were brought, in these small trinkets. Any amount which one had would be gratefully exchanged for a hawk's bell.

The admiral was invited to dine with Guacanagari. He was deeply impressed with the unaffected dignity and refinement which the chief manifested on this occasion. The entertainment abounded with every luxury the island could afford. The king ate slowly and with moderation, like one accustomed to the usages of good society. The attendants served the prince and his guest with great politeness. The sovereignty on the island was hereditary; and the people seemed to be deeply impressed with the dignity of illustrious birth.

After dinner the chief conducted Columbus to the lovely groves which surrounded his truly beautiful home. A thousand of the natives, respectfully, and with every mark of affectionate interest, attended them. It did indeed appear like a scene in Eden. Though all were entirely naked, there was not the slightest sign of any indecorum. Several very interesting games were performed, by direction of the chief, to amuse his guest, who was evidently much oppressed by anxiety.

Columbus endeavored to requite these attentions by the exhibition of a military parade. There was a Castilian on board, a veteran soldier, who could rival William Tell in the accuracy with which he could throw an arrow. These natives were men of peace. They lived upon fruit. They had neither cultivated the arts of war nor of the chase. The Castilian brought to the entertainment his Moorish bow, and quiver of arrows. The chief was astounded in witnessing the force and accuracy with which the steel-pointed and deadly weapon could be thrown.

Columbus informed the chief that he had weapons of far more terrible power. He ordered a large

6

cannon to be discharged, directing the ball against a tree at some distance. When they saw the lightning flash, and heard the thunder peal, and perceived the path of the invisible bolt through the forest, crashing and rending the trees, their consternation threw them prostrate upon the ground. When they had, in some degree, recovered from the shock, Columbus arrayed all his available force for a military display. His men were marshalled, in burnished armor, and with keen-edged, polished swords, which glittered in the rays of the setting sun. They wheeled to and fro, keeping time to the music of the trumpet and the drum; they performed manœuvres as beautiful as they were intricate. With loud yells they rushed forward in the charge. With unbroken ranks they fell back in the retreat.

The natives clearly understood that these were all arrangements and movements for deadly war. To their mind it was clear that the Spaniards were invested with supernatural powers, for the destruction of men. The thoughtful must have been perplexed to decide whether they were angels or demons. Their power seemed to indicate that they had aid from heaven. But why were they so armed with weapons of destruction, and so skilled in their use? They began to look upon their formidable guests with awe and terror.

Gradually Columbus, saddened by the wreck, regained serenity of mind. He and his men were living in the luxurious enjoyment of a delightful climate
and of delicious fruits. Every day his stores of gold
were increasing. The loving-kindness with which
the Spaniards were treated by the natives could
not well have been exceeded. And to crown all, he
became convinced that there were inexhaustible
mines of gold in the interior of the island.

The Spanish sailors were quite fascinated with
the easy and voluptuous life to which they had been
introduced. They had escaped all the cares and toils
of civilization. Fruit, of delicious flavor and fragrance, hung from almost every bough. The rivers
and the coast abounded with fish. They spent the
day in indolent repose, beneath the shade of the
groves; and in the coolness of the evenings they engaged with the amiable natives in their games, or
danced, now to the music of the drum, and again to
that of the native bands. In view of these scenes
of apparent happiness, so seldom witnessed by the
care-worn sons of Adam, Mr. Irving writes:

" Such was the indolent and holiday life of these
simple people ; which, if it had not the great scope
of enjoyment, nor the high-seasoned poignancy of
pleasure which attends civilization, was certainly destitute of most of its artificial miseries. The venera-

ble Las Cases, speaking of their perfect nakedness, observes, it seemed almost as if they were existing in the state of primeval innocence of our first parents, before their fall brought sin into the world. He might have added, that they seemed exempt likewise from the penalty inflicted on the children of Adam, that they should eat their bread by the sweat of their brow."

Many of these adventurers had no disposition ever to return to the solicitudes and toils of European life. Here they wanted for nothing. Columbus was besieged with applications for permission to remain upon the island. It would indeed be very uncomfortable, for so large a crew as that of both vessels united, to be crowded into one small caravel, for the return voyage. This suggested to the admiral to form the germ of a future colony, on the magnificent and beautiful island of Hispaniola. Leaving a small party behind to explore the island, to search out its sources of wealth, and to obtain all the additional gold in their power, he decided to return to Spain with the tidings of his great discovery, intending to come back with new ships and reinforcements.

Guacanagari had informed him that there were hostile Indians, called Caribs, who occasionally made descents upon Hayti, and carried off many captives.

This furnished an excuse to Columbus for building a fortress. The natives aided him with hearty goodwill. It would afford them a grand protection against the Caribs. He armed the fort with the cannon which had been rescued from the wrecked ship. A small garrison was left, with ammunition and supplies for a year.

No reliable tidings were heard from the *Pinta*. Columbus thought it very probable that she was lost. In that case but one small shattered bark remained, of the three which had sailed from Palos. Should that be lost, the great discovery would remain unknown. Columbus would be remembered only as a wild enthusiast, who had foolishly thrown away his life. He therefore decided no longer to expose his frail craft to the peril of navigating unknown seas, but to return to Spain.

There was no end to the kindness which Guacanagari lavished upon Columbus. While the admiral was superintending the erection of the fortress, the chief assigned to him the largest house in the village. The floor was carpeted with ingeniously woven palm leaves, and furnished with seats of polished jet black wood, resembling ebony. Whenever he received Columbus, in his own residence, he met him with the dignity of a monarch, and invariably hung upon his neck a jewel of gold, or some other valuable present.

At one time the chief visited the admiral, acpanied by five subordinate chiefs. Each one brought a present of a coronet of gold. Guacanagari had a regal crown, wrought of this precious metal. He took it from his own head, and placed it upon the head of his guest. Columbus, in return, hung a string of brilliantly colored beads upon the neck of the sovereign, invested him with his own crimson mantle of finest fabric, gave him a pair of colored boots, and placed upon his finger a silver ring, which the natives prized more highly than gold, as silver was not found upon the island.

Columbus became quite elated with the prospect of obtaining a large quantity of gold. He began to regard his shipwreck as an indication of divine favor. He writes in his journal, describing his anticipations at that time:

"I hoped that, upon my return from Spain, I should find a ton of gold, obtained in traffic by those I had left behind; and also mines and spices discovered in such quantities, that the sovereigns, before three years, would be able to undertake a crusade for the deliverance of the Holy Sepulchre."

Aided by the natives, the fortress, in ten days was erected and its armament placed in position.

Columbus had now such perfect confidence in the natives, that he deemed he had nothing to fear from them. Indeed he considered the fortress mainly necessary to hold his own lawless men in subjection. There was danger otherwise, that they would wander everywhere over the island, committing acts of licentiousness which might exasperate the inhabitants. He named the fortress The Nativity, in grateful commemoration of the fact that he had escaped from shipwreck on Christmas day.

Thirty-nine men were carefully selected to remain in the garrison.* These included a physician, and several mechanics skilful in their various callings. The command was intrusted to Diego de Arana. He was a cavalier, from Cordova, of eminent rank and of commanding powers. A strong boat was left to aid in fishing; seeds for the culture of the ground, and an abundant supply of articles for traffic with the natives.

The hour for the departure arrived. Columbus assembled the garrison before him, and, in an earnest address, enjoined upon them the duty to treat with the utmost respect and friendship their illustrious benefactor, Guacanagari, and his chieftains. He

---

* Helps says that they were forty in number, and that among these there were one Irishman and one Englishman.—*Life of Columbus*, p. 110. Other accounts give thirty-seven, thirty-eight, and thirty-nine.

urged upon them to be always gentle and just in their intercourse with the natives; and especially to be circumspect in their treatment of the native wives and daughters. He warned them not to scatter asunder, but to keep together. The commander, Arana, was instructed to make every effort to procure gold, to search for mines, and to make himself acquainted with all the productions of the island.

On the 2d of January, 1493, Columbus gave a parting feast to Guacanagari and his chieftains. The whole crew was brought on shore, and his guests were entertained with military evolutions and sham fights. The Indians gazed with inexpressible amazement and awe upon the long, glittering, keen-edged sword. And when the artillery was discharged, and the balls of stone, which were then used, shivered the trees, the thousands of natives, whom the occasion had assembled, trembled and rejoiced. They trembled in contemplating such tremendous powers of destruction; rejoiced at the thought that they no longer need fear the Caribs.

The next morning the signal gun for setting sail was fired. Responsive cheers rose from the garrison and the departing crew. A fair wind swept the ship beyond the curve of the eastern horizon.

Through storms and perils the *Nina* ploughed its way toward Spain. The garrison was left to a fate hereafter to be described.*

* The capital of Guacanagari was called Guarico. It is where the village of Petit Anse now stands ; about two miles south-east of Cape Haytien. Punta Santa was probably the present Point Picolet. The fort of the Nativity must have been erected near Haut du Cap. The locality of the town of Guacanagari has always been known by the name of Guarico.—*Letter of T. S. Heneken, Esq.*

6*

CHAPTER VI.

The Return Voyage.

The Nina meets the Pinta—Rio de Gracia—A fierce tribe encoun-
tered—The first conflict—Peace established—Life at sea—
Terrific storm—Vows of the Admiral and crew—Distress of Co-
lumbus—The parchment and cask—They reach the Azores
—Troubles at St. Mary's—Continued storms—Enters the Tagus
—Honors at Lisbon—Court intrigues—Reception at Palos—Ex-
citement throughout Spain—Sad fate of Pinzon—Columbus at the
Spanish Court.

ON the 4th of January, 1493, Columbus sailed
from Hayti for Spain. With a gentle breeze he
glided almost beneath the shadow of a lofty and
bald promontory, to which he gave the name of
Monte Christo; and which name it still retains.
Baffled by calms and head winds, they made slow
progress, still creeping along the shore of the island,
whose grandeur and beauty seemed to be increasingly unfolded. They had advanced but about fifty
miles when, on the 6th, the lookout at the mast-
head shouted, "The Pinta, the Pinta."

It was even so. By a singular chance the vessels
had met. Pinzon obeyed the signal of the admiral,
and followed him into a small bay, a little west of

Monte Christo, where both vessels cast anchor.
Pinzon made a lame excuse for his desertion, attribut-
ing it to stress of weather. Columbus, though not
deceived, deemed it politic to accept the apology.
One of the seamen on board the *Pinta* stated that an
Indian had very emphatically declared to the captain
of the *Pinta* that, at the distance of but a few leagues
to the eastward, there was a mine whence immense
amounts of gold could be obtained. The cupidity of
Pnizon was aroused. He thought he could load
his ship speedily, and return to Spain with the precious freight; and that he could defend his conduct
by alleging that he had been separated from Columbus in a storm.

But the mine was sought for in vain. Pinzon
found his vessel entangled in the midst of a number
of small islands and shoals. He became alarmed.
Should his vessel encounter any accident, by which
it became disabled, it was scarcely possible that
he could ever return to Spain. He therefore again
directed his course toward Hispaniola: and it
is probable that he was anxiously looking for the
admiral. He had, however, during the separation,
entered a river where, in a three weeks' sojourn, he
had opened traffic with the natives, and had obtained a considerable quantity of gold. One-half
of this, it was said, he retained for himself, and the

rest he distributed among the sailors to purchase their secrecy.

On the evening of the 9th, the two vessels again set sail in company. The next day they cast anchor in the mouth of the river, where Pinzon had been trading. Columbus named it Rio de Gracia. It is now called Porto Caballo. The natives complained that Pinzon had violently carried off four men and two young girls. Columbus found them on board the *Pinta*. It was evident that Pinzon intended to sell them as slaves in Spain. Columbus ordered their immediate release. He also loaded them with presents, as some recompense for the wrongs which they had endured. Pinzon was greatly offended, and yielded with reluctance and with angry words.*

As they again weighed anchor, a gentle, but favorable wind wafted them along as far as what is now called Cape Cabron. Here they came upon a race of fierce savages. Their warriors were hideously painted like the *braves* of the North American Indians. They were armed with war-clubs, and had bows of great strength. Their arrows were tipped with bone, or with very hard wood, and would penetrate the body with almost the force of a rifle-ball. They had also swords made of exceedingly hard wood, almost as heavy as iron. " They

* Irving's " Columbus," vol. i. p. 246.

were not sharp," writes Las Casas, "but broad, of nearly the thickness of two fingers, and capable, with one blow, of cleaving through a helmet to the very brains." *

These natives did not venture to make any attack upon the Spaniards. On the contrary, one of them went pleasantly on board the ship, and sold bows and arrows. Columbus probably misunderstood him to say, in the obscure language of signs, that there was an island, near by, inhabited exclusively by women. The Caribs occasionally visited them. Of the children that were born, the males were taken from the island, and the females were left with their mothers. Undoubtedly Columbus misunderstood the man. It is hardly to be supposed that the savage had a sufficient spirit of roguery to attempt thus to *hoax* the strangers.

Columbus also understood that there were mermaids, *maids of the sea*, in those waters. He saw some of these animals which they described. They were probably sea-calves. Their heads, when slightly elevated above the waves, somewhat resembled the human face. The admiral treated his intrepid guest with great kindness. He hoped thus to open friendly intercourse with the tribe. But it would appear that the bold savage had gone on board as a

* Las Casas, " Hist. Ind." lib. i. cap. 77. MS.

spy. He was sent on shore, with many presents, in one of the ship's boats.

The moment he landed he gave a whoop, which instantly summoned a war party, from ambush, to his side. They endeavored to capture the boat's crew. Quite a fierce battle ensued. The Spaniards were much better armed than the natives. Having wounded two they put the rest to flight. This was the first contest, between the Europeans and the Indians, in the New World. Would that it had been the last. The conflict, thus commenced, raged, in subsequent years, with increasing violence, until the soil of nearly every island was crimsoned with blood, and the natives were entirely exterminated.

Columbus was much grieved at this misadventure. He feared that it might result in a sanguinary attack upon his garrison by a resistless band of these fierce warriors. The next day a large party of the Indians appeared upon the beach. They made no hostile manifestations, but appeared friendly and confiding. A boat's crew, well armed, was sent on shore with a string of shell beads, which Columbus understood to be, with the Indians, like a flag of truce with civilized nations.

The chief, with trust which seems astonishing under the circumstances, entered the boat, accompanied by three attendants, and was rowed out to the admiral's ship. They were cordially received, and were feasted on the choicest viands which the ship afforded. All the wonders of the ship were exhibited to them, and they were returned to the shore with many gifts, which gathered around them, throngs of admiring natives.. The chief, in polite acknowledgment of these favors, sent to Columbus his crown of gold. It is to be inferred from subsequent narratives, that the name of this chief was Mayonabex, and that his tribe was called the Ciguayans.

Kindness proved successful. Columbus remained in the bay two or three days. Friendly relations continued uninterrupted. The people, though always thoroughly armed, brought freely on board the ships, cotton, and a great variety of vegetables and fruit. There were four intelligent and affectionate young men to whom Columbus became much attached. They voluntarily accompanied him, when he sailed, to some islands which they described as situated a few leagues to the east.

On the 16th of January the ships sailed. The bay they left, now known as the Gulf of Samana, Columbus called the Gulf of Arrows. After sailing about sixty miles, as the ships were approaching Porto Rico, a very favorable breeze sprang up for the homeward voyage. The sailors, as they saw the ships diverging from the route to Spain, to visit the island, began to murmur, and to insist upon a return home. Columbus was conscious that he had no time to lose. His ship was in a leaky condition. The seamen were on the eve of insubordination He could place but little reliance in the good faith of Pinzon. Should shipwreck come, all his records might be buried, with himself, in the ocean; and the knowledge of the great discovery would be lost to the world.

He therefore, to the great joy of the crew, shifted sail and turned his course toward Spain. Probably he encountered but little difficulty in reconciling the four young Indians to this course, as he could prom ise, after showing them all the wonders of the old world, to bring them speedily back to their homes. The winds are proverbially fickle. During all the remainder of January there were light breezes, with occasional calms. The Indians would frequently plunge into the glassy water, and swim like fishes around the ships.

These calms, as ever in human life, were succeeded by storms. Black tempests swept the ocean and the roaring billows threatened to engulf them. It was often necessary for the admiral to slacken sail, that the *Pinta* might keep pace with him. Amidst. clouds and darkness and rushing billows they lost their reckoning. Pinzon and the two pilots differed

from Columbus as to their position. They thought
that the ships were four hundred miles nearer Spain
than Columbus thought them to be. Columbus was
right. Las Casas makes the remarkable statement,
that Columbus allowed them to remain in their
error, and even endeavored to add to their perplexity, that they might have confused views of the voyage, and that he alone might retain a clear knowledge of the route to be pursued.*

We cannot credit this strange statement. Pinzon and the three pilots were veteran seamen.
Having been to the New World and back again, they
could not be ignorant of the route to be pursued.
On the 12th of February, as they were drawing near
the end of their long voyage, a terrific storm arose,
which continued, with increasing violence, for three
days. In this storm the *Pinta* was lost sight of. Columbus had every reason to fear that the frail caravel,
with all it contained, was engulfed in the angry sea.†

After a dreadful night, a dismal morning dawned
lurid and tempestuous. The ocean was lashed into
fury, and nothing was to be seen but the maddened
waves, and nothing to be heard but their threaten-

* Las Casas, " Hist. Ind.," lib. i. cap. 70.

† " Columbus, during this voyage, sought to confuse the pilots in
their reckoning, so that he alone might possess a clear knowledge of
the route ; a proceeding which elicits anything but censure from his
biographers."—*Life of Columbus*, by Aaron Goodrich, p. 211.

ing roar. In accordance with the religion, or superstition, of the times, lots were drawn to see who, if
saved from the tempest, should make a pilgrimage
to the shrine of the Virgin Mary at Gaudaloupe,
bearing a wax taper of five pounds weight. Beans
were placed in a cap, upon one of which a cross was
marked. Columbus was the first to put in his hand.
The lot fell on him. Lots were again cast for a pilgrimage to the shrine of the Virgin, at Loretto. It
fell upon a seaman, by the name of Pedro de Villa.
The admiral promised to bear all the expenses of
his journey.

The Virgin did not seem to pay much heed to
these vows, for the storm continued to rage with
unabated fury. To offer her a still higher reward, if
she would interpose in their behalf, Columbus and all
his crew united in a vow, that wherever they might
first land, where there was a church dedicated to the
Virgin, they would all go to her shrine, in solemn
procession, barefooted and in their shirts only, to
offer her prayers and praises. It is difficult to conceive why the Virgin could take any pleasure in seeing them present themselves before her in costume
so disgraceful, that it would exclude them from every
earthly court.

Still the storm raged and howled. In these
dreadful perils, when Columbus thought far more of

the loss of his great discovery than the loss of his life, his agitated feelings can be best expressed in his own words, addressed to the king.

"I could have supported this evil fortune," he writes, "with less grief, had my person alone been in jeopardy; since I am debtor for my life to the Supreme Creator, and have, at other times, been within a step of death. But it was a cause of infinite sorrow and trouble to think that, after having been illuminated from on high, with faith and certainty to undertake this enterprise; after having victoriously achieved it : and when on the point of convincing my opponents, and securing to your highness great glory and vast increase of dominions, it should please the Divine Majesty to defeat all by my death. It would have been more supportable also, had I not been accompanied by others, who had been drawn on by my persuasions, and who, in their distress, cursed not only the hour of their coming, but the fear inspired by my words, which prevented their turning back, as they had at various times determined.

"Above all, my grief was doubled when I thought of my two sons, whom I had left at school in Cordova, destitute, in a strange land, without any testimony of the service rendered by their father, which, if known, might have inclined your highness to befriend them. And although on the one hand I was comforted by faith that the deity would not permit a work of such great exaltation to his church, wrought through so many troubles and contradictions, to remain imperfect ; yet on the other hand, I reflected on my sins, as a punishment for which he might intend that I should be deprived of the glory which would redound to me in this world."*

In these hours of anxiety, Columbus wrote, on parchment, a brief account of his discovery. This, carefully sealed, was addressed to the king and queen. It was superscribed with the promise of a thousand ducats, about two thousand dollars, to whomsoever should deliver the packet unopened to their majesties. This was wrapped in a waxed envelope, and placed in a cake of wax. The whole was deposited in a strong water-tight cask, and cast into the raging sea. It is not known that this memorial was ever found.†

But gradually the storm abated. A gleam of golden light, in the western sky, indicated, that the fury of the tempest was over. In the night the stars

* "Hist. del Almirante," cap. 36.

† About the year 1852, a paragraph went the rounds of the newspapers, announcing the discovery of this cask on the coast of Africa, by the captain of a barque, called the *Chieftain*, from Boston, Massachusetts. The account was very circumstantial, and was credited by the French historian Lamartine, and many others. But, as it has never since been authenticated, it is now supposed that the story was invented by some ingenious newspaper correspondent.—See Helps' *Life of Columbus*, p. 117, note.

came out in all their brilliance. And in the morning, though tumultuous waves still raged, the sun
rose in a cloudless sky, and a favoring breeze swelled
the sails. Just as the sun was rising, the joyful shout
of "Land" was heard.

It proved, as Columbus supposed, one of the
Azores, and was distant but about fifteen miles.
But a strong head wind arose, which rapidly increased
into another tempest. Thus baffled and driven back,
it was not until the evening of the 17th that he cast
anchor under the shelter of the northern side of St.
Mary's Island, which was the most southern of the
Azores group. The inhabitants were astonished
that two such frail caravels could have survived the
severity of the gales which, for fifteen days, had
swept the ocean with almost unexampled fury.

The devout Columbus reminded the crew of their
vow, to repair, in procession, to the first church dedicated to the Virgin which they could find, wherever
they might land. Faithfully the vow, not strange in
those days, was fulfilled. One-half of the ship's
company went first, with a priest to perform mass.
All were destitute of clothing, save only their shirts.

St. Mary's was a Portuguese island. When the
first procession appeared, in such unseemly guise, all
the rabble of the village was gathered around them.
The governor, surprised at the exhibition, and not

knowing what it signified, headed a squadron of dragoons, and arrested them all. The naked men were in no condition to fight. The chapel was hid from the sight of Columbus by an intervening point of land. But when he ascertained what had taken place, he attributed it to the hostility which the Portuguese court had already manifested toward him and his enterprise.

He had an interview with the governor. Angry words were interchanged. The governor, Castaneda, was not in an amiable mood. Assuming a defiant air, he declared that all he had done was in conformity with the commands of the king. Columbus greatly feared that war had broken out, during his absence, between Spain and Portugal. He armed all his men, and made vigorous preparations to resist any attempt to capture him. A strong wind rose, blowing directly upon the shore. The anchorage was not safe. He was compelled to stand out to sea. For two days he continued beating about, in much peril, with half of his crew arrested.

The weather moderated on the evening of the 22d. Returning to his anchorage, a Portuguese boat came to the ship, bearing two priests and an important officer of government.

This governmental official was much more conciliatory in his demeanor than Casteneda had been.

In the name of the governor he requested a sight of the ship's papers. It seems that the governor had taken them for pirates, with which all seas were then infested. Columbus, still suspicious that he was treacherously pursued, showed his letters of commission. This gave entire satisfaction. The naked pilgrims were then liberated.

Another explanation of this difficulty, but not so plausible, is suggested both by Las Casas, and by Ferdinand, the son of Columbus. It is said that the King of Portugal, jealous of the renown which her great rival Spain, would gain, should Columbus prove successful, had sent orders to all her distant ports that the admiral should be arrested wherever he might be found. Castaneda hoped to surprise Columbus in the chapel. Failing in that, he endeavored to get possession of his person by stratagem. He was prevented from accomplishing this, by the fact that Columbus had armed his crew, and was on his guard. The improbability of this explanation must be obvious to every intelligent reader.*

Matters being thus settled, Columbus, barefooted and bareheaded, led the other half of the crew, in the fulfilment of his vow, to the shrine of Our Lady. No tidings were heard from Pinzon. It was prob-

* "Hist. del Almirante." cap. 39 ; Las Casas, "Hist. Ind.," lib. i. cap. 72.

able that he was lost.   After the delay of about five
days at St. Mary's, Columbus, on the 24th of February, again set sail.   When within about three
hundred miles of Cape St. Vincent, another gale
was encountered.   At length a few murmurs escaped
the lips of the heroic admiral.   He seemed to think
it hard that, after struggling against so many storms,
he should again be assailed so fiercely, when at the
very door of his house.

In the tropical paradise which he had discovered,
scarcely a rude blast had assailed him.   There he
had enjoyed sunny skies, balmy breezes, and an ever-
tranquil sea.   He rode out the storm in safety.
"Whom the Lord loveth He chasteneth."   The
truly good Las Casas suggests that these many
trials were intended to save the illustrious discoverer
from undue pride, in the contemplation of his marvellous achievement.   Thus he might be prevented
from arrogating to himself the glory of a discovery
which was all due to God.   And thus he might be
taught that he was only a humble instrument in the
hand of the Almighty.*

At day-break on the 4th of March, the eyes of
Columbus were cheered by the familiar sight of the
rock of Cintra, just off the mouth of the Tagus, in
Portugal.   Though he had many fears of treachery,

* Las Casas, "Hist. Ind.," lib. i. cap. 73.

COLUMBUS BEFORE THE COMMISSIONERS.

on the part of the Portuguese court, the tempestuous weather compelled him to run into the river for shelter. At three o'clock in the afternoon he reached safe anchorage, opposite the Rastello. The people on the shore had been all the morning watching the frail caravel struggling against the storm. Every moment they had expected to see it engulfed by the huge billows which were assailing it. They crowded on board, congratulating the ship's company upon their miraculous preservation. The most experienced mariners testified that they had never known a winter of such continuous and terrific storms.

Columbus immediately sent a courier to the Spanish court, to announce his arrival. He also wrote to the Portuguese court, soliciting permission to enter the port of Lisbon. There was a large Portuguese man-of-war at anchor in the roadstead. It was stationed there, on guard. The next day, the Portuguese captain summoned the Spanish admiral on board his ship. Columbus stood upon his dignity, asserted his rights, and refused either to go himself or to send any one in his stead. As soon as the captain, Don Alonzo de Acuna, learned the rank of Columbus, and the extraordinary voyage he had made, he treated him with all the homage with which one brave man could regard another. He manned his largest boat, decorated it with banners,

7

placed on board his well-trained musical band, and taking his seat in the stern, paid the admiral a visit. Fully recognizing his rank, and the great service he had rendered the world, he politely placed himself and his ship at the disposal of the great discoverer.

When the tidings reached Lisbon, that Columbus, who had so long and unavailingly implored the aid of the Portuguese court, had actually discovered a new world, and that, returning from his triumphant voyage, he was safely anchored in the Tagus, the excitement almost surpassed all conceivable bounds. Barges and boats of every kind crowded the river, and swarmed around the caravel, which was freighted with inhabitants and productions as strange as if they had been brought from the remotest star in the firmament. All ages, both sexes, and all conditions of society, shared in the boundless curiosity.

From morning till night the ship was thronged with visitors. All the energies of Columbus and his crew were taxed, in telling over and over again the story of their adventures. First of all, the Indians, who were dressed in the glittering costume of bril-liantly colored fringes and plumes, which constituted their dress on a gala-day, attracted the gaze of the multitude. The accumulated gold seemed wonderful. The plants and animals were different from any which had before been seen. The regret was intense,

with both the court and the people, that so immense
an acquisition had been lost to Portugal.*

King John was then at Valparaiso, about thirty
miles from Lisbon. On the 8th of March, a Portuguese grandee came from the king to Columbus, to
congratulate him upon his arrival, and to invite him to
his court. A royal order was also issued, that everything the admiral required, for himself, his vessel, or
his crew, should be furnished without cost. Columbus immediately set out for Valparaiso. The king
had made arrangements that he should be sumptu-
ously entertained on the way.

When he approached the palace, all the principal
members of the royal household came out to meet
him, and to escort him to the presence of the king.
The monarch received him with all possible honor,
gave him a seat by his side, as though he were a
prince with royal blood in his veins, and assured
him that everything in his kingdom, which could be
of service to him, was at his command.

---

* Mr. Goodrich writes: "And then he wrote to the King of Portugal, informing him of his discoveries, and demanding permission to
go on to Lisbon, averring that he would be more safe, as the report
concerning the gold might tempt the people where he then was, to
rob him. We are not surprised, knowing the boastful false pride of
the man, to find him contemptibly elated at being thus able to flaunt
his discovery in the face of a prince who had refused to engage in it ;
but the arrogance and boastfulness of the pirate become admiral,
exceed all belief."—*Life of Columbus,* p. 215.

The king listened with commingled feelings of pleasure and of intense regret, to his recital of the wealth and beauty and vast population of the wonderful world which Columbus, by his discovery, seemed to have presented to the Spanish monarchy.   Columbus was, that night, assigned to the hospitality of one of the highest nobles of the court.   The next day the king sought another interview.   During the night he had apparently prepared himself with a series of the minutest questions, in reference to the route taken in the voyage, the climate, soil, and productions of the regions he had visited, and the prospect of obtaining gold.

A mean spirit of envy and jealousy pursued the admiral.   Those who had derided his enterprise, now endeavored, in every way, to underrate his services.   They attributed his actions to the most ignoble motives.   They decried the value of the discovery.   They accused him of a boastful and vainglorious spirit, and held him up to ridicule in every way in their power.   The quotations we have made from the book of Mr. Aaron Goodrich will show the kind of representations which the enemies of Columbus might make, of his conduct and career.

Mr. Irving writes:

"Seeing the king much perturbed in spirit, some went even so far as to propose, as a means of impeding the prosecution of these enterprises, that Columbus should be assassinated; declaring that he deserved death, for attempting to deceive and embroil the two nations, by his pretended discoveries. It was suggested that his assassination might easily be accomplished, without incurring any odium; advantage might be taken of his lofty deportment, to pique his pride, provoke him into an altercation, and then despatch him, as if in a casual and honorable encounter.*

This fact is asserted by several historians, both Portuguese and Spanish. Indeed, there was hardly any wickedness which, in those dark days, could not find advocates in the courts of Europe. But King John II. rejected the infamous proposal, though he was chagrined beyond measure, in contemplating the loss Portugal had incurred, and the wealth and renown Spain had gained, in consequence of his rejection of the enterprise of Columbus.

Some of the king's council proposed that Columbus should be permitted to return to Spain, and that a powerful armament should be immediately despatched, to take possession of the newly discovered countries in the name of Portugal, by extending the explorations and establishing colonies. The king ignobly accepted this suggestion. Vigor-

* Irving's "Life of Columbus," vol. i. p. 272.

ous but secret measures were pursued for fitting
out the squadron, and one of the most distinguished
captains of the age, Don Francisco de Almeida, was
placed in command.

Columbus was escorted to his ship by a numerous train of cavaliers. The queen was at a convent
at Villa Franca. At her earnest request Columbus
stopped there, and was received with the most flattering attentions. The queen was surrounded by
the most distinguished ladies of the kingdom. With
intensest interest they listened to the recital of Columbus, which was more full of romantic adventure
than the fictitious narratives of the most admired
novelists.

The admiral, returning to the *Nina*, put to sea
on the 13th of March. A two days' sail brought
him to Palos. It was mid-day when his solitary
caravel entered the harbor. He had left the port
on the 3d of August of the preceding year. Thus
he had been absent not quite seven months, on
this most memorable voyage which had ever been
undertaken.*

---

* From Lisbon Columbus wrote to Ferdinand and Isabella a letter,
which closed with the following words. " Let the king and queen,
our princes, and their most happy kingdom, and all the other provinces of Christendom, render thanks to our Lord and Saviour Jesus
Christ, who has granted us so great a victory, and such prosperity.
Let processions be made, and sacred feasts be held, and the temples

The return of Columbus to Palos, with proof which could not be questioned of his amazing discovery, created a scene of excitement such as has rarely been witnessed on this globe. As the months passed slowly away, and no tidings were heard, it was generally supposed that all engaged in this expedition had perished, in the midst of the mysterious perils of an unknown sea.

The appearance of the storm-beaten caravel, slowly ascending the harbor, conveyed the first news of the adventurers since their departure. The *Nina* was alone. Both of the other vessels had disappeared. The terrible storms, which had raged during the winter, had increased the popular apprehension that both of the other vessels had been swallowed up by the angry billows. Terrible was the suspense. There was hardly a family in Palos who had not some friend or relative in the expedition. As soon as the vessel reached her anchorage, and it was announced that the voyage had been entirely successful, that the crew of the *Santa Maria* were on board the *Nina*, and that they had parted company with the *Pinta*

be adorned with festive boughs. Let Christ rejoice on earth, as He rejoices in heaven, in the prospect of the salvation of the souls of so many nations hitherto lost. Let us also rejoice, as well on account of the exaltation of our faith, as on account of the increase of our temporal prosperity, of which not only Spain, but all Christendom, will be partakers."—*Select Letters of Christopher Columbus*, p. 17.

only a few days before, the joy was indescribable. One of the first acts of this devout man was to repair, with his whole ship's company, to the church, to offer thanks to God for their safe return.

The glad tidings swept over Spain like fire on the prairies. Bonfires blazed on every eminence, salutes were fired from every fortress, and from every church steeple the bells rang exultant peals. To add to the joy, on the evening of this very day, and while the bells were ringing, the cannon booming, and the populace shouting, the *Pinta* entered the harbor. Driven before the gale, Pinzon had succeeded in making the port of Bayonne, in the Bay of Biscay, where he awaited the subsidence of the storm.

When he entered the port of Palos, and witnessed the enthusiasm with which Columbus was received, it is probable that his consciousness of his crime, in deserting the admiral, oppressed him in the deepest degree. It was his one fault. It was like the desertion of a soldier on the field of battle, and exposed him to arrest and severe punishment. So deep was his chagrin, that he took a boat, landed privately, and repairing to his home, did not show himself in the streets until after the admiral's departure, on his journey to the court.

This unhappy defection is greatly to be regretted.

It cannot be denied that the success of the expedition was in no inconsiderable degree due to Martin Alonzo Pinzon. He was one of the first, in Spain, to appreciate the plans of Columbus. He aided the poor adventurer liberally, with his purse and his personal influence. He assisted effectually in procuring and fitting out ships. And finally he embarked with his brother and friends, in the expedition, thus staking, not only his property but his life, on the event.

It should also be said, in mitigation of too severe a judgment, that he was a seaman of great professional experience and skill. In that respect, he was not inferior to Columbus. He was a man of high position, and inspired by a lofty ambition. Well does Mr. Irving say:

"His story shows how one lapse from duty may counterbalance the merit of a thousand services; how one moment of weakness may mar the beauty of a whole life of virtue; and how important it is for a man, under all circumstances, to be true, not merely to others, but to himself."

Pinzon was in disgrace. He was forbidden to appear at court. He was soon seized by a fatal malady, which was probably aggravated by mental suffering, and died. Subsequently, the Emperor Charles V., in recognition of his eminent services,

7*

granted the family the rank and privileges of nobility.
A coat-of-arms was also conferred upon them, em-
blematical of the great discovery.

The king and queen were at Barcelona, a distance
of about seven hundred miles from Palos. A despatch was immediately sent to Columbus, requesting
him to repair to the court. This rendered it necessary for him to traverse the long route, which, under
the circumstances, could not fail to prove a triumphal
march. He had taken with him, from the island,
ten Indians. One had died on the voyage. Three
were left sick in Palos. Six accompanied him to
the court.

The season of the year, for this long journey
through the heart of Spain, was delightful. Nearly
every mile of the way Columbus received a jubilant
welcome, such as no mortal probably ever received
before. The Indians, who accompanied him, were
gorgeously decorated with golden ornaments and
coronets, and with brilliantly colored plumes. All
the most showy products of the new world were displayed to the admiring thousands.

The cavalcade was very imposing. Columbus
rode a fine horse, and was accompanied by a large
retinue. The country, all along the road, poured
forth its thousands to witness the pageant. Eager
spectators filled the streets, windows, and balconies.

Never did imperial triumph surpass this show. It was about the middle of April when he reached Barcelona. Most of the nobles of Castile and of Aragon were assembled there to do him honor. As the cavalcade approached the city, they all came forth, in a large procession, to escort him to the presence of the sovereigns.

Ferdinand and Isabella, with their royal son, Prince John, were seated beneath a silken canopy, in a vast saloon prepared for the occasion. The nobles and the illustrious personages of the two realms crowded the apartment. As Columbus entered, every eye was riveted upon him.

"He was conspicuous," writes Las Casas, "for his tall and majestic person, his dignified bearing, and his expressive features. His long gray locks added to his venerable appearance. A modest smile played upon his countenance, showing that he was not insensible to the homage he was receiving." *

As Columbus approached the sovereigns they paid him the remarkable respect of rising, and inviting him to take a seat at their side. This was an honor conferred only on persons of the highest rank. Columbus, in accordance with court etiquette, kneeled, and offered to kiss their hands. With some hesitancy they yielded to the ceremony. Being

* Las Casas, " Hist. Ind.," lib. i. cap. 78. MS.

seated, the admiral gave an account, to the royal
pair and the immense audience, of the remarkable
events of his voyage.   He displayed the birds of the
country, of wonderfully-gorgeous plumage, some living and others stuffed.   Gold-dust, gold nuggets,
golden ornaments, and especially golden coronets,
wrought with all the ingenuity barbaric art could
give, attracted the eager attention of monarchs and
nobles, who alike hungered and thirsted for gold.
The natives, tall, with forms which no statuary could
surpass, with pleasing smiles and affectionate manners, and carefully dressed in the picturesque garb
of their courtly festivals, attracted intense and inexhaustible interest.

It is worthy of comment that, at the close of the
narrative, the king and queen, and the whole united
audience, fell upon their knees, clasped their hands,
and thus united in the thanksgiving breathed forth
by the choir, in the majestic anthem, " *Te Deum Lau-
damus* "—Thee, God, we praise.   There were no
shouts, no noisy demonstrations.   The feelings excited were too deep for mirth.   Tears dimmed many
eyes.   Las Casas writes :

" The souls of the auditors were, in that solemn
hour, so borne up to heaven that it seemed as if
they communicated with celestial delights."

Alas ! for man.   This discovery, which might

have been an immeasurable blessing to all, had the
fatherhood of God and the brotherhood of man been
recognized, proved, through the depravity of our
fallen race, a curse to the inhabitants of the new
world, the enormity of which can never be known,
until, at the Day of Judgment, the secrets of all
hearts shall be revealed.

It was an age of darkness. Scarcely an individual could be found who had risen above the fanaticism and superstition of the times. Columbus must
be judged by the light of the fifteenth, and not by
that of the nineteenth century. He was still pondering his grand scheme for the deliverance of the Holy
Sepulchre. To this enterprise he was to devote all
the wealth he might gain from his great discovery.
Gold and renown were nothing to him, only as instruments for the furtherance of his pious plan, upon
which he could not doubt that God was looking with
approbation. His anticipations were so sanguine
that he made a vow that, within seven years, he
would furnish an army of fifty thousand foot, and
four thousand horse, for the rescue of Palestine from
the Turks.

This visionary project had become entwined
with all the fibres of his intellectual and moral nature,
He deemed himself raised by heaven, and divinely
inspired for his great discovery, in order that he

might successfully prosecute this holy crusade, for the glory of God and the welfare of man. "It shows," writes Mr. Irving, "how much his mind was elevated above selfish and mercenary views; how it was filled with those devout and heroic schemes, which, in the time of the crusades, had inflamed the thoughts and directed the enterprises of the bravest warriors and the most illustrious princes." *

* Irving's " Life of Columbus," vol. i, p. 236.

CHAPTER VII.

The Second Voyage.

Excitement throughout Europe—The Coat-of-Arms—Pension adjudged to Columbus—Anecdote of the Egg—The Papal sanction—Religious zeal of Isabella—Designs of Portugal—The new
armament—General enthusiasm—Sailing of the fleet—The pleasant voyage—Electric phenomenon—Cruise through the Antilles—
Lost in the woods—Conflict between the boats—Porto Rico—
The Caribbee Islands—The approach to Hayti—The Gulf of
Samana—La Navidad reached—Fate of the colony.

THE excitement created by the discovery of
Columbus spread through the whole civilized world.
Genoa exulted in the boast that she had given birth
to the great discover.   England was then but an inferior maritime power.   When the tidings reached
London, the event was declared to be more divine
than human.   Sebastian Cabot was then in London.
The news inspired him with intense desires to emu-
late achievements so heroic.   Thus he was led to the
renowned voyages which have given immortality to
his name.   In illustration of the emotions excited in
the minds of the learned of that day, I will give
abrief extract from a letter from Peter Martyr,

to his philosophic friend, Pomponius Laetus. He
writes :

"You tell me, my amiable Pompònius, that you
leaped for joy, and that your delight was mingled
with tears when you read my epistle, certifying to
you the hitherto hidden world of the antipodes.
You have felt and acted as became a man eminent
for learning ; for I can conceive no aliment more
delicious than such tidings to a cultivated and ingen-
uous mind. I feel a wonderful exultation of spirits,
when I converse with intelligent men who have
returned from those regions. It is like an accession
of wealth to a miser. Our minds, soiled and debased
by the common concerns of life and the vices of
society, become elevated and ameliorated by contemplating such glorious events." *

Still no one comprehended the real significance
of the discovery. It was universally believed, by
Columbus, and by all others persons, that he had
found a new route to vast realms of India, which had
never yet been visited by civilized men. The idea
had as yet entered no mind, that the newly discovered countries were parts of an entirely unknown
continent, separated from India, as well as from Europe and Africa, by thousands of miles of ocean.
The lands were therefore called the West Indies.
And as the region had never been explored before,

* " Letters of Peter Martyr," let. 153.

and was, apparently, of measureless magnitude, it was entitled to the appellation of a New World.

While Columbus was at Barcelona, he was the object of universal attention. The king and queen were continually showing him the most remarkable proofs of their favor. Ferdinand often rode on horseback, with Columbus on one side, and the king's son, Prince John, on the other. A coat-of-arms was assigned him, to perpetuate the memory of his achievements. The astonishing honor was conferred upon him of quartering the royal arms of Castile and Leon, with a group of islands surrounded by waves, with the motto annexed:

> To Castile and Leon,
> Columbus gave a New World.

To Columbus was adjudged the pension which the sovereigns had promised to the one who should first discover land. Many thought that this was not a just decision. It is not certain that the light which Columbus saw, "which appeared like a candle, and went up and down," was from the island. Indeed there are pretty strong arguments to indicate that it could not have been. Mr. Helps writes:

"Their highnesses had promised a pension of ten thousand marevedi,* to the fortunate man who

---

* This was about three thousand dollars ; but considerably more. if we estimate the comparative value of money in those days. A ma·revedi was a small coin, worth about three mills of our currency.

should see land first. The *Pinta* was the foremost vessel. It was from her deck, at two o'clock in the morning, that land was first seen by Rodrigo de Triana. We cannot but be sorry for this poor common sailor, who got no reward. The pension was adjudged to the admiral." *

Mr. Irving writes, " It may, at first sight, appear but little accordant with the acknowledged magnanimity of Columbus, to have borne away the prize from this poor sailor; but this was a subject to which his whole ambition was involved, and he was doubtless proud of the honor of being personally the discoverer of the land, as well as projector of the enterprise." †

This may explain his conduct, but does not excuse it. It would have redounded far more to the reputation of Columbus, if he had said, "There is some uncertainty about the light I saw, but none whatever about the land first seen by Triana. Therefore the sailor is entitled to the pension." ‡

It was while Columbus was at Barcelona, that the

* " Life of Columbus," by Arthur Helps, p. 92.
† " Life of Columbus," vol. i. p. 290.
‡ Oviedo, in his " Cronico de las Indias," lib. ii. cap. 2, says that Rodrigo de Triana was so chagrined at the injustice which he thought had been done him, that he renounced his country and faith. Going to Africa he turned Mussulman. We do not, however, find any corroboration of this statement ; and Oviedo does not enjoy the reputation of a reliable historian.

well-known incident in reference to the egg is said to have taken place. According to the story, Pedro Gonzales de Mendoza, Grand Cardinal of Spain, and in rank the first subject of the realm, invited Columbus to a banquet. The admiral was assigned the most honorable seat at the table. One of the courtiers, jealous of the honors which were showered upon the discoverer, asked him whether he thought, if he had not discovered the Indies, no one else could have done so. Columbus made no reply. But taking an egg, invited each one of the company to try if he could make it stand upon one end. All attempted it in vain. Columbus struck the egg gently upon the table, so as to break the end, leaving it standing upon the broken part. Thus he illustrated the fact that it would be very easy to follow the path to the New World, now that he had pointed out the way.*

The doctrine was, at this time, established by the Papal Church, that its emissaries had a right to invade and take possession of all the territories of heathen nations, that the sway of the church might

* Mr. Irving comments as follows upon this statement. "This anecdote rests on the authority of the Italian historian, Benzoni. It has been condemned as trivial. But the simplicity of the reproof constitutes its severity; and it was characteristic of the practical sagacity of Columbus. The universal popularity of the anecdote, is a proof of its merit."—*Life of Columbus*, vol. i. p. 291, note.

be extended. The Spanish sovereigns immediately
applied to the Pope for his sanction of their claim
to all the realms they had discovered. Pope Martin
V. had conceded to the crown of Portugal, all the
lands it might discover, from Cape Bojador to the
Indies. The King of Portugal endeavored to found a
claim, upon this grant, to the realms Columbus had
discovered. In the application which the Spanish
monarchs made to Pope Alexander VI., they stated
that the present discoveries did not interfere with
the Portuguese possessions.

Ferdinand and Isabella were considered devoted
children of the Church. Their expulsion of the
infidel Moors from Spain was deemed a holy crusade. The Pope readily granted their request. To
prevent any conflicting claims, an ideal line was
drawn, from the north to the south pole, three hundred miles west of the Azores. All land, west of
this line, which the Spanish navigators might discover, was to belong to the Spanish crown ; all east,
to Portugal. In reference to this division, several
obvious difficulties arise, which were not at the time
considered.*

* There can be no question of the correctness of the following
account of Isabella, by Mr. Arthur Helps. " Methinks I can still see
her beautiful majestic face, as it looks down upon the beholder from
one of the chapels of the cathedral in Grenada ; a countenance too
expressive and individual to be what painters give as that of an angel,

Great exertions were immediately made to fit out
a Second Expedition.   In this world, virtue and vice
are found in strange blending.   The funds for this
expedition were raised, part from the church tithes
and part from the confiscated property of the Jews,
who, simply because they were Jews, had been ex-
pelled from Spain and robbed of all their possessions.   The conversion of the heathen was deemed
one of the most important objects of the enterprise.
No candid man will say that this was hypocrisy on
the part of the Spanish monarchs.

Twelve learned ecclesiastics were selected to
accompany the expedition.   Bernardo Boyle was
appointed over them, as the apostolical vicar.   Isabella, from her own purse, supplied him with ornaments and vestments, to give brilliance to the ceremonies of the church.

"Isabella, from the first," writes Irving, "took
the most warm and compassionate interest in the
welfare of the Indians.   Won by the accounts given
by Columbus, of their gentleness and simplicity, and

and yet the next thing to it.   What she would say, in her defence,
were we to interrogate her, is, that she obeyed the voice of heaven,
taking the wise and good men of her day as its interpreters.   Oh, that
she had persisted in listening to it, as it spoke in her own kindly
heart.   But at least the poor Indian can utter nothing but blessings
on her.   He might have needed no other protector, had she lived.
Nor would slavery have found, in his fate, one of the darkest **and**
most fatal chapters in its history.—*Life of Columbus*, p. 96.

looking upon them as committed, by heaven, to her especial care, her heart was filled with concern at their destitute and ignorant condition. She ordered that great care should be taken of their religious instruction; that they should be treated with the utmost kindness; and enjoined Columbus to inflict signal punishment on all Spaniards who should be guilty of outrage or injustice toward them." *

The six Indians, who were brought to Barcelona, were baptized, with very imposing ceremonies, in the cathedral. The royal family were all present, and the king and queen officiated as sponsors. One of the natives soon after died. In accordance with the cruel theology of the age, Herrera writes: "We are bound, by our faith, to believe that he was the first of his nation that entered heaven." †

The court confirmed Columbus in his titles, prerogatives, and emoluments, as Viceroy, Admiral, and Governor of all the countries he had or might discover. On the 28th of May, Columbus left Barcelona for Seville. Spies announced that Portugal was making hurried preparations for an expedition to seize upon the newly discovered countries. Very unfriendly relations began to spring up between the two governments. Ferdinand sent a letter to the

---

* "Life of Columbus," vol. i. p. 301.

† Herrera, "Hist. Ind." decad. i. lib. ii. cap. 5.

Portuguese court, prohibiting the Portuguese navigators from visiting the newly discovered lands. A
very curious and keen diplomatic contest ensued,
which we have not space to describe. Intrigue and
cunning, on both sides, took the place of fair, honest,
and honorable dealing.

Columbus seems to have been a stranger to these
court intrigues. All his energies, at Seville, were
concentrated upon fitting out his new armament. A
fleet of seventeen vessels, large and small, was prepared. Arrangements were made for the establishment of a colony, of farmers, mechanics, and professional gentlemen. Horses, cattle, and domestic animals of all kinds, were provided, to stock the settlement. Plants and seeds were gathered ; and all articles of traffic which experience taught them would
be in demand by the Indians. General enthusiasm
was aroused. There was scarcely any end to the
applications to join the expedition. Many of the
highest grandees, and prominent officers in the army
and the navy, sought for passage, at their own cost.
An army of European adventurers was thus upon the
eve of falling, like an avalanche, upon the helpless
natives. There was perhaps, no power, in the court,
or in the truly good men of the expedition, to protect the Indians from their encroachments.

It is not strange that this enthusiasm should have

swept wildly over the land. The world-weary and
the care-worn were told that here were islands as of
the blessed. Here there was no winter, no toil.
Bowers, as of paradise, invited to repose. The bloom
of Eden was everywhere around. Delicious fruit
hung from the boughs, amply sufficient to satiate all
hunger and all thirst. Beneath those sunny skies, life
was but a continuous gala day. It is not to be
wondered at that hundreds and thousands should
have been lured, by these visions, to seek refuge
from labor and care amidst the groves, bowers, fruitage, and songs of this earthly paradise.

One of the most distinguished men who embarked on this expedition, was Don Alonzo de
Ojeda. We shall often have occasion to refer to his
name. He was of illustrious birth, being closely
related to the Grand Inquisitor of Spain, and having
been brought up under the patronage of the Duke
of Medina Celi, who, in wealth, pride, and power,
rivalled the Spanish monarchs. He was a fearless,
reckless cavalier, rejoicing in the most perilous adventures, and a man without fear.

The whole company which embarked in the
ships amounted to fifteen hundred. Columbus was
provided with a gorgeous retinue, that he might
maintain, with suitable dignity, his high position as
viceroy. On the 28th of September, 1493, the fleet

commenced its voyage from the bay of Cadiz. It was a lovely morning. A propitious breeze swelled the sails. All hearts were glad. On the 1st of October the fleet touched at the Canaries. Here Columbus laid in a stock of calves, goats, sheep, and domestic fowls. It is also said that oranges, lemons, melons, and various other fruits were introduced to the soil of Hispaniola from the Canaries.* When again they put to sea the captains of all the vessels were instructed to direct their course to the harbor of the Nativity, on the island of Hispaniola. Here the friendly chief Guacanagari resided, and here the garrison had been left.

They soon struck the trade winds, and were borne rapidly forward over a quiet sea, and beneath cloudless skies. Having made about twelve hundred miles west of Gomera, the fleet encountered a severe thunder-storm. The phenomenon was witnessed, not unusual under such circumstances, of flames of electric fluid playing upon the tops of the masts. Fernando Columbus comments as follows upon this spectacle, thus exhibiting the philosophy of that superstitious age.

"On the same Saturday, in the night, was seen

---

* Humboldt says that there were small, bitter wild oranges and lemons in the West India Islands, when discovered by Columbus. —Humboldt, *Essai Politique sur l'Isle de Cuba,* tom. i. p. 68.

8

St. Elmo, with seven lighted tapers, at the topmast There was much rain and great thunder. I mean to say that those lights were seen, which mariners affirm to be the body of St. Elmo; on beholding which they chant litanies and orisons, holding it for certain that, in the tempest in which he appears, no one is in danger. Be that as it may, I leave the matter to them. But if we may believe Pliny, similar lights have sometimes appeared to the Roman mariners, during tempests at sea; which they said were Castor and Pollux, of which likewise Seneca makes mention.*

On Sunday morning, November 3d, a lofty island was seen far away in the west. It was greeted with shouts of joy from all the ships. Columbus named it Dominica. By order of the admiral the crew of all the ships were assembled upon their decks, and religious services were held, giving especial thanks to God for their prosperous voyage, in prayers and in chanting anthems. In these external observances this was certainly a far more religious age than the present.†

---

* " Hist. del Almirante," cap. 45.

† " The pilots of the fleet reckoned, on that day, that between leaving Ferro and first reaching land, we had made eight hundred leagues; others said seven hundred and eighty; thus the difference was not great. There were three hundred more between Ferro and Cadiz, making in all eleven hundred leagues. I do not therefore feel

The fleet had now entered the beautiful group of islands called the Antilles. Of this cluster, the magnificent island of Porto Rico is one of the most western. As the fleet glided along, six islands were passed, whose tropical verdure elicited continued exclamations of delight. Upon one of these, called Marigalante, Columbus landed. The island, which was covered by a dense forest, appeared to be uninhabited. Columbus raised upon it the banner of Spain, and took possession in the name of his sovereigns.

Another island, which appeared much larger, was in sight. Columbus landed, with a boat's crew. He found the island inhabited, and witnessed many strange sights. He called the island Estremadura. The Indians fled in terror. There was a pleasant village of about thirty houses, surrounding a public square. Each house had a portico, where the family could sit, sheltered from the rays of the sun. One of these was decorated with grotesquely carved wood. Hammocks, neatly woven of strong cotton cord, were suspended within, and several very useful vessels were found, formed of calabashes, or earthenware. There were domesticated geese, and tame

as one who had not seen enough of the water."—*Select Letters of Columbus, Second Voyage*, p. 21. Dr. Chanca, who wrote the above was physician to the fleet.

parrots in the yards. Here, for the first time, the Spaniards found the delicious and fragrant pine-apple.

Returning to the ship, they sailed along the coast of this island a few miles, when they cast anchor in a good harbor for the night. They saw many villages along the coast, but the panic-stricken inhabitants fled at the sight of the ships. The next morning a boat was sent on shore. The sailors caught a boy and several women, and brought them on board. From the arms which the sailors found, and a revolting spectacle of human bones which was seen, and also from what he could learn from the women, through his Indian interpreters, Columbus inferred that this was one of the islands of the famous Carib cannibals.* Their arrows were sharp-pointed with bone, and the tips poisoned with the juice of a certain herb. In strong predatory bands they ravaged other islands, killing the aged, retaining the most beautiful girls as servants and companions, and cooking and eating the young men. Human limbs were found suspended from the beams of the houses, as

---

* Dr. Chanca writes: "These women also say that the Caribbees treat them with cruelty as would scarcely be believed. They eat up the children which they bear to them, and only bring up those which they have by their natural wives. They say that man's flesh is so good that there is nothing like it in the world."—*Select Letters of Columbus, Second Voyage,* p. 31.

if undergoing some process of preparation for food. In one of the houses the bleeding head of a young man was seen, recently cut off. Other portions of a human body were roasting before the fire.*

A captain of one of the caravels, with eight men, had, without permission, ventured on an exploring tour, and was missing. Columbus was greatly alarmed. He had reason to fear that they had been cut off by these fierce savages. After waiting anxiously through the day and the succeeding night, and hearing no tidings of them, he sent parties in various directions, to blow trumpets and fire guns. But the search was fruitless. Many of the natives were caught sight of; but they fled, with fleet steps, as soon as approached.

The chivalric Alonzo de Ojeda volunteered to take forty men and make a thorough exploration of the island. The little band pushed far into the interior. They waded large streams, and forced their

* Mr. Goodrich indignantly rejects the idea that any cannibals existed in the Indies. He writes : " This is the first time the grave charge of cannibalism is preferred against the natives of the New World ; a charge which investigation and the laws of nature alike prove to be false."

He assigns, as a reason why Columbus should have fabricated the story, " Columbus, still bent on the establishment of slavery, sought some excuse ; and the most plausible was to represent his victims as monsters, feeding upon human flesh, whom to enslave was to civilize."—*Life of Columbus*, p. 230.

way through almost impenetrable thickets. Arquebuses were fired, and the loudest blasts of trumpets
blown. From this exploration Ojeda returned without any tidings of the lost ones. Several days had
elapsed since their disappearance. There was no
longer any hope of their discovery. With a sad
heart Columbus was raising his anchors, when a feeble shout was heard from the dense forest on the
shore, and the men appeared upon the beach. Their
ragged clothing and haggard features told too plainly
what they had suffered. They had been lost in the
thickets of a tropical forest so dense as almost to
exclude the light of day. It was with the utmost
difficulty that they could force their way through
the tangled network of canes, vines, and thorns.
Vast trees, which overshadowed them, excluded the
sight, even of the stars.

To add to their sufferings, they were agitated by
the dreadful fear that the admiral, thinking them
dead, might proceed on the voyage, and thus abandon them to the most dreadful fate. In that case
they could never hope to see friends or home again.
In all probability they would be killed and devoured
by the savages. At length they found the sea-shore.
Anxiously they followed it along, with scarcely any
hope that the fleet would have delayed its voyage
so many days for them. To their inexpressible joy

they found the harbor, and the ships still riding at anchor.

They brought with them, one or two girls and boys. They had not seen a single man. It was said that all the warriors were absent, on a plundering expedition to some distant island. Columbus justly deemed this departure of the captain and his men from their ship, without permission, a grave offence. It had delayed the whole fleet for several days, had required great toil in the search for them, and had caused, throughout the ships, much anxiety. Thus, notwithstanding all they had suffered, the offenders were placed under arrest.*

On the 10th of November, the fleet weighed anchor, and sailed prosperously along, through the most beautiful archipelago of islands to be found upon the globe. As the fleet glided by these green and blooming Edens, emerging from a tranquil sea, Columbus gave them names, as Adam, in the morning of creation, named the animals which passed in procession before him. On the 14th, he cast anchor in the harbor of an island, which the Indians called Ayay, but to which he gave the name, now so widely

* The comment upon this transaction, by Mr. Goodrich, is : " The truants found their way back to the ship ; and so greatly was our humane admiral incensed, at their having lost their way, that he ordered them to be put in irons, and their allowance of food re- trenched."—*Life of Columbus*, p. 232.

known, of Santa Cruz, or the Holy Cross. A well-manned boat was sent on shore. As usual, the natives fled. In a deserted village they captured one or two men and a boy. These were prisoners, whom the ferocious natives had taken from another island. A canoe was seen, with several Indians in it, coming round a point of land. The boat's crew, vigorously plying their oars, overtook them.*

The Caribs, as they were called, seized their bows and arrows, and fought with almost demoniac desperation. But the Spaniards, protected by bucklers, generally shielded themselves, though two were soon wounded. Two of the natives were women. They fought as fiercely as the men. One of them threw an arrow with such force, that it pierced entirely through a Spanish shield. The frail canoe was overturned. The savages fought in the water, throwing their arrows as rapidly and as dextrously as when in the boat.

At length they were captured. One was mortally wounded, and died as he was brought on board the ship. Several others were wounded. One of the women seemed to be a chief of high rank. She was

* " When the Caribbees saw that all attempt at flight was useless, they most courageously took to their bows, both women and men. I say most courageously; because they were only four men and two women, and our people were twenty-five in number."—*Letter of Dr. Chanca.*

accompanied by her son. He was a young man of wonderful physical strength, with a ferocious countenance and lion-like courage. All were hideously painted, and their hair was black, long, and coarse. Though strongly bound, they still maintained a bold and defiant air. They appeared like caged tigers, whose palpable strength and menacing aspect caused all to regard them with emotions of terror. One of the Spaniards was mortally wounded in the fray, and died in a few days.

Continuing the voyage, the fleet soon arrived within sight of another cluster of islands. Some of them were covered with luxuriant vegetation. Some were naked, sterile rocks, blackened by the winds and waves of centuries. The fertile islands seemed to be generally inhabited. They were so near together that it was dangerous for large ships to endeavor to pass between them. The group still retains the name of the Virgin Islands, which Columbus gave them. The largest of the group he called Santa Ursula.

Still the fleet pressed its way westward toward its destined port, on the island of Hispaniola. In the evening of a cloudless day a magnificent island rose before them, crowned with forests and indented with bays. It was Porto Rico. The natives had called it Boriquen. Columbus, at first, gave it the

8*

name of San Juan Bautista.   It had been supposed
that this was the central island of the dreaded Caribs.
Columbus was now informed that it was a place of
refuge from their sanguinary raids.   Here a single
chief reigned over a large population.   They were
warriors from necessity, and fought only for self-pro-
tection.   They devoured their prisoners in revenge.

For a whole day the fleet coasted along the beautiful shores of the island, and, in the evening, anchored in a bay near the western extremity, where
fish filled the waters in the greatest abundance.   The
admiral landed.   He found a pleasant Indian village,
surrounding, as usual, a public square.   A good road
led from the village to the sea.   On each side of the
road there were fruitful gardens, enclosed in substantial fences of reed.   At the end of the road, near the
shore, there was reared upon an eminence, an observ-
atory or look-out, which commanded quite an extensive view of all the approaches by sea.   Nothing
equal to this village, in neatness, comfort, and civilization, had thus far been seen upon the islands.*

* Dr. Chanca gives quite a different account of the homes of the
natives generally, from that which Columbus was accustomed to give.
He writes from La Navidad. "These people are so degraded that
they have not even the sense to select a fitting place to live in. Those
who dwell on the shore build for themselves the most miserable hovels
tha. can be imagined. All the houses are so covered with grass and
dampness, that I wonder how they can contrive to exist."—*Letter of
Dr. Chanca*, p. 50.

But solitude, like that of Thebes or Palmyra, reigned throughout those habitations. Not a living being was seen. The natives, at sight of the squad· ron, fled into the interior. The fleet remained here two days. During all that time, not an Indian ven- tured to show himself.

The account which Columbus sent home, of this cruise among the Caribbee Islands, was read through- out Europe with intense interest. It seemed to settle the mooted question whether the human race had any where sunk so low as to feed on human flesh. Still it is not doubted that much of the information which Columbus received from the natives, was obscure, and that their ignorance and superstitions were so great that full reliance could not be placed even in their most positive statements. Mr. Irving very judiciously remarks:

" The evidence adduced of their cannibal propen- sities must be received with large allowances for the careless and inaccurate observations of sea-faring men, and the preconceived belief of the fact which existed in the minds of the Spaniards. It was a custom, among the natives of many of the islands, and of other parts of the New World, to preserve the remains of their deceased relatives and friends; sometimes the entire body; sometimes only the

head, or some of the limbs dried at the fire ; sometimes the mere bones."*

On the 22d of November, the eastern cliffs of
Hayti appeared in the distance.   The greatest excitement prevailed on board all the ships, when it was
announced that Hispaniola was in view.   With well-
filled sails the fleet glided along the beautiful shores,
while all were entranced with the scenes of sublimity
and loveliness which were continually opening before
them.   A seaman, who had been wounded in the
fray at Porto Rico, died.   A well-armed crew was
sent on shore to bury him.   The funeral ceremonies
were performed upon the beach.

There was no disturbance.   The natives had
heard of Columbus and his friendly disposition.   A
canoe unhesitatingly approached the admiral's ship,
with an invitation from the chief of that part of the
island, that he would visit him.   Columbus declined
the invitation, but loaded the envoy with presents.
The fleet, proceeding on its way, cast anchor in the
Gulf of Samana.   It will be remembered that Columbus, on the first voyage, was attacked by the natives,
at this place ; that by a conciliatory course he had
won their friendship, and that four of the young
Indians had accompanied him to Spain.

One of these, who had been baptized, and who
* " Life of Columbus," vol. i. p. 336.

was professedly a convert to Christianity, Columbus put on shore. He dressed him in rich apparel, and loaded him with those trinkets which the Indians most highly regarded. He did not return. No tidings were ever heard of him. There was now but one Indian remaining in the fleet, of all whom Columbus had taken to Spain. This young man, who had been baptized with the name of Diego Colon, seemed to be a true Christian.

On the 25th of November the fleet anchored in the harbor of Monte Christo. It will be remembered that a large stream flowed into this bay, which Columbus called Rio del Oro, or the Golden River, but which is now called the Santiago. They were greatly alarmed by finding on the coast four bodies of dead men, with very decisive indications that they were Europeans. They must therefore have been members of the garrison which Columbus had left at La Navidad, only a few leagues further west.* The most gloomy anticipations were thus awakened respecting the fate of the colony.

Still several natives came on board the ship, with a frank and friendly bearing, which did not imply any consciousness that hostilities had arisen between the natives and the Spaniards. The short twilight

* It is said that the precise distance is seven leagues.—See *Second Voyage of Columbus*, by the Hakluyt Society, p. 45.

of the tropics was fading away on the evening of the 27th, when Columbus cast anchor, about three miles off the port of La Navidad. He did not venture to enter the harbor in the dark. Impatient to receive tidings of his garrison, he ordered two of the largest cannon to be discharged. The reverberations rolled along the forest-covered shores and the cliffs, but no response came back. Sadly and silently the hours of the night passed away. No light was seen; no shout was heard. The stillness of the primeval forest seemed to reign through the awful solitude.

About midnight a small canoe was dimly seen in the distance, cautiously approaching one of the vessels. The canoe paused, and an Indian, who had perhaps acquired some slight knowledge of the Spanish language from the soldiers in the garrison, stood up hailing the vessel, and inquiring for Columbus. The admiral's ship was pointed out to him. Slowly he paddled toward it. But when he drew near he would not venture on board until Columbus had made his appearance, and a torch was held up to his face, to show that there was no deception.

He then, with a companion, entered the ship, stating that he was a cousin of the illustrious chief Guacanagari, and that he had brought from him a present of two coronets of gold. To the anxious inquiries of Columbus respecting the fate of his colony, his answers seemed to be confused and obscure. Indeed it was very difficult for him, both by signs and words, to make his meaning plain. Columbus understood him to say that several of the Spaniards had died of sickness; that a quarrel had arisen among themselves, and that a number had been killed; and that the others had taken Indian wives and had dispersed throughout the island.

He also gave the melancholy intelligence that a band of fierce warriors, from what he called the mountains of Cibao, had assailed the beautiful village of Guacanagari, laid all the houses in ashes, killed many of the inhabitants, and carried others away captive. Guacanagari, though he had escaped the massacre, was lying sick and wounded in a neighboring hamlet; else he would have come, in person, to pay his respects to the admiral.

Sad as was this intelligence, Columbus was comforted by the thought that the garrison had not perished through the perfidy of the natives. These incidents gave very decisive evidence that the New World was by no means an uncontaminated Eden of innocence and bliss. It was inhabited by the fallen race of Adam, and here, as everywhere else, man's inhumanity to man was the most dreadful scourge of the human race. The Indians, having been fed and rewarded with many presents, returned to the shore. They assured Columbus that it was the intention of the chief, who was recovering from his wounds, to be brought on board the next morning.

Columbus, ever attentive to all the ceremonial observances of courts, as the morning dawned, waited hour after hour for the promised visit from the prince. Silently the day passed. Not a canoe was in sight. A painful aspect of desolation and desertion was spread everywhere around. Not even a column of smoke could be seen, rising from the forest, with its indication of human life.

As evening approached, Columbus, anxious and weary, sent a boat to the shore to reconnoitre. The crew hastened to the fortress. It presented an appalling scene of violence and ruin. By some cruel foe it had been sacked, burned, and utterly destroyed. They caught sight of one or two Indians lurking in the distance, but no one of them ventured to draw near. When the sailors endeavored to approach them, they ran, as if oppressed by conscious guilt. With this disheartening report the seamen returned to the admiral.

Columbus was greatly troubled. Having entered the harbor, and safely anchored his fleet, he, the following morning, went on shore himself. No traces of the garrison remained; but only a spectacle of devastation, indicating a terrible conflict, and an exterminating massacre. The timbers were thrown down; the windows were dashed in; fragments of garments soiled and storm-worn, fluttered in the breeze. But nothing could be discovered which would throw any additional light upon the awful tragedy which had there taken place. The mournful spectacle revived suspicions, with most of the company, that Guacanagari had been treacherous. But Columbus adhered to his conviction of the good faith of the chief. He was confirmed in this opinion by the smouldering ashes to which the native village had been reduced.

Having concluded this search, Columbus, with the boats, ascended the river, to find out, if possible, what had become of the men. They had rowed about three miles, when they came to a small collection of huts, from which all the inhabitants had evidently fled, as they saw the approach of the Spaniards. Here they found several European articles, which had undoubtedly been taken from the garrison. This confirmed the fears of those who suspected Guacanagari. In this uncertainty they returned to the ruins of the fortress.

It will be remembered that about forty men had been left behind. They were Spanish veterans, accustomed to war, and with their gleaming swords and death-dealing muskets, they would fight to the last gasp. The fortress was strongly built and, being defended by cannon, was apparently impregnable to any force the natives could bring against it. It seemed difficult to imagine how such a garrison could have been taken, by men marching to the assault with bows and arrows only. The perplexity was somewhat increased by finding, during the day, the graves of eleven of the Spaniards.

In the afternoon of this day a small band of Indians was seen hovering about at a distance. They were, however, evidently afraid to draw near the Spaniards.

Columbus gradually succeeded in dispelling their fears, so that he opened intercourse with them, and they soon became quite communicative. Some of them had acquired a slight knowledge of the Spanish language, and thus, with the additional assistance of an Indian interpreter, Columbus probably obtained a pretty correct account of the destruction of the colony.

Whatever may be said of the celestial character of the natives, there can be no question respecting the earthly character of the Spaniards. The common seamen were men of the lowest order, ignorant, fanatical, and depraved. It required all the energies of Columbus, with his official dignity and his unlim-

ited powers, to hold them in restraint. Don Diego
Arana, who was left in command, was a well-mean-
ing man, though he was not capable of triumphing
over the vast difficulties he soon encountered.*

Scarcely had the admiral's ship disappeared in
the eastern horizon, when these sailors, forgetful of
all the counsel they had received, commenced treating the natives with wanton abuse. In small bands,
and well-armed, they wandered freely among the
dwellings of the Indians, robbing them of their gold,
taking ruffianly possession of their homes, and trampling mercilessly upon all their domestic relations.
The natives had supposed that the Spaniards descended from the skies. Their conduct showed
rather that they came up from the abodes of fiends.
Demons could hardly have conducted themselves
more atrociously than did those Spaniards, when
freed from all restraints.

They took possesion of the best houses: selected
any number of female companions they pleased,
especially seizing, by violence, in defiance of all pro-
testations, the wives and daughters of the chiefs.
Wherever they could find gold, they grasped it.
Brawls frequently arose over their ill-gotten gains ;
daggers were drawn, and blood flowed. Arana lost

* Oviedo, in his " History of the Indies," book 2d, chapter 12
describes the characters of these ruffianly men.

all control of his men. The fortress was virtually abandoned. Quarrels arose as to the supreme command. Factions sprang up. In a violent affray one man was killed.

A party of nine Spaniards, under two leaders of the revolt, set out in search of distant mines of gold. They directed their steps to the mountains of Cibao, in the interior of the island. A renowned and intelligent chief, Caonabo, reigned there, over a warlike tribe. The atrocities practised by the Spaniards had reached his ears. He attacked the desperadoes as they entered his dominions, and put them all to death. He then formed an alliance with another tribe, whose chief was Mayreni, and in a well-con-concerted attack, fell upon the fortress.

Their march was secret. The garrison was taken by surprise. Many were absent. At the dead of night, two bands, with hideous yells, rushed into the unguarded fortress ; set fire to the barracks, and with clubs dashed out the brains of the astounded Spaniards, springing from their beds. Some were driven into the sea and drowned. All perished. The faithful Guacanagari rallied his forces for the rescue. It was too late. The fortress was demolished. Every Spaniard was dead. Still Guacanagari fought bravely. But the force against him was overwhelming. His village was burned to the ground.

Many of the warriors were slain. Guacanagari, severely wounded by the hand of Caonabo himself, escaped from his utterly desolate home. He was not pursued. The great object of the allied chiefs was the extermination of the Spaniards.*

* There can be no doubt respecting the general accuracy of this narrative. It is authenticated by Herrera, Peter Martyr, the History of the Admiral, by Fernando Columbus, and by many other ancient annalists.

CHAPTER VIII.

Life at Hispaniola.

THE account which the natives gave of the tragical fate of the colony was confirmed by statements received from other quarters. One of the caravels, commanded by Melchoor Maldonado, was sent along the coast to search out a more favorable location for a new colony. He had advanced but a few leagues, when a canoe with two Indians was seen approaching his vessel. One of these was a brother of Guacanagari. He entreated Maldonado to come ashore and visit the chief, who was at his house, confined by wounds. They found the chief unable to leave his hammock, and carefully tended by seven of his wives.

Guacanagari expressed great regret that it had been out of his power to visit the admiral. Minutely he related the events of the great disaster. His

account was in entire harmony with that which we
have already given. He generously entertained the
Spanish captain and the two or three companions
who accompanied him. Upon their departure he
presented each one with a valuable coronet of gold.
The next morning, Columbus in person visited his
old friend. Wishing to impress the cacique and his
retinue with a sense of his dignity and power, the
admiral appeared in his most brilliant court dress,
accompanied by a numerous train of officers, all encased in glittering coats of mail.*

Guacanagari was in his hammock. He manifested
deep emotion in again meeting his old friend, and
shed tears as he gave an account of the fate of the
Spaniards. The admiral did not question the sincerity of his friendship, or the truth of his narrative.
But the Spaniards generally looked upon the chief
with an evil eye. It was evident that he had been
shocked by the atrocities committed by the Spaniards, and that he was by no means desirous that
they should settle within his bounds. The interview
was friendly, and an exchange of presents took place.
The golden gifts received from the chief surpassed,
in the European estimate of value, more than a hun-

* " The admiral went on shore, accompanied by all the principal
officers, so richly dressed, that he would have made a distinguished appearance even in any of our chief cities."—*Letter of Dr. Chanca*, p. 54.

dred-fold the trinkets which he received from Colum.
bus in return.   It may, however, be said that the gifts
received far exceeded, in native estimation, the value
of those they gave.

A surgeon examined the wounded leg.   While
he thought it possible that there might be some bruis-
ing of the nerves, which might cause severe pain,
others thought that the chief was feigning a far
more severe wound than had been inflicted.   But
Columbus defended his friend.*   In the evening, the
cacique, though apparently suffering, was conveyed
on a visit to the ships.   When Columbus first
entered the harbor, he came with two small and
shattered caravels.   There was now a proud fleet, of
seventeen vessels, floating in the bay.   The admiral's
ship was one of the most massive of the Spanish
navy.

* " The surgeon of the fleet and myself being present, the admiral
wished he would show us his wound.   He said he was willing.   The
surgeon approached him and began to untie the bandage.   He then
said that the wound was made with a stone.   When the wound was
uncovered, there was no more wound on that leg than on the other ;
although he cunningly pretended that it pained him much.   Ignorant
as we were of the facts, it was impossible to come to a definite conclusion.   There were certainly many proofs of an invasion by a hostile
people, so that the admiral was at a loss what to do.   He, with many
others, thought that, for the present, and until they could ascertain the
truth, they ought to conceal their distrust, for, after ascertaining it,
they would be able to claim whatever indemnity they thought proper."
—*Letter of Dr. Chancaa,* p. 56.

Guacanagari was astonished at the spectacle of
grandeur, wealth, and power, which met his eye.
He seemed lost in wonder and thoughtfulness, as he
gazed upon the fruits, plants, and animals of the old
world. There were sheep, swine, and cows, all of
which were new. The size, strength, and terrible
aspect of the horses astonished him. He was still
more astonished in seeing their docility, and the ease
with which they were managed.*

On board the admiral's ships there were ten
young women. One of them, who was called Catalina, was exceedingly beautiful. She had the distinguished air of a princess, and would anywhere have
attracted attention and admiration. These girls
were prisoners of the Caribs, who had been rescued
by Columbus. The chief looked upon them with
much sympathy. They were now captives of the
Spaniards. Guacanagari had witnessed an appalling
exhibition of the atrocities which the Spanish sailors
could perpetrate. He spoke to Catalina in tones
of remarkable gentleness, and in a very affectionate
manner. It would seem that, though different dia-

* " No four-footed animal has ever been seen in this or any of the
other islands, except some dogs of various colors, as in our own country, but in shape like large house dogs ; and also some little animals,
in color, size, and fur like a rabbit, with long tails, and feet like those
of a rat."—*Letter of Dr. Chanca*, published by the Hakluyt Society,
p. 41.

9

lects were used on the various islands, there was
such a general resemblance in the language, that
the natives could easily make themselves understood.

It is not improbable that Guacanagari still considered the Spaniards as coming from another world.
But he no longer regarded them as angelic visitants.
They seemed to him like fiends, whose atrocities
excited his loathing.   The chief was evidently em-
barrassed, and all the efforts to restore past ease
and cordiality were unavailing.   When Columbus
suggested the idea of coming to live with him, the
cacique was evidently troubled, and remarked that
the place was unhealthy, which was indeed the fact.

Unfortunately, the chief regarded the symbols
of the Christian religion with feelings of repulsion.
He had at first considered them as constituting
parts of the worship of a class of beings whom he
deemed far superior to all ordinary humanity. Now,
to his mind, they indicated the fiend-like conduct of
men whom he loathed.   Notwithstanding his fond-
ness for ornament, the admiral found it difficult to
pursuade Guacanagari to wear an image of the Virgin suspended around his neck.   The chief returned
to the land, troubled in spirit, and followed by the
suspicious looks of the Spaniards generally.

The next morning the chief sent to inquire when
Columbus intended to sail; and was informed that

he would leave the harbor the next morning. In the afternoon the brother of Guacanagari came on board. He was observed to converse privately with the women, particularly with the beautiful Catalina. At midnight, when the crew were generally asleep, Catalina and her companions stealthily dropped themselves down, from one side of the vessel, into the water. The ship was anchored three miles from the shore and the sea was rough.

The watch on deck overheard them. The alarm was given. A boat was instantly manned and gave chase. A small fire was burning on the shore, evidently serving as a beacon, to guide them. The women swam like ducks, and were not overtaken until they landed. Four, however, were caught upon the beach. The rest with Catalina, escaped. It was found, in the morning, that Guacanagari and all his followers had departed. This increased the suspicions of many of the Spaniards, that he had been a traitor. But he could not have been blind to the angry looks of the sailors the day before. Some had clamored for his arrest, that he might be held as a hostage. He certainly acted wisely in not leaving himself any longer in their power.

Gloom overshadowed everything at La Navidad. The fortress was in ruins. The graves of the Spaniards were constant memorials of violence and blood.

luxuriously soft and genial. Trees were in full foliage and full flower. The melody of bird songs filled
the air with sweetest music. "They had not yet
become familiarized with the temperature of this
favored island, where rigors of winter are unknown,
where there is a perpetual succession, and even inter-
mixture of fruit and flower, and where smiling verdure reigns throughout the year." *

Here Columbus decided to establish his colony.
As an additional inducement, he had been informed
that the mountains of Cibao, where, it was said, rich
gold mines existed, were not far distant. Great was
the joy, on board the ships, in being released from
the long imprisonment. Every vessel was anchored
as near as possible to the shore. Every boat was
called into requisition. Every man was busy. Cattle, domestic fowl, provisions, guns, ammunition, furniture, were transported to the shore, and placed
under temporary shelter upon the plain, near a lake-
let of crystal water. Here, about forty miles east of
Cape Haytien, Columbus established the first city
built by Europeans in the new world. It was called
Isabella, in honor of his royal patroness.

The streets were laid out scientifically, and
the buildings so arranged as to surround public
squares. The three most important buildings were,

Irving's " Life of Columbus," p. 359.

a church, a public store-house, and a residence for
the admiral.* These were all of stone. Skilful
architects planned them; well-trained mechanics
built them. The private houses were built of tim-
ber or reeds, with plastered walls. There was a brief
scene of sunshine, hope, gladness, as all engaged,
with alacrity, in rearing new homes, amidst the bloom
and fruitage of this garden of nature.

But the storm came ; the storm which seems ever
destined to desolate the homes of the fallen children
of Adam. An epidemic sickness broke out. The
rank soil exhaled malarious vapors. The enervating
climate rendered even ordinary toil exhausting.
Many thoughtless men had embarked in the enterprise, with the most silly impression that they were
bound to a real Eden, where nature would rear for
them the most lovely bowers, and feed them with
the most delicious fruits ; where gold could be picked
up like pebbles, and where this mortal life, redeemed
from the penalty of the fall, would prove but one
continuous gala day.

The novelty of the tropics soon vanished. Languor invaded the body. Homesickness oppressed
the mind. Disappointment soured the disposition.

* Mr. Goodrich thus comments upon these transactions. " He
proceeded to build a church, a magazine, and a *house for himself;* a
triad which illustrates the ruling traits of his character, hypocrisy,
avarice, and selfishness."—*Life of Columbus,* p. 236.

Murmurs rose, followed by quarrels. Change of place had not changed the heart. Serene skies had not diffused their peace into the troubled soul of man Even Columbus did not escape the general doom. The colony, from which he had anticipated so much, was in ruins. The tons of gold, which he had intended to send to Spain in the return ships, to astonish and delight Ferdinand and Isabella, had no longer any existence, even in his imagination. The natives had become unfriendly, and avoided all intercourse with the Spaniards. The care of the squadron ; the peril of unknown seas ; the heterogeneous character of the mass of men, whom he with difficulty controlled, weighed heavily upon him. Notwithstanding all his efforts to bear his burdens gracefully, and to maintain a cheerful air, he could not conceal the gloom which oppressed him. For several weeks he was confined to his bed. But mental energies at length triumphed over bodily weakness. He girded himself with new strength to go forth to life's great battles.*

The ships which had discharged their cargoes, were immediately sent back. All in Spain were looking eagerly for their return, freighted with gold, and other of the treasures, which Columbus had portrayed in such glowing colors, as abounding in

* See " Letter of Dr. Chanca ;" also Herrara, " Hist. Ind." decad i. lib. ii. cap. 10 ; ' Hist. del Almirante," cap. 50.

the New World. It was inexpressibly mortifying to him to be compelled to send them back empty. He could not even give any account of the interior of the island, of mines discovered, of new realms penetrated by their explorations. The sovereigns were expecting wonderful returns. It would be a bitter disappointment to them, and would greatly diminish their confidence in Columbus, to receive only tidings of disaster.

Under these circumstances Columbus felt impelled to make the most strenuous exertions, that the ships, on their return should, in some way, justify the magnificent representations which his sanguine spirit had honestly led him to make. He had learned that the so-called mines of Cibao were situated at the distance of but about three or four days' journey in the interior. He sent out an exploring expedition. It would be some comfort to be able to transmit the news that the golden mountains had been reached ; and that the mines, so full of promise, would immediately be worked.

The chivalric Alonzo de Ojeda was selected to lead this enterprise. He loved adventure and peril, and exulted in the thought that he was to penetrate the realms of the all-powerful chief Caonabo. Early in January, 1494, Ojeda, with a well-armed band of picked men, set out for the interior. For two days

9*

they traversed a deserted country. All the inhabitants had fled before them. They reached the
mountains, and by a narrow zigzag defile ascended
to the summit of the ridge. The morning sun exhibited to them as magnificent a panorama of tropical splendor as earth's surface can exhibit. Beneath
their feet there extended apparently a limitless
expanse of verdant fields, luxuriant groves, and winding streams, with the scattered cottages and villages
of the natives decorating the whole plain.

Descending from these heights they fearlessly
entered the villages beyond. It would seem that
the fear of the Spaniards had not reached that
remote district. The inhabitants received them
kindly, and regaled them with profuse hospitality.
But they found that it was still quite a long journey
to the mountains of Cibao. The face of the country
was rugged with occasional ravines and unbridged
rivers, and forests, whose dense underbrush could
only be penetrated by cutting their way with
hatchets.

For six days they toiled along, not suffering from
thirst, or cold, or hunger, but blistered by the rays
of a torrid sun. The natives were naked and corre-
spondingly uncivilized in all their bearing. Still
they generally appeared to be lamb-like, not wolfish
in nature. But the explorers saw, or thought they

saw, signs of great mineral wealth. Particles of glittering gold were, according to their representations, scattered through the sands of the mountain streams. Peter Martyr testifies that Ojeda brought back a nugget of pure gold, which weighed nine ounces, and which he himself had picked up in one of the brooks. He also saw stones streaked with veins of gold. It was deemed that these were mere surface washings; and that, beneath the soil, vast deposits of solid gold would be found.*

Ojeda was of as ardent imagination as Columbus. He returned with a glowing report. We easily credit that which we wish to believe. Columbus eagerly accepted all, and, in his sanguine disposition, added new colors to the picture. Indeed the spirits of all the colonists were reanimated by these flattering accounts. Inexhaustible sources of wealth were opening before them. Columbus retained five ships for his own service, and returned the rest, laden with these golden promises. A few specimens of the gold which had been found by Ojeda were sent back, and a few curiosities in the way of plants and fruits.†

* Peter Martyr, decad. i. lib. 11.

† " An enemy of Columbus, one Fermin Cedo, who is represented as a conceited and ignorant man, but who had come to the island as an assayer of metals, asserted, with persistence, that gold could not be found upon the islands, in quantities to repay the search. He declared

With the return fleet, Columbus wrote to the king and queen. He assured them of his confident anticipations that he should soon be able to make more abundant shipments of gold, and of the most valuable drugs and spices. The powers of language were exhausted in his description of the beauty and fertility of the island of Hispaniola. The skies were brilliant, the climate genial, the mountains glorious, the scenery surpassingly lovely, the soil fertile, the fruit delicious, and the bloom perpetual. The sugar, cane, which he brought from Europe, grew with amazing luxuriance.

A colony of over a thousand hungry people, accustomed to the European style of living, consumes a vast amount of food. These men could not live upon fruit alone. Their provisions were rapidly vanishing. It required considerable time to break the soil and raise crops, in field and garden. The animals were all to be carefully preserved that the stock might be increased. Many of the colonists were sick. The medicines were exhausted. The *gentlemen* could not work. More laborers were needed to dig in the mines and smelt the ore. Many of the horses had perished, and more were

that the nuggets obtained from the natives had been melted, and had been the slow accumulation of many years."—*Cura de los Palacios* cap. 120.

greatly needed for public works and military services. Thus it became necessary that large supplies should be promptly sent to him.

The letter, which Columbus wrote to the Spanish sovereigns on this occasion, indicates earnestness and honesty of mind. There was no intentional misrepresentations of anything. He truthfully related all the facts, as they appeared to him. He faithfully depicted their difficulties and their prospects. He sent to Spain, in the ships, several natives, men, women, and children, whom he had captured in the Caribbee Islands. They were cannibals, taken from the most cruel scenes of depravity and degradation. The letter was addressed to Antonio de Torres, stating the information which he was to communicate to Ferdinand and Isabella. The admiral wrote:

"You will tell their highnesses that, as we are not acquainted with the language of these people, so as to make them acquainted with our holy faith, as their highnesses and we ourselves desire, and as we will do so soon as we are able, we send, by these two vessels, some of these cannibal men and women, as well as some children, both male and female. Their highnesses can order them to be placed under the care of the most competent persons to teach them the language; giving instructions at the same time, that they may be employed in useful occupations; and that, by degrees, more care be bestowed upon them than would be given to other slaves, in order that afterward, one may learn from the other.

" By not seeing or speaking to each other for a long time, they will learn much sooner in Spain than here, and they will become much better interpreters. We will, however, do what we can. It is true that, as there is but little communication between one of these islands and another, there is some difference in their mode of expressing themselves; which mainly depends on the distance between them. But as among all these islands, those inhabited by the cannibals are the largest and most populous, I have thought it expedient to send to Spain, men and women from the islands which they inhabit, in the hope that they may one day be led to abandon their barbarous custom of eating their fellow-creatures.

" By learning the Spanish language in Spain, they will much earlier receive baptism, and insure the salvation of their souls. Moreover, it will be a great happiness to the Indians who do not practise the above cruel custom, when they see that we have seized and led captive those who injure them, and those they dread so much that their name alone fills them with horror.*

* " Such arguments must be allowed to have much force in them. And it may be questioned whether many of those persons who, in

"You will assure their highnesses that our arrival
in this country, and the sight of so fine a fleet, have
produced the most desirable effect and insured our
future safety. For all the inhabitants of this great
island and of those around it, when they see the
good treatment that we shall show to those that do
well, and the punishment we shall inflict on those
who do wrong, will hasten to submit; and their
highnesses will shortly be able to reckon them among
the number of their subjects."

To this portion of the letter, the sovereigns
replied, "Let Columbus be informed of what has
transpired to the cannibals that came over to Spain.
He has done well; and his suggestions are good.
But let him endeavor by all possible means to convert them to our holy Catholic religion. And do
the same to the inhabitants of all the islands to
which he may go."

But Columbus continues to write, upon the same
subject: "You will tell their highnesses that, for the
good of the souls of the said cannibals, and even of
the inhabitants of this island, the thought has suggested itself to us, that the greater the number that

these days, are the strongest opponents of slavery, would then have
had that perception of the impending danger of its introduction
which the sovereigns appear to have entertained, from their answer
to this part of the document."—*Life of Columbus*, by Arthur Helps,
p. 136.

are sent over to Spain the better; and that good
service may result to their highnesses in the following manner. Considering what great need we have
of cattle, and of beasts of burden, both for food and
to assist the settlers in their work, their highnesses
will be able to authorize a suitable number of caravels to come here every year, to bring over the said
cattle, in order that the fields may be covered with
people and cultivation.

"These cattle might be sold at moderate prices,
for account of the bearers, and the latter might be
paid with slaves, taken from among the Caribbees,
who are a wild people, fit for any work, well pro-
portioned, and very intelligent, and who, when they
have got rid of the cruel habits to which they have
become accustomed, will be better than any other
kind of slaves. When they lose sight of their
country, they will forget their cruel customs. And
it will be easy to obtain plenty of these savages, by
means of row boats that we propose to build. Their
highnesses might fix duties on the slaves that may
be taken over, on their arrival in Spain. You will
ask for a reply on this point, and bring it to me, that
I may be able to take the necessary measures, should
the proposition merit the approbation of their highnesses."

This suggestion, that the court of Spain should

thus energetically embark in the slave trade, evidently startled Ferdinand and Isabella. They were led to pause and think. Somewhat vaguely they replied. "The consideration of this subject has been suspended for a time, until other measures may be suggested, with reference to the islands. The admiral will do well to write what further he thinks upon the subject." *

These sentiments of Columbus, so abhorrent to the enlightened Christian views of the nineteenth century, were quite in accordance with the opinions generally cherished throughout Christendom four hundred years ago. Such mistaken views of human-rights were almost universally prevalent in that day. The conversion of the souls of the heathen was deemed so important that it was to be effected by whatever means the Church could devise, whether fair or foul. Candid judgment will make allowance for the darkness of the age in which Columbus lived. The admiral undoubtedly thought that he was advocating a measure of mercy, which would prove a great blessing to the poor Caribs, and to humanity in general ; and that it would be well pleasing in the

* The whole of this exceedingly interesting letter together with the replies which the Spanish sovereigns returned to each portion, may be found in the "Select Letters of Christopher Columbus," issued by the Hakluyt Society, London.

sight of God. Men of upright intentions may often
deceive themselves by the strangest sophistry.

It is pleasant to record that Ferdinand and Isabella, upon mature reflection, rejected the flattering
proposal. There was in it much to commend itself
to their approval. The colony could thus, not only
free of expense but with profit, be amply supplied
with live stock from Spain. The peaceful islanders
would be rescued from the ravages of these fierce
cannibals, who were keeping them ever in a state of
terror. The royal treasury would be greatly en-
riched, enabling the ambitious sovereigns to do much
for the promotion of the interests of their realms.
And best of all, a large number of savages might be
brought under the influence of the institutions of
Christianity, and thus their souls might be saved.*

The return fleet put to sea on the 2d of February,
1494. Three and a half centuries after the founda-
tions of the city of Isabella were laid, T. S. Heneken,
Esq., visited the place. The following is his interesting account of the aspect the city then presented:

"Isabella, at the present day, is a city quite
overgrown with forests; in the midst of which are

---

* "It is but just to add that the sovereigns did not accord with
his ideas, but ordered that the Caribs should be converted like the
rest of the islanders ; a command which emanated from the merciful
heart of Isabella, who ever showed herself as the benign protectress of
the Indians."—Irving's *Life of Columbus*, vol I. p. 369.

still to be seen, partly standing, the pillars of the church, some remains of the king's store-houses, and a part of the residence of Columbus, all built of hewn stone. The small fortress is also a prominent ruin. A little north of it is a circular pillar, about ten feet high, and as much in diameter, of solid masonry, nearly entire ; which appears to have had a wooden gallery or battlement round the top, for the convenience of room ; and in the centre of which was planted the flag-staff. Having discovered the remains of an iron clamp, imbedded in the stone, which served to secure the flag-staff itself, I tore it out, and now consign to you this curious relic of the first foot-hold of civilization in the New World, after it has been exposed to the elements nearly three hundred and fifty years." *

The energies of Columbus pressed forward the work, and the city of Isabella rapidly rose, in quite imposing proportions. We infer that the buildings could not have been very elaborate. Columbus entered the harbor on the 7th of December. In two months, on the 6th of February, the church was completed, and dedicated. Twelve ecclesiastics, under their spiritual head, Friar Boyle, assisted in the imposing ceremonies.

The departure of the fleet was a gloomy hour for

* From the Letter of T. S. Heneken.

those who remained. A general feeling of discontent pervaded the little colony. All were disappointed. Some blamed themselves for their folly in
leaving homes in Spain, for a wilderness inhabited
only by savages. Other denounced the admiral,
whose false representations, they said, had lured
them to destruction. Murmurs were heard on all
sides. These increased to upbraidings and bitter
quarrels. — Many sad eyes watched the departure of
the ships. And denser clouds of gloom seemed to
settle over the colony when the last sail vanished
beneath the horizon.*

Among the adventurers there was a proud, arrogant man, from the court of Spain, whose assump-
tions had several times brought him into collision
with the admiral. His name was Bernal Diaz de
Pisa. He organized an insurrection, with quite a
number of the disaffected. Their plan was to seize
one or all of the remaining ships, and return to Spain,
where they would unite in weighty charges against

* "Mr. Goodrich gives vent to his own feelings, and probably to
those of some of the colonists, when he writes, " As the unhappy Spaniards awakened from their dreams of splendor, to the reality of a
country in which was found neither food nor shelter, dissatisfaction
daily increased. Hatred for the pirate admiral, who had so craftily
allured them to destruction, became more and more apparent. Nor
were the harsh measures and tyrannical conduct of Columbus calcu-
tated to conciliate. Bitter complaints were made against him."—
Life of Columbus, p. 239.

Columbus. They hoped to enlist so many in the conspiracy as to seize all the five ships.

The mutiny was discovered, and the ringleaders arrested. In the investigation which took place, a very atrocious libel was found, in the handwriting of Bernal Diaz, full of slanders and misrepresentations. Diaz was a man of high rank. Columbus very prudently declined bringing him to trial, before one of his own courts, where his own influence might be deemed paramount, but sent him to Spain, with his seditious memorial. Some of the inferior mutineers were punished, but more mildly than their offence merited. To guard against any renewal of the attempt, the guns and ammunition were removed from all the ships but one; and that was intrusted to persons whose fidelity could not be questioned.*

Columbus was not a Spaniard, but a citizen of Genoa. National prejudices rose against him as a foreigner. The haughty Spaniards combined for his overthrow. He had no natural friends to rally to his support. Though the general safety rendered it necessary that the disturbers of the public peace should not go unpunished, and though he was humane and lenient in the extreme in his dealings with transgres-

* "Historia del Almirante," cap. 50; Herrera, " Hist. Ind.," decad. i. lib. ii. cap. ii.

sors, still his opponents assailed him as arbitrary and vindictive. It is not possible for any one, invested with power, to escape denunciation. George Washington, throughout the whole of his career, was assailed as if he were a fiend. The hostility engendered against Columbus increased in rancor, until he found repose in the grave. And the envenomed assaults still pursue him, after the lapse of three and a half centuries.

Columbus decided to take a working party, and go to the mines in person, that he might superintend operations there. He intrusted the government at Isa bella, during his absence, to his brother, Don Diego. Las Casas, who was familiarly acquainted with him, represents him as a very amiable, upright man, a lover of peace, gentlemanly in his bearing, frugal in his habits, simple in his attire.*

As Columbus was to enter the territory of a renowned warrior, who had already manifested his deadly hostility to the Spaniards, it was necessary that he should take a force, not only sufficient to repel assaults, but also one of such a character as to convince the natives of the resistless power of the new-comers. It would be easy for those left behind in their fortress, to defend themselves against any attack. He therefore took nearly all the able-bodied

* Las Casas, " Hist. Ind.," lib. i. cap. 32.

men, and all the horses which could be spared.
Experience had taught him how deeply the savages
were impressed by external appearances. He therefore arrayed his force in with all the military splendor he could command.*

The expedition, consisting of four hundred men,
set out, on the 12th of March, 1494. The company,
encased in dazzling armor, with highly polished
weapons and gilded banners, and with the notes of
the trumpets reverberating through the forests, must
have impressed the natives with ideas of supernatural and resistless power. All the prominent men
were in rich uniform, and mounted on gayly capari-
soned horses. It was a serene and lovely day, as
the band crossed the flower-enamelled plain toward
the distant hills. In the early evening they reached
the entrance of a rocky defile among the mountains.
On the turf, breathing the balmy air, they slept
sweetly. A narrow Indian trail led through the
rugged defiles.

Several high-spirited cavaliers rode forward as
pioneers to remove obstructions. The road thus

---

* " Columbus had already discovered the error of one of his opinions concerning these islanders, formed during his first voyage. They
were not so entirely pacific, nor so ignorant of warlike arts as he had
imagined. He had been deceived by the enthusiasm of his own feelings, and the gentleness of Guacanagari and his subjects."—Irving's
Life of Columbus vol. i. p. 389.

opened was called the Gentleman's Pass, in honor
of the cavaliers who constructed it. When they
reached the height of land, the same prospect of
fairy-like loveliness was opened before them, upon
which Ojeda and his companions had gazed with
delight. The pen of Irving has portrayed the scene
with almost the vividness of the landscape painter's
pencil.*

" Below lay a vast and delicious plain, painted
and enamelled, as it were, with all the rich variety of
tropical vegetation. The magnificent forests presented that mingled beauty and majesty of vegetable
forms, known only to those generous climates.
Palms of prodigious height, and spreading mahogany
trees, towered from amid a wilderness of variegated
foliage. Freshness and verdure were maintained by
numerous streams, which meandered gleaming
through the deep bosom of the woodland ; while
various villages and hamlets, peeping from among
the trees, and the smoke of others rising out of the
midst of forests, gave signs of a numerous population.
The luxuriant landscape extended as far as the eye
could reach, until it appeared to melt away and
mingle with the horizon. The Spaniards gazed with

* The Spanish name was El Puerto de los Hidalgos, or The Pass
of the Hidalgos. *Hidalgo* is said to be derived from *Hijo de Algo*, the
" Son of Somebody." This was to distinguish him from one of obscure
birth, who was said to be a *Son of Nobody.*

rapture upon this soft, voluptuous country, which
seemed to realize their ideas of a terrestrial paradise;
and Columbus, struck with its vast extent, gave it
the name of the Vega Real, or Royal Plain." *

This now solitary route is still occasionally traversed by the tourists of modern days. It remains a
lonely, rugged footpath, winding among rocks and
precipices; the only practicable defile across the
Monte Christo range of mountains. It is called the
Pass of Marney. The beautiful island has been
crushed beneath the scourge of the kind of civilization which the Spaniards introduced. Solitude,
desolation, and gaunt poverty reign where the smiling villages of the Haytiens formerly enlivened the
scene, leading Columbus to think that he was gazing
upon an earthly Eden.†

With great pomp of military display, and the
clangor of trumpets, the glittering host emerged
upon the plain. The natives could not refrain from
regarding the wonderful pageant as a supernatural
vision.‡ Las Casas says that, at first, they consid-

* " Life of Columbus," vol. i. p. 399. Irving gives, as his authority for this description, Las Casas, " Hist. Ind. lib. i. cap. 90. MS..

† " Letter from T. S. Heneken, Esq.," dated Santiago (St. Domingo), 20th of September, 1847.

‡ Perhaps historic justice demands that we should give Mr. Goodrich's comments upon the march. He writes: " The progress
through the country, on this expedition, was characteristic. His band
was sickly, wearied, and disheartened. Yet he must needs enter every

ered the horse and his rider as one animal. Generally, the Indians fled in terror. The kindness of
Columbus eventually overcame their fears. Native
interpreters were sent forward to assure them that
no harm was intended. Presents were also distributed, which the natives received with amazement
and delight. Food was considered by them as free
to all. One could enter any house and eat at his
pleasure. But we are told, in apparent contradic-
tion to some previous statements, that other private
property was held sacred. Theft was punished with
great severity.

A march of fifteen miles brought them to a large
stream, which Columbus named the River of Reeds.
It proved to be the upper waters of that stream,
which, near its mouth, he had called the River of
Gold. Upon these green banks, and bathing in
these still waters, the adventurers passed a night of
luxurious encampment. The next morning they
crossed on rafts, swimming the horses. For two
days the march was continued through this magnificent plain. They passed many villages, from all of
which the natives at first fled. On the evening
of the second day they reached the northern decliv-

Indian hamlet, with trumpets sounding and banners flying ; so irre-
pressible were his vanity and delight in exhibiting his newly acquired
rank."—*Life of Columbus*, p. 240.

ities of what were called the Golden Mountains of Cibao.

The next morning they commenced the ascent, through gloomy ravines and craggy rocks, where the horses were with difficulty led. They reached the summit. An entrancing view again met their eyes. The plain lay spread out before them like a " verdant lake." According to the estimate of Las Casas, it was two hundred and forty miles in length, and about seventy miles in breadth. They had now reached the centre of the famous gold region. The summits of the mountains presented but a dreary scene of barrenness and desolation. Scarcely a flower bloomed. All vegetation was scanty. Gloomy pines were on the hill-sides. But the Spaniards were consoled for the cheerlessness of the scene, in finding, among the sands, glittering particles of gold, which seemed to give assurance that there were inexhaustible mines of wealth locked up within the mountains.

The exploring party was then about fifty or sixty miles from Isabella. Columbus selected a pleasant site for his encampment. He erected a wooden fort, which he, perhaps playfully, called St. Thomas, in gentle reproof of those unbelieving ones, who would not believe that any gold was to be found, until they had seen it with their eyes and touched it with their hands.

CHAPTER IX.

The Coast of Cuba Explored.

The fortress of St. Thomas—Extravagant expectations of the Spaniards—The exploring expedition—The arrest of thieves—Com-
mencement of the maritime cruise—The harbor of Guantanamo—
Interesting scene with the Indians—Jamaica—Its grandeur and
beauty—Naval scene—Events at Santa Gloria—Native canoes—
Events of the voyage—Testimony of Humboldt—The decision—
The Island of Pines—Speech of the chief—The return to Hispaniola—Incidents of the voyage.

WHILE building the fortress of St. Thomas, Columbus sent out a small band to explore the surrounding country. The men were thoroughly armed,
and were led by a chivalric young cavalier, by the
name of Juan de Luxan. They traversed the province of Caonabo, and judged it to be about equal in
extent to the kingdom of Portugal. Particles of
gold-dust were found in the sands of all the streams.
Language could hardly exaggerate the fertility and
beauty of the country.

A garrison of fifty-six men was left at the fortress.
Mining operations were commenced, and Columbus
returned to Isabella. On the 29th of March, he
reached the colony, bearing a very flattering report

of the prospect of obtaining gold. Soon a report reached him that the Indians, at St. Thomas, were becoming unfriendly. The fact was that, as soon as the restraint of the presence of Columbus was withdrawn from the Spaniards, the unprincipled men began to rob the natives, and to subject their wives and daughters to intolerable insults. Caonabo knew them well. With great impatience he saw them establishing themselves in the midst of his mountains.

Columbus did not think that there was much to be feared from their hostility. He contented himself with sending to the fort a small reinforcement, with provisions and supplies. But he had cause to be greatly troubled, in view of the discontent and murmurings ever increasing at Isabella, and the manifestation of hostile feelings toward himself. Very many were sick. They had no proper food, and their medicines were exhausted. We read, with some surprise, that the colonists could not accustom themselves to the food of the natives. Threatenings of famine rendered it necessary to put the people upon short allowance. This caused increasing murmurs. No one was more turbulent in these complainings than the Spanish chief of ecclesiastics, Father Boyle.

The ecclesiastics and the grandees were irritated

because Columbus made no distinction of rank in civil duties. The very existence of the colony required that mills should be erected, and that other labors for the public welfare should be performed. All were alike required to aid. The haughty hidalgos rose in indignant remonstrance. Columbus was denounced as a foreign upstart, and he found himself without a friend.

Columbus was a strict disciplinarian. He was not theoretically versed in the science of political economy, or popular rights; but was guided by the honest instincts of his own strong mind. It is not improbable that, coming from industrious Genoa, where labor was honorable, he did not sufficiently appreciate the amazing pride and haughtiness of the Spanish nobles. They regarded all labor as the ignominious doom of the " sons of nobody." Many young cavaliers, who had been reaping renown upon the military fields of Grenada, had entered upon the expedition to the New World, with the most romantic ideas of the wealth which was to roll in upon them. They were to dwell in castles, bestride their war-horses, and eclipse the splendor even of Spanish imperialism, in the grandeur of their feudal establishments and the obsequiousness of their crowds of attendants. Mr. Irving writes:

" Many of these young men had come out hoping, no doubt, to distinguish themselves by heroic achievements and chivalrous adventure, and to continue, in the Indies, the career of arms which they had commenced in the recent wars of Grenada. Others had been brought up in soft, luxurious indulgence, in the midst of opulent families, and were little calculated for the rude peril of the seas, the fatigues of the land, and the hardships, the exposures, the deprivations which attend a new settlement in the wilderness. When they fell ill, their case soon became incurable. The ailments of the body were increased by sickness of the heart. They suffered under the irritation of wounded pride, and the morbid melancholy of disappointed hope. Their sick bed was destitute of all the tender care and soothing attention to which they had been accustomed. And they sank into the grave in all the sullenness of despair, cursing the day of their departure from their country." *

Ferdinand and Isabella were pressing Columbus to continue his voyages of discovery. Apparently there was a wide and unknown world opening before him, and no one could imagine what wonders might be revealed. The growing troubles at Isabella led Columbus to judge it wise to disperse the colonists, on these tours. He therefore fitted out a strong

* Irving's " Life of Columbus," vol. i. p. 406.

expedition to explore the interior of the island. The force included every healthy man who could be spared from tending the sick, and from performing pressing public duties. There were, in the band, two hundred and fifty cross-bow men, one hundred and ten arquebusiers, sixteen horsemen, and twenty officers. Peter Margarite, a friend of Columbus, and one of the most illustrious knights of the Order of Santiago, was placed in command. Ojeda was left as superintendent of the mines.

Columbus gave Margarite very minute written instructions. They develop his sound judgment, his humanity, and his noble ambition not to live in vain. The sincerity of the admiral cannot be questioned. In this document he says : " Treat the Indians with the utmost kindness. Protect them from all wrong and insult. Pay liberally for everything you receive from them, for the support of the troops. Do all in your power to win their confidence and friendship. Should the absolute necessities of the army compel you to take from them anything which they are unwilling to sell, do it as gently as possible ; endeavoring to soothe them by kindness and caresses. And ever bear in mind that their majesties are more desirous of the conversion of the natives than of any riches to be derived from them." *

* " Letter of Columbus," Navarette Colec., tom. ii. doc. No. 72.

All these judicious instructions Margarite disregarded. Prosperity and happiness would have attended their faithful observance. The vileness of this band of Spaniards brought on war and misery. The Indians were exterminated. Spain was disgraced. Humanity was dishonored. And Columbus himself was pursued with the most intense vituperation which language could coin.

The cacique, Caonabo, was an intelligent, artful, and determined foe. His expedition for the destruction of the Spanish garrison at La Navidad, had been executed with great skill and entire success. The evidence was decisive that he was now organizing a force to destroy the Spaniards who had invaded his territory, and who were fortifying themselves at Fort St. Thomas. Deplorable is the lot of man. No one can blame the chief for his desire to drive from his country the Spaniards, who had already developed a demoniac character, in their treatment of the natives. On the other hand, no one can blame Columbus for sending an expedition into the interior of the island, in search for gold. Columbus could conscientiously pray to God to protect his colony. With equal sincerity could Caonabo implore the deities he worshipped to aid him in driving out the intruders.*

* " Columbus was wrong in the impression he first received, that

10*

Ojeda accompanied the expedition of nearly four hundred men, to St. Thomas, where he was to relieve Margarite, and surrender the explorers to him. Five Indians had robbed, it was said, three Spaniards. Their chief was accused of sharing their spoil, instead of punishing them. Ojeda caught an Indian, who was declared to be one of the thieves. He cut off his ears, in the public square of the Indian village. Arresting the chief, his son and his nephew, he sent them all in chains to Isabella.

A neighboring chief, who had proved friendly to the Spaniards, accompanied the terrified captives, to plead for their forgiveness. Columbus paid no heed to these friendly intercessions. He sent the three prisoners to the public square, with their hands tied behind them ; directed the crier to proclaim their crime, and then ordered their heads to be struck off. Oviedo says, in palliation of the order, that it was important to strike awe into the minds of the natives, in respect to the property of the white men ; and that the crime of theft was punished, by the Indians, with impalement.*

It, however, is not probable that Columbus had

the natives had no religious belief. They had a vague and simple creed. There was, in their view, one Supreme Being, who dwelt in the sky. He employed inferior deities. To these subordinate gods, only, was prayer addressed."—*Historia del Almirante.*

* Oviedo " Hist. Ind." lib. v. cap. 3.

any intention of executing the cruel penalty. At the assigned place of execution the friendly chief wept bitterly, and in the most pathetic tones implored the admiral not to take the lives of his friends; assuring him that there should be no repetition of the offence, and pledging his own life as the forfeiture, if there should be. The admiral yielded, and the prisoners were set at liberty.

Columbus had for some time been making preparations to set sail, with his squadron, in search of new realms. It will be remembered that he supposed Cuba to be, not an island, but a portion of the continent of Asia. His present plan was to cruise along the southern coast of this vast promontory.

The little squadron sailed on the 14th of April, 1494. Don Diego Columbus was left in command at Isabella. Cruising to the westward, a short tarry was made at Monte Christo, and the fleet cast anchor in the gloomy bay of La Navidad. On the 29th, passing the extreme western cape of St. Domingo, the ship came in sight of the extreme eastern cape of Cuba, which Columbus had named Alpha and Omega. It is now known as Point Maysi. The channel between the two islands is about fifty-four miles wide. Crossing this channel, he ran along the southern coast of Cuba, about sixty miles, when he

cast anchor in a capacious harbor, which he named
Puerto Grande.   It is now called Guantanamo.

Cottages and fires, on the shore, indicated the
presence of inhabitants. Columbus, with a well-
armed party, landed.   But not an Indian could be
found. All had fled to the mountains.   The Spaniards found food in abundance, which they eagerly
devoured.   Just as they had closed their feast, they
saw, upon a distant eminence, about seventy Indians,
looking down upon them apparently with awe and
astonishment.   Upon approaching, all but one fled
with the utmost precipitation.   One bold young man
ventured to tarry behind, though apparently ready in
an instant to bound away.

Columbus sent forward an Indian interpreter
with presents.   The bold young man came forward,
to meet the native envoy.   Upon receiving the presents, and assurances of the kind intentions of the
Spaniards, he ran after his companions, to communicate to them the intelligence. Slowly, and with timid,
hesitating footsteps, they returned.   They had been
sent to the coast, to procure fish for a great banquet,
which the chief was to give to a neighboring chieftain.   The fishes had been roasted, to preserve
them.   The hungry Spaniards had devoured all.
The gentle, friendly natives said that it was of no
consequence, as one night's fishing would replace the

loss. But Columbus, with characteristic justice, insisted that full payment should be made. Thus the Spaniards and the Cubans parted, well-pleased with each other.*

Still continuing his cruise to the west, the country seemed to grow more fertile and more populous. Natives—men, women and children—crowded the shore, to gaze upon the fleet, gliding gently by, at the distance of about a mile from the land. At length the fleet entered another large bay, surrounded by beautiful scenery. It was probably the harbor now called St. Jago. The fleet anchored, and passed the night. The natives seemed to have lost all fear of the strangers. They came, in crowds, to the ships, in their canoes, lavishing upon the Spaniards the most generous hospitality.

Everywhere Columbus inquired for gold. Generally, in reply, the natives pointed south ; intimating that there was a large island there, abounding with the precious ore. On the 3d of March, Columbus turned the prows of his ships in a southerly direction ; and abandoned the coast of Cuba, in search of the reported island. After a few hours' sail, magnificent mountains began to rear their heads, like clouds, in the horizon. As they drew near, a vision of wonderful beauty was unveiled before

* " History of the Discoveries of Columbus," by Peter Martyr.

them. Accustomed as they were to these luxuriant
Edens, emerging from the sunny waves, exclamations of admiration burst from all lips, as the ships
glided along. the shores, where mountains, valleys,
groves, and picturesque villages in ever-varying loveliness, charmed the eye.

When quite near the shore, the wind died away,
and the ships floated almost motionless, as upon a
sea of glass. Instantly, about seventy canoes, crowded
with warriors, pushed out from the shore. These
truly intrepid men, painted, plumed, and brandishing their lances, uttered loud yells as they advanced,
in war-like array, to attack an apparation which, to
them, one would think must have been invested with
supernatural terrors.

When one of the canoes was within hailing distance, a native interpreter called out to the crew.
They understood him. His assurance of the friendship of the strangers, and the potent influence
of some presents of marvellous value, in their eyes,
which were tossed into their boat, disarmed their hospitality. They paddled back. The little fleet of
canoes gathered around them to listen to their
strange report. While they were thus conferring,
lost in amazement, the wind freshened, and the squadron, unassailed, pursued its course. It is altogether
probably, that had not Columbus been on board,

the Spanish sailors would have amused themselves
in seeing what effect a few discharges of grape-shot,
from their heavy cannon, would produce upon the
dense throng of the natives huddled together in this
group of canoes.

A short sail brought them to a spacious harbor,
where Columbus cast anchor. He named the bay
Santa Gloria. Landing, he raised the Cross of Christ,
and the banner of Spain, and took possession of the
island in the name of his sovereigns. One of the
ships had sprung a leak. It was necessary to careen
and calk it. He sent a boat in search of a suitable
spot. Two large canoes, filled with warriors, approached, hurling their javelins at the crew; but from
such a distance that they fell harmless. Soon the
beach was covered with Indians, brandishing their
weapons like frantic men, and uttering hideous yells·

These natives seemed to have none of the gentle
character of those of Cuba and Hayti, but manifested
all the ferocity of the Caribs. It was absolutely necessary to careen the ship. Columbus deemed it essential that the natives should be overawed, so that they
would not take advantage of the opportunity, and
attack him with overwhelming numbers. Whether
he pursued a wise course is a question upon which
good men may differ. No candid man will assert
that any love of cruelty inspired his action.

The shoal-water prevented the caravels from drawing near the beach. He therefore sent several boats toward the shore, well-manned and armed. We do not learn that they waited to be attacked. When within bow-shot of the land, they discharged a volley of arrows from their cross-bows, which wounded a number of the Indians, and put all the rest to flight. The Spaniards, cased in coats-of-mail impervious to the arrows of the natives, sprang upon the beach, and threw another volley of their sharp-pointed and barbed arrows upon the fugitives. At the same time they let loose, upon the almost naked natives, a powerful blood-hound, who pursued them with the resistless strength and ferocity of a tiger and mangled them with bloody fangs.

This is the first account we have of the employ-ment of the terrible blood-hound in the butchery of the Indians. The terrified natives, being thus dis-persed, with no fear of their returning, Columbus took formal possession of the island. He gave it the name of Santiago. Fortunately, it has retained the far more beautiful Indian name of Jamaica. It is a melancholy reflection that the first approach of Chris-tendom to this barbaric isle was accompanied with terror, wounds, slaughter, and the manglings of the blood-hound.*

* Cura de los Palacios, cap. 125

For the remainder of that dismal day, not an Indian was to be seen. But the next morning, just as the sun was rising, six of the natives were seen at a distance, cautiously approaching, and apparently making signs of friendship. The admiral received them kindly, and learned that they were sent, by several of the chiefs, with offers of peace. Columbus assured them of his earnest desire to live on friendly terms with all the people; but that he had power to punish them with the most terrible severity, should they be guilty of any treachery. In proof of his wish for fraternal intercourse, he sent the chiefs many presents, which they must have regarded as of inestimable value. Who can imagine the worth of a substantial sharp-edged knife to a savage, who has been accustomed painfully to carve out his bow and his arrows with pieces of flint?

The Indians were like children. All their animosity was at once laid aside. In crowds they came to the encampment, where Columbus was repairing his ships. For three days the most friendly intercourse prevailed. But these Indians were manifestly a warlike race. Their military weapons were quite formidable, and their war canoes were constructed with much artistic skill. They were made of the single trunk of a species of mahogany tree. Columbus measured one of these canoes, which was ninety-six feet long, and eight broad.

The ship being repaired, and a supply of water taken in, the cruise was continued along the coast of the island, to the west. The breeze was very light, and the water so transparent that the pebbles could be seen at the depth of several fathoms. As the caravels glided slowly along, within a few rods of the shore, they were, at times, entirely surrounded by the canoes of the natives. They shot out from every bay, river, and headland. The island seemed to be thronging with inhabitants, all friendly, and all eager to get some European trinket at whatever price.

Columbus still called for gold. None could be found. None could be heard of. Much disappointed, he turned back to what he considered the main land of Cuba. It was still uncertain whether Cuba was an island or a continent. That question he wished to solve. As they were spreading their sails, a very interesting Indian young man came on board the admiral's ship, and implored that he might be taken to the country of the Spaniards. Curiosity was apparently the motive which inspired him—an intense desire to visit the homes from which the wonderful strangers came. The relatives of the young man, with the most pathetic lamentations, entreated him to desist from his purpose. Though the tender-hearted youth wept, he still persisted in his plan; and, having obtained the consent of the admiral, hid himself in a secret part of the ship, that he might not witness the distress of his friends. Unfortunately, we hear nothing more of this youthful adventurer.

On the 18th of May Columbus reached the coast of Cuba, at a point which he called Cabo de la Cruz. The name is still retained. There was a large village here. The inhabitants had heard of the first voyage of Columbus, and received the Spaniards with the greatest kindness. The admiral made many inquiries, of the most intelligent chiefs, whether Cuba was an island or a continent. Invariably they gave the contradictory reply that it was an island, but of limitless extent. No one, they declared, had ever been able to find any end to it. This gave confirmation to the opinion that Columbus was on the great continent of Asia. By continuing his course further west, he thought that he should soon reach the renowned and resplendent dominions of the great Khan. As he cruised along the southern shore he entered a wonderful archipelago, where there seemed to be thousands of islands clothed in richest verdure, and of every variety of size and picturesque form. Most of the islands were uninhabited. The narrow channels between them were as still as the placid waters of the most secluded mountain lake. Flowers were in richest bloom. The groves, meadows, and waters abounded with tropical birds of splendid plumage.

Upon one of the largest of the islands, which Columbus called Santa Marta, he landed. It was the 22d of May. There were inhabitants here, but they had abandoned their houses. It afterward appeared that they were absent on a fishing excursion. Slowly working his way through the narrow channel of these islands, he continued his course about fifty miles beyond, when, on the 3d of June, he came to a large Indian village. The inhabitants received the strangers with that kindness which was almost invariable on the island of Cuba.

Here again Columbus was assured that there was no western end to Cuba. A prosperous breeze filled his sails, and the admiral was quite sanguine, as he pressed onward toward the setting sun, that he should soon reach the civilized realms of Asia. There was now before him an expanse of nearly a hundred miles, unbroken by a single island. The densely wooded coast of Cuba was on his right. On the left was the broad and open sea. The weather was delightful ; and the fleet kept so near the coast, that the natives came off in great numbers, some swimming and some in canoes. Through the night the songs of the natives, and their rude music, were wafted by the gentle breezes to their ears. It was supposed that the natives were thus celebrating the advent of the celestial visitants.

That region, then so populous, is now a dreary solitude. Not a single descendant of the Indians, whose peaceful homes then adorned the hills and the valleys, now remains. Humboldt, but a few years ago, passed a night on this coast. He writes:

"I passed a great part of the night upon the deck. What deserted coasts! not a light to announce the cabin of a fisherman. From Batabano to Trinidad, a distance of one hundred and fifty miles, there does not exist a village. Yet, at the time of Columbus, this land was inhabited even along the margin of the sea. When pits are digged in the soil, or the torrents plough open the surface of the earth, there are often found hatchets of stone, or vessels of copper, relics of the ancient inhabitants of the land." *

After two days' sail, the fleet reached another group of islands, through whose intricate channels it was with difficulty and danger that the vessels threaded their way. Still Columbus pressed onward to the west. Every hour he hoped to meet with some indications that he was approaching the great

* Humboldt, " Essai Pol. sur Cuba," tom. ii. p. 25.

eastern empire. But day after day he encountered only naked savages and their lowly huts. The dialect of the Indians, in these remote regions, had become unintelligible to the native interpreters from Hayti. But little could be learned from them, by the language of signs. But Columbus so interpreted their signs, as to receive constant confirmation that he was cruising along the shores of the vast Asiatic continent.

All the companions of Columbus agreed with him in this opinion. And among these were several learned scholars, and experienced navigators. The ships were crippled by the long voyage. The rigging was worn, and the sails tattered. Their provisions were nearly exhausted. The sailors were discontented and murmuring. There was no longer any novelty in the scenes presented. All wished to return. Columbus himself did not deem it safe to continue the voyage longer. He assembled all the officers, and the most intelligent men. With one voice they declared that Cuba could not be an island ; that it was impossible but that so vast a continuity of land should be a continent.

The admiral deemed it of the utmost importance that his opinion should be sustained by the corroborative evidence of all on board the ships. As he had already ample evidence that he had hosts of ene-

mies, who were disposed to dispute his statements
and depreciate his discoveries, he wished to establish
the fact that he had discovered a continent by proof
which would command universal confidence. He
therefore sent an accredited officer to every ship in
the little squadron, to take the opinion, under oath,
of every person, from the captain to the ship-boy.
To every one the statement was made, that if he had
any doubt whatever, that the land before them was
the continent of India, he should state that doubt,
and give the reason for it; that it might then and
there be considered.

Lest some, from caprice or malice, should hereafter
declare that they had not given an honest opinion;
that from compulsion or policy they had signed a false
statement, thus convicting Columbus of fraud, and
of attempting to deceive his sovereigns by pretended
discoveries, sustained by documents which fear had
extorted, it was proclaimed that should any one hereafter declare that he had given, from interested
motives, a false opinion, and that he did not believe
that a continent had been reached—if an officer, he
should pay a penalty of ten thousand marevedi; *
if a common sailor, he was to receive a hundred
lashes, and have his tongue cut out.

* Marevedi ; a small copper coin of Spain, equal to three mills
of American money ; less than a farthing sterling.— *Webster.*

This awful penalty, to be inflicted upon the ignorant, fanatic sailors, who could be easily bribed to
make any declaration the enemies of Columbus
might desire, indicate how deeply his feelings were
exasperated by the conspiracies which were continually formed against him, as an upstart foreigner, the
" son of nobody." Though it is undoubtedly true
that Columbus never intended that the cruel penalty
should be executed, it is unfortunate that it should
have been announced. It put a new weapon in the
hands of those who were ever eager to assail the
admiral.*

The experienced navigators and geographers on
board the vessels carefully examined the maps and
charts. After mature deliberation, they unanimously
gave it as their opinion that they had reached the
main land. Upon oath they declared that they had
no doubt upon the subject. They stated that, in
the sinuosities of their voyage along the coast of
Cuba, they had already traversed an extent of over
a thousand miles, and that the land still continued
to stretch out interminably beyond them. Every
individual on board the ships united in the general

* This document still exists. It may be found entire, in the collection of Martin Fernandez de Navarette. He was secretary of the
Royal Academy of History at Madrid. All subsequent historians of
the great discoverer are much indebted to the valuable collection he
made of documents relative to the Voyages of Columbus.

statement. Columbus cherished not a doubt that he had reached the Asiatic continent. In this conviction he lived and died.*

It is thought that this important statement was drawn up in the bay of Philippina, though some place it in the bay of Cortez. The ships were then so near the western end of the island, that a sail of three days would have dissolved the illusion, and would have introduced the fleet to the almost boundless waters of the Mexican gulf.

The squadron commenced its return, following along the coast in a south-east direction. They soon came to a group of small islands and barren rocks, which the Spaniards called *cayos*, or keys.† In the

---

* Mr. Aaron Goodrich comments upon this movement as follows: "That he knew that he was not in Asia, is evident from the extraordinary measures he took to convince the world he had reached that continent. Had he been assured of that fact, he would have trusted to further investigation to establish its verity. On the other hand, if he knew he was practising a fraud, he would endeavor to procure as much testimony as possible to insure the fraud's gaining credence.

"Here Columbus, not content with speaking and writing a falsehood, *is guilty of subornation of perjury.* He manufactures perjury wholesale, which felony he would perpetrate by the barbarous means of scourging, and cutting out the tongues of those who speak the truth. Thus, by a system unknown to Thales and Ptolemy—original, if not scientific, did the much-lauded navigator and astronomer, the pious and humane 'admiral,' determine the latitude and the longitude of the island of Cuba."—*Life of Columbus*, p. 243.

† *Cayo*, or key; sandbank, rock, or islet in the sea; an island rising a little above the surface of the water, as in the West Indies.— *Webster.*

midst of them majestic mountains rose towering to
the skies, indicating an island of imperial grandeur.
Columbus had no time to explore it. In one of the
harbors he anchored, for a few hours, to take in wood
and water, and to raise upon it the cross of our cru-
cified Saviour, and the banner of Spain. Columbus
gave the island the name of Evangelista. It is now
called the Island of Pines.

Through many perils and occasional disasters in
navigating these unknown seas, where rock and sand-
bars abounded, they followed along the coast of
Cuba, toward the east. His crew had become greatly
enfeebled by the enervating climate, the unaccustomed food, and the incessant toil and watchings
which had been necessary. For two months they
struggled against difficulties and dangers. The heat
of the sun destroyed all fresh provisions in a few
hours. Fish must be cooked and eaten as soon as
caught. The crew, at sea, were reduced to a pound
of mouldy bread a day, and a small portion of wine.

On the 7th of July, Columbus ran into an allur-
ing harbor to refresh his exhausted men. The Indians regaled them with all abundance. As usual,
Columbus raised the cross and the banner. It was
Sunday morning. Mass was performed with great
solemnity. A crowd of natives gazed, with intensest
interest, upon the pageant. A venerable chief, four-

score years of age, seemed impressed with awe and
reverence, as he listened to the chanting of the robed
priests, and witnessed the lighted tapers, the wreaths
of incense, and the mysterious gesticulations.   When
the service was ended he approached Columbus and,
taking him by the hand, addressed him in the following extraordinary speech :

" This, which thou hast been doing, appears to
be thy manner of giving thanks to God.   I am told
that thou hast lately come to these lands, with a
mighty force, and subdued many countries, spreading great fear among the people.   But be not therefore vainglorious.   Know that, according to our
belief, the souls of men have two journeys to perform, after they have departed from the body.   One
to a place dismal and foul, and covered with darkness, prepared for those who have been unjust and
cruel to their fellow-men.   The other, pleasant and
full of delight, for such as have promoted peace on
earth.   If then thou art mortal, and dost expect to
die, and dost believe that each one shall be rewarded
according to his deeds, beware that thou wrongfully
hurt no man ; nor do harm to those who have done
no harm to thee." *

The speech was interpreted by the Haytien

* This remarkable speech is recorded by all the early annalists of
Columbus: by Herrera, Ferdinando Columbus and Peter Martyr.

interpreter. Columbus' was surprised in hearing such noble sentiments from the lips of the aged chief. In reply he assured the venerable Indian that he agreed with him in his views as to the future state of the soul; that it was his wish to teach them the true religion, and to protect them from all injury; and that consequently all innocent people might look to him as a friend and protector. The aged chieftain seemed suddenly seized with an intense desire to visit the wonderful country from which the Spaniards came. His wife and children, however, pleaded with the good old man with such lamentations and tears, that he was persuaded to desist from his purpose.

"Of a truth I perceive that God is no respecter of persons. But in every nation he that feareth Him and worketh righteousness, is accepted with Him."*

The name of Rio de la Misa, River of the Mass, was given to the spot where these events took place. On the 16th of July he again weighed anchor. Steering to the south, he sailed over a broad and open sea, directing his course for Hispaniola. Several tropical gales were encountered, of such se r y that the escape of the fleet seemed almost miraculous. Fierce and contrary winds drove the squadron across to Jamaica. Nearly a month

---

St. Peter, as quoted in the Acts of the Apostles, x. 34.

was spent in beating eastward, against head-winds, on this coast. Almost every evening Columbus cast anchor in some one of the numerous harbors which indented the shore. Often, at night, he anchored near the same spot which he had left in the morning.

The natives were no longer hostile. They brought supplies profusely to the ships. Though all the novelty of tropical scenery had long since passed away, Columbus was increasingly delighted with the beauty and productiveness of the noble island. We give one of the scenes witnessed on this cruise, as described by the graphic pen of Washington Irving.

"The next morning the ships were under way, and standing along the coast, with a light wind and easy sail, when they beheld three canoes, issuing from among the islands of the bay. They approached in regular order. One, which was very large, and handsomely carved and painted, was in the centre, a little in advance of the two others, which appeared to attend and guard it. In this was seated the cacique and his family, consisting of his wife, two daughters, two sons, and five brothers.

"One of the daughters was eighteen years of age, beautiful in form and countenance. Her sister was somewhat younger. Both were naked, according to the custom of these islands; but were of modest demeanor. In the prow of the canoe stood the standard-bearer of the cacique, clad in a mantle of variegated feathers, with a tuft of gay plumes on his head; and bearing in his hand a fluttering white banner. Two Indians, with caps or helmets of feathers, of uniform shape and color, and their faces painted in a similar manner, beat upon tabors. Two others, with hats curiously wrought of green feathers, held trumpets of a fine, black wood, ingeniously carved. There were six others, in large hats of white feathers, who appeared to be guards to the cacique.

" Having arrived alongside of the admiral's ship, the cacique entered on board with all his train. He appeared in full regalia. Around his head was a small band of small stones of various colors, but principally green, symmetrically arranged, with large white stones at intervals, and connected in front with a large jewel of gold. Two plates of gold were suspended to his ears, by rings of very small green stones. To a necklace of white beads, of a kind deemed precious by them, was suspended a large plate, in the form of a fleur-de-lys,* of guanin, an inferior species of gold. A girdle of variegated

---

* *Fleur-de-lys*, flower of the lily. The royal insignia of France. Whether originally representing a lily, or the head of a javelin, is disputed. — *Webster.*

stones, similar to those around his head, completed his regal decorations.

" His wife was adorned in a similar manner ; having also a small apron of cotton, and bands of the same round her arms and legs.   The daughters were without ornaments, excepting the oldest and the handsomest, who had a girdle of small stones, from which was suspended a tablet, the size of an ivy leaf, composed of various-colored stones, embroidered on network of cotton.

" When the cacique entered on board the ship, he distributed presents of the productions of the island, among the officers and the men.   The admiral was at this time in his cabin, engaged in his morning devotions.   When he appeared on deck the chieftain hastened to meet, him with an animated countenance, and said :

" ' My Friend: I have determined to leave my country and to accompany thee.   I have heard, from the Indians who are with thee, of the irresistible power of the sovereigns, and of the many nations thou hast subdued in their name.   Whoever refuses obedience to thee is sure to suffer.   Thou hast destroyed the canoes and dwellings of the Carib ; slaying their warriors, and carrying into captivity their wives and children.   All these islands are in dread of thee.   For who can withstand thee, now thou knowest the secrets of the land and the weakness of the people. Rather, therefore, than that thou shouldst take away my dominions, I will embark with all my household in thy ships, and will go to do homage to thy king and queen, and to behold their country.'

" When this speech was explained to Columbus, and he beheld the wife the sons, and the daughters of the cacique, and thought upon the snares to which their ignorance and simplicity would be exposed, he was touched with compassion, and determined not to take them from their native land. He replied to the cacique, therefore, that he received him under his protection as a vassal of his sovereigns ; but having many lands yet to visit before he returned to his country, he would, at some future time, fulfil his desire. Then, taking leave with many expressions of amity, the cacique, with his wife and daughters and all his retinue re-embarked in the canoes, returning reluctantly to the island, and the ships continued on their course." *

There was still a long voyage before Columbus. He was assailed by tempests; the shattered fleet was dispersed, and many perils and sufferings were encountered. Columbus was utterly exhausted by anxiety and toil. He had shared the scanty fare and

* " Life of Columbus," vol. i. p. 456.

all the hardships of the most humble sailor.   While,
amid the howlings of the tempest others slept, he,
with heavy eyelids and a care-worn heart, faced the
peltings of the storm through sleepless nights.   The
lives of all depended upon him ; and the world was
anxiously watching the result of his enterprise.   A
sudden paralysis struck him down.   He was instantly
deprived of memory, sight, and of all his faculties.
In a state of utter unconsciousness—in a lethargy
resembling death—the heroic admiral was borne into
the harbor of Isabella.   Apparently, well would it
have been for him if he could have passed from that
stupor into that sleep which has no earthly waking.
Appropriate would have been the motto :

> " Life's labor done, securely laid
> In this his last retreat,
> Unheeded o'er his silent dust
> The storms of life shall beat."

CHAPTER X.

The Return to Spain, and the Third Voyage.

Arrival of Bartholomew Columbus—Outrages of Margarite—Conspiracy against Columbus—Friendship of Guacanagari—Feat of Ojeda—Enslaving the natives—A bloody battle—Despotism of Columbus—Mission of Juan Aguado—The return to Spain—Weary months of disappointment—Unfortunate ebullition of passion—The third voyage commenced—Incidents of the voyage—The administration of Bartholomew Columbus—Anarchy at Hispaniola.

IT was the 29th of September, 1494, when the little fleet entered the harbor of Isabella, bearing the almost lifeless body of the admiral, in a state of utter helplessness and unconsciousness. Though Columbus had bitter enemies at Isabella, he had also many friends. His friends had been greatly disquieted by his long absence, and greatly rejoiced at his return, though in a state of such extreme debility. During the absence of the admiral, his tenderly beloved younger brother, Bartholomew, came out from Spain to join him, with three ships, freighted with supplies. As Columbus regained consciousness he was overjoyed to find his brother at his side.

Bartholomew was a far more efficient man than his mild and amiable elder brother, Diego. His person and address were as commanding as were the energies of his mind. He was well educated in the science of the times, and could write fluently in the Latin language. Columbus immediately appointed him lieutenant-governor over his domains, which were then nominally so vast as to have no recognized limits. His duties were, however, mainly confined to the settlements at Isabella and St. Thomas.

Hayti consisted of five territorial divisions, each occupied by an independent tribe or nation. Over each an absolute hereditary chief reigned, aided by many minor chiefs. The population of the island was perhaps extravagantly estimated at one million. It will be remembered that Don Pedro Margarite, with a force of four hundred men, had entered upon a tour to explore the island. Regardless of the instructions he had received, and apparently seeking self-indulgence only, he entered the luxuriant plains of the Vega, where he and his men indulged in every imaginable excess.

They robbed the Indians. They caroused through their dwellings. They treated matrons and maidens with every conceivable outrage. Tidings of these atrocities reached the ears of the amiable Diego

Columbus, during the absence of the admiral. He summoned his council. A severe reproof was sent to Margarite, and he was ordered immediately to proceed on his exploring tour. But the haughty Spanish noble affected to despise the Genoese adventurers —*sons of nobody.* He paid no heed to the warning, and plunged more deeply into all diabolical excesses. Ten Spaniards, in their impenetrable coats of mails, could put to flight a hundred naked Indians. The poor natives, goaded to desperation, attempted resistance. Fearfully they were slaughtered.

Caonabo organized a confederacy. With a thousand warriors he marched against the Spanish fiends, who, like demons, were rioting through the homes of his people. Blood deluged the land. Many Spaniards were killed. It does not speak well for Guacanagari that he refused to join the alliance of the other four chiefs against the Spaniards. But his love for Columbus was such that he remained, through all these scenes of horror, his firm friend. Though one of his own wives had been murdered by the Spanish soldiers, and another had been carried off by them, he even offered to fight by the side of the Spaniards against the coalition of Caonabo. Perhaps he was, in some degree, incited to this by revenge for the injuries he had received from

Caonabo, who had laid his town in ashes when he destroyed the Spanish garrison.

Ojeda was a skilled and terrible warrior. He was never more at home than amid the tumult and carnage of the battle-field. Cased in armor from head to foot, he plunged into the thickest bands of the enemy, as recklessly and pitilessly as a fanged wolf would leap into a fold of lambs.

Margarite was not only of ancient family, but was a favorite of the king. The Spanish nobles, in Hispaniola, generally rallied to his support. Friar Boyle, who was at the head of the religious fraternity, joined them. Thus there was a very powerful aristocratic faction formed against Columbus and his brothers. They could not forget that Columbus, in a time of emergency, had compelled hidalgos and ecclesiastics to share in the toils and deprivations of the common people.

The haughty Margarite assumed that he was military commander of the island. Leaving the army in the care of Ojeda, he returned to Isabella, to plot against the admiral, who was then on his cruise along the coast of Cuba. He did not even condescend to call upon Diego Columbus, who was then in command, or to recognize his authority in any way. Concerting with the grandees, he and Bishop Boyle, who was also in high favor with the king, took pos

session of some ships, and with a large band of malcontents, sailed for Spain. All were agreed to present
at the Spanish court the loudest possible clamor
against Columbus.

Such was the deplorable state of affairs when the
admiral was brought, in a state of utter insensibility,
into the port of Isabella. Columbus had scarcely
recovered consciousness, before his firm friend Guacanagari came, with brotherly sympathy, to his bed-
side. All suspicion of the good faith of the cacique
was now banished entirely from the mind of the admiral and his friends. Columbus, though a man of
intense emotions, was not a passionate man. He
was calm, thoughtful, sedate. No provocations
could rouse him to a fury of rage. As he listened
to the story of the atrocities of the Spaniards, and
witnessed the ruin wrought upon the colony,
though his soul was agitated to its inmost depths, it
was with grief rather than with wrath.

All his thoughts were directed to the question
of what was to be done to restore tranquillity. But
this was impossible. An archangel from heaven
could not have accomplished this, with the Spanish
soldiers as the instruments with which he was to
work. The forces of Columbus were small. Many
had died of their excesses. Many had been killed,
in their straggling bands, by the natives. And quite

a number had returned in the ships. The natives were justly in the highest state of exasperation. The coalition was very formidable. It could bring many thousand warriors into the field.

An Indian chief, by the name of Guarionex, was sovereign cacique of the Royal Vega. Columbus sent a friendly embassy to him, and assured him that the excesses of the Spaniards were contrary to his express orders, and that it was his earnest desire to live on friendly terms with the natives. He made the chief rich presents; treated him in all respects with brotherly kindness, and induced him to give his daughter in marriage to the Indian interpreter, who was in high favor with Columbus, and to whom he had given the Christian name of Diego Colon. The amiable cacique was won over by these kindnesses.

Caorabo was, above all others, the dreaded warrior of those wilds. Ojeda's chivalric deeds of daring had won his admiration. The young Spaniard formed a plan to capture the Indian chief. It was wild, romantic, and perilous in the extreme. The story could not be credited, were it not sustained by the most unquestionable authority. He selected ten companions. All were in glittering armor, and mounted on powerful horses. Plunging into the forest, they rode about one hundred and fifty miles, to Maguana, one of the principal towns of the chief, and where he then resided.

Ojeda approached the chief with great deference. Addressing him as a sovereign prince, he assured him that he had come from Columbus with rich presents, and to implore that cruel war might cease and that friendly relations might be established. Caonabo, who, with his people, had suffered terribly, and was despairing of his power to resist the Spaniards, not unwillingly listened to his proposals. Ojeda and his companions were hospitably entertained. The perfidious young Spaniard exerted all his powers of attraction to win the confidence of the chief.

He proposed that Caonabo should accompany him to Isabella, where he assured him that he should receive the highest honors from Columbus; should be loaded with gifts; and that the admiral would become his firm friend and ally, to aid him in all his plans.

There was a bell in the chapel of Isabella. As it was daily rung for church services its tones swept far and wide over hill and valley, exciting the amazement of the natives. There was nothing the Spaniards possessed which so deeply impressed the Indians. Even Caonabo himself had often prowled about the settlement, listening to its wondrous tones.

Ojeda told Caonabo that Columbus, anxious to prove the sincerity of his friendship, had decided to make the chief a present of that bell, which he would aid him to suspend upon a tower at his palace. This lure was irresistible. The chief consented to accompany the treacherous Spaniard to Isabella.

When the time for departure came, Ojeda was surprised to find that Caonabo had a very large force of warriors ready to accompany him. Upon inquiring the reason, the chief replied :

" It is not becoming that a great prince, like myself, should visit the Spanish admiral with a scanty attendance."

Ojeda began to fear that the chief was also playing a perfidious game ; and that he was plotting either to capture the admiral, or to take the garrison by surprise. The march, however, was commenced. They encamped upon the banks of a stream, where they had high festivities, in the intermingling of Spanish and Cuban sports. Ojeda had a set of manacles, of highly polished steel. To the natives they appeared like the richest ornaments they had ever seen. Ojeda told Caonabo that they were decorations such as the Spanish monarchs wore when they wished to appear in greatest splendor. He suggested that the chief should mount the horse of Ojeda, behind him, and, being adorned with the manacles, should ride into the camp, exciting the astonishment and admiration of all his people.

. The chief consented ; the little band of horsemen was instructed how to act. The cacique was manacled, and mounted on a powerful steed behind Ojeda. After a few evolutions, the cavaliers, all mounted, closed around, and putting spurs to their chargers, vanished through the paths of the dense forest with their prize. With drawn swords they threatened the chief with instant death should he make any resistance. They had before them a journey of nearly one hundred and fifty miles. It was safely accomplished. The captive was conveyed in triumph to the fortress of Isabella.*

Columbus forgot the treachery of the act, in the satisfaction he felt in having the most formidable foe of the Spaniards in his power. The high-spirited Carib chief was held in close confinement. He maintained an imperial air of defiance, scorning to ask any favors or to manifest any spirit of submission. He seemed to regard the feat performed by Ojeda with great admiration, notwithstanding he was the victim of the stratagem. When Columbus entered his apartment, he paid him no reverence

---

* This remarkable exploit is recorded by Las Casas, Herrera, Fernando, Pizarro, Charlevoix, Peter Martyr, and others. Apparently it is well authenticated.

When Ojeda entered, he rose and saluted him with the most profound respect. Upon being asked why he thus neglected the supreme governor, and manifested homage to one of his subjects, the haughty cacique replied:

" The admiral never dared to come, in person, to the heart of my territories to seize me. It is only through the valor of Ojeda that I am a prisoner. To him I owe reverence, and not to the admiral."

The subjects of Caonabo bitterly deplored his captivity. One of his brothers raised an army of seven thousand men, and marched to his rescue. Ojeda, with a squadron of steel-clad horsemen, plunged upon them by surprise, and put them to flight in a terrible panic. Their gleaming swords, their armor, which neither arrow nor javelin could penetrate ; the blood-hounds, who seized the naked Indians by the throat and dragged them to the earth ; and, most dreadful of all, the ferocious beasts the Spaniards strode—as frightful, in their view, as lions and tigers to women and children—enabled a few hundred men to scatter ten times their number in utter rout. Ojeda was merciless. The poor natives, fighting in the most righteous cause, were massacred as dogs devour lambs.*

* Oviedo, "Cronica de los Indias," lib. iii. cap. 1 ; Charlevoix " Hist. St. Domingo," lib. ii. p. 131.

About this time four ships arrived from Spain
with ample supplies. They brought very complimentary letters to Columbus from both Ferdinand
and Isabella. Margarite and Friar Boyle had not
yet reached Spain, to poison the minds of their
majesties with their atrocious libels. A proclamation was issued by the sovereigns, commanding the
colonists to obey Columbus as implicitly as they
would the king and queen. The admiral was also
invited to return to Spain to assist the court, with
his experience, to adjust the geographical line which
would separate the discoveries of Portugal from those
of Spain.

Columbus did not feel that he could then safely
leave the colony. Everything was in confusion.
The working of the mines had entirely ceased. The
severe sickness with which he was attacked still
confined him to his bed. He therefore decided that
his brother Diego should return to Spain to attend
to his interests there. As he had no gold to transmit
to the sovereigns, he sent five hundred kidnapped
natives, who, he suggested, might be sold as slaves
at Seville. Mr. Irving, commenting upon this
atrocious act, very judiciously remarks:

"It is painful to find the brilliant renown of
Columbus sullied by so foul a stain. The customs
of the times, however, must be pleaded in his

apology. The precedent had been given, long before, by both Spaniards and Portuguese, in their
African discoveries, wherein the traffic in slaves had
formed one of the greatest sources of profit.   In
fact the practice had been sanctioned by the Church
itself; and the most learned theologians had pronounced all barbarous and infidel nations, who shut
their eyes to the truths of Christianity, fair objects
of war and rapine, of captivity and slavery." *

It is manifestly right that these considerations
should have some weight in palliating the great
crime of Columbus, in thus enslaving the natives.
But the deed will ever remain an indelible stain
upon his character. Columbus ought to have known
better. There were men, in those days, who did
see the iniquity of the practice, and remonstrated
against it. The good Las Casas vehemently denounced the atrocity. And yet with candor which
does him honor he writes:

"If pious and learned men, whom the king and
queen took for guides and instructors, were so ignorant of the injustice of this practice, it is not strange
that the unlettered admiral should not be conscious
of its great wrong." †

* "Life of Columbus," vol. ii. p. 42.

† "Las Casas, by a singular inconsistency, in his zeal for the Indians, became the author of the slave trade, by proposing to purchase
negroes from the Portuguese in Africa to supply the planters with

All the inhabitants of the island, with the exception of the few whom Guacanagari could influence,
were now roused to the highest pitch of indignation
against the Spaniards. Columbus, prostrate upon
his bed, in the extreme of languor, with his military
force and his whole colony suffering greatly from
sickness, exerted all his powers of conciliation to dis-
pel the hostility which was roused against him. But
the outrages which had been inflicted upon the natives they could not easily forget.

A combined army of the natives was assembled
in the Vega, within two days' march of Isabella.
Columbus rose from his bed to repel the approaching assault. He could muster only two hundred
infantry, and twenty horsemen. They were armed
with weapons far superior to those of the natives.
They had many arquebuses. These were very formidable weapons, like large muskets, which threw a
heavy ball, and which were supported on forked
rests when in use. They had also twenty blood-
hounds, as fierce as tigers. Nothing daunted them.
With inconceivable ferocity they plunged upon the

laborers. This was unfortunately put in execution. He composed
several works, which have never been published, among which is a
'General History of the Indies.' All his works evince profound
learning, solid judgment, and piety. Notwithstanding his great inconsistency with regard to the negroes, he must be regarded as a very
benevolent man, and a lover of mankind."—*Encyclopædia Americana
Article Las Casas.*

naked bodies of the Indians, grasped them by the throat, and with bloody fangs tore them to pieces.

On the 27th of March, 1495, Columbus, with his little army, issued from Isabella, and marched to attack the foe by surprise. The Indians, by their scouts, learned of his approach. Las Casas states that the native army numbered one hundred thousand men.* This is doubtless an exaggeration. It is not probable that any accurate estimate of their numbers could be made. The battle took place near the present city of St. Jago. It was an awful scene of slaughter. The steel-clad cavaliers hewed down the natives with sinews which seemed never to tire. The blood-hounds seized them with a grip which nothing could loose, and tearing out their bowels, sprang from one to another with satanic energies. The victory of the Spaniards was entire. The natives were crushed beyond all retrieval.

The cruelty with which Columbus followed this scene of carnage and woe, is utterly inexcusable. With his steel-clad dragoons he made a military tour through the provinces. In important places he reared fortresses, which he garrisoned with blood-hounds, and with mailed warriors no less ferocious and pitiless. Ojeda was eager for any enterprise of rapine and slaughter. At the slightest menace of

* Las Casas, " Hist. Ind.," lib. i. cap. 104, MS.

resistance, he would fall upon the doomed point like a thunderbolt.

That he might send gold to the Spanish court, and thus silence the calumnies which his enemies were fabricating against him, he endeavored to raise an extravagant revenue, by imposing the most intolerable burdens of taxation. Every individual native, above the age of fourteen, was required to pay, every three months, an amount of gold dust equivalent to five dollars of our money ; or, if we estimate the superior value of gold in those days, equal to fifteen dollars of our time.* Thus these naked, native children were compelled to pay a tax amounting to sixty dollars a year, in gold. A much larger sum was extorted from the chiefs. Manicaotex, the brother of Caonabo, was obliged to pay, every three months, gold to the amount of one hundred and fifty *pesos*, or six-hundred dollars a year.† It would seem that nothing but the terrors of the bloodhounds' fangs could have driven the poor natives to the toil of collecting gold dust sufficient to pay such enormous taxation. A copper medal was suspended around the neck of each one who had paid the tax. If any were found without the medal, he was liable to arrest and severe punishment. In those provinces

* Las Casas " Hist. Ind.," lib. i. cap. 105.
† *Peso ;* the Spanish dollar of exchange.

where there was no gold dust, twenty-five pounds of cotton for each person were demanded every three months.*

The ruin which had fallen upon the inhabitants of Hispaniola was like that which befell Eden when Satan entered it. Utter despair overwhelmed the people. Sounds of woe filled the air. The simple-hearted natives, living upon fruit, and in bowers of bloom, all unused to labor, were reduced to the most deplorable slavery, and doomed to anxiety and toil which rendered life a burden. There was no escape, and no hope. Their pleasant island life was at an end. The gloom of utter despair settled down over Hispaniola, and from this gloom there was no refuge, until the perishing inhabitants were silent in the grave. The history of the world is full of tragedies. But we know not where to look for one more deplorable than the fate of the inhabitants of the West India Islands.

* We find ourselves in entire sympathy with Mr. Goodrich in his comments upon these atrocities. He writes : " Leaving the hideous and ghastly scene of butchery, and assuming the air of a conqueror, Columbus now traversed the island, and proceeded to extort an immense revenue from the unoffending inhabitants. In vain the poor islanders, crushed by this imposition, remonstrated. In vain the chiefs, in lieu thereof, offered to cultivate, for him, a breadth of land stretching across the island from sea to sea—enough, according to Las Casas, to furnish all Castile with bread for ten years. Columbus was inexorable. Gold he must have, if it cost the life of every Indian in the island to procure it."—*Life of Columbus*, by Aaron Goodrich, p. 250.

Many, in their despair, fled to the scarcely pene-
trable wilderness, and to caves in the mountains.
But the blood-hounds, with unerring scent, pursued
them ; and they perished miserably. Parents saw
their children emaciate with starvation, or torn to
pieces by the merciless beasts. The subjects of
Guacanagari fared no better than the rest. His
countrymen hated him for refusing to unite with
them against the detested Spaniards. Overwhelmed
with the opprobrium of all the chiefs, and utterly
impoverished by the extortion of the Spaniards, he
endeavored to hide himself in a wild and sterile
retreat, where he died, in neglect and misery, pitied
by none.*

In the meantime, Margarite and Bishop Boyle
were busy in the Spanish court, striving to under-
mine the reputation of Columbus. Their representations were sustained by the malcontents who had
accompanied them to Spain. The government
appointed Juan Aguado, as commissioner, to go to
Hispaniola, and investigate these serious charges.
At the same time they issued a proclamation, grant-
ing to any Spaniard the privilege of fitting out
private expeditions for discovery and for traffic
in the New World. This was very annoying to
Columbus. He considered it a palpable violation

* Charlevoix, " Hist. de St. Domingo," lib. ii.

of the agreement which the sovereigns had made with him.*

It is difficult to reconcile the enormous extortion which Columbus was practising upon the natives, with the intense solicitude he professed, and often manifested, for the conversion of the natives. But man is often a bundle of inconsistencies. Virtue and vice are frequently found in strange companionship. Herrera, in his History of the West Indies, writes:

"Columbus, like a discreet man, being sensible that the wealth he sent to Spain must be his support, pressed for gold ; though in other respects he was a good Christian, and feared God."

Upon this strange statement, Mr. Goodrich comments very truthfully, " This may be rightly interpreted thus : Columbus was cruel, avaricious, dishonest ; but in other respects, except where he failed, he was a good Christian." †

The loving heart of Isabella had been deeply moved by the accounts she had received of the gentle and hospitable character of the islanders. She regarded them as intrusted by God to her peculiar

* " The permission was granted without consulting the opinion or wishes of the admiral. It was loudly complained of by him, as an infringement of his privileges, and as disturbing the career of regular and well-organized discovery, by the licentious, and sometimes predatory enterprises of reckless adventurers."—Irving's *Life of Columbus* vol. ii. p. 59.

† " Life of Columbus," by Aaron Goodrich. p. 250.

protection. When the five hundred slaves arrived
an order was issued for their sale. Isabella coun-
termanded the order; and summoned a council of
the most learned men, and of ecclesiastics of the
highest repute, to decide if such a deed could be jus-
tifiable in the sight of God. The council was probably not agreed.* Isabella ordered that the captives
should be returned to their own land. And she sent
a special injunction that the natives should be treated
with the utmost kindness.† But it was too late for
her benevolence to rescue the island from those billows of blood and woe which were surging over it.

Juan Aguado sailed from Spain with four caravels, the latter part of August, 1495, and landed at
Isabella in October. He was, intellectually and
morally, a weak man. Though he had been the
friend of Columbus, he was exceedingly puffed up
with the brief authority with which he had been intrusted. Assuming the most intolerable airs of supe-
riority, he summoned Columbus, the acknowledged
viceroy of all those realms, before him, as a criminal, to be questioned, and to be acquitted or condemned by his judge. The Spanish grandees were

* The historian Munoz, after the most thorough research among
documents relating to Spanish America, declares that he can find no
evidence that the question was decided.

† Letter of the Sovereigns to Fonseca, in Navarette's "Collection
of Voyages," doc. 92.

delighted with the thought that Columbus, the up-start foreigner, the "son of nobody," and who had ventured to exercise authority over the hidalgos of Spain, was about to be crushed.*

Under these adverse circumstances, Columbus conducted himself with such dignity, with such punctilious courtesy and lofty self-respect, as greatly to embarrass his feeble foe. It is worthy of notice that no charge seems to have been brought against Columbus, at the court of Spain, for any oppression of the natives. It was said that Columbus had deceived the sovereigns, by extravagant descriptions of the wealth of islands which were steeped in poverty; that he had forced excessive labor on the Spanish colonists; and that he had heaped indignities on Spanish gentlemen of noble birth. The charges brought against him were unquestionably meritorious acts. The one great condemning crime of Columbus, in plunging a million of people into unutterable woe, in his greed for gold, they were silent about. For the natives they had no pity. Columbus was continually interposing to pro·tect them from the demoniac cruelty of the haughty nobles and the brutal sailors.†

---

* "Every dastard spirit, who had any lurking ill will, any real or imaginary cause of complaint, now hastened to give it utterance; perceiving that, in vilifying the admiral, he was gaining the friendship of Aguado."—Irving's *Life of Columbus*, vol. ii. p. 66.

† The estimate that there were a million of inhabitants in Hayti,

On the 14th of March, 1496, Columbus set sail
for Spain.   He took the captive Caonabo with him.
The unhappy chief died on the way.   After a long
and very uncomfortable voyage, he landed at Cadiz,
on the 11th of June.   The king and queen received
him with kindness, which he had not anticipated.
They immediately wrote, congratulating him upon
his safe return, and inviting him to court.   No mention was made to him of the bitter accusations with
which he had been assailed by Margarite and Boyle.
Columbus, thus encouraged, proposed that he should
be intrusted with six ships for another voyage of
discovery.   This was promised him.   But the treasury was drained.   The intrigues of men in office in-
terposed delays.   Columbus was doomed to infinite
mortifications.   Weary months lingered away, and
nothing was accomplished.

The king's counsellors were the enemies of Columbus.   The king himself, influenced by their incessant reproaches, began to regard him with an
unfriendly eye.   The queen alone remained faithful
to the admiral.   Isabella caused an hereditary title
of nobility to be conferred upon him, which, with his
estates, was to descend to his heirs.   The admiral,
though deeply in debt, had not yet relinquished the

was probably an exaggeration.   Still such was the opinion of the
Spaniards.

idea that vast wealth was to be accumulated, as the result of his discoveries. In his will, he made very liberal provision for his relatives; gave marriage portions to the poor females of the family; directed that the heirs of his title, and consequently of the bulk of his estates, should, in all time, do everything in their power to promote the prosperity of his native city of Genoa. And especially he ordered, that whoever should inherit his estates, should, from time to time, invest such money as he could spare, to form a permanent fund for a crusade to recover Jerusalem.

A great reaction had taken place in public sentiment, in reference to the New World. No one was willing to engage in a voyage to islands, which all recent reports declared to be the abodes of sickness, poverty, and misery. The crown, to obtain seamen, resorted to the desperate measure of commuting the sentence of criminals sent to the galleys, to transportation to the new settlements. All malefactors at large were offered pardon if they would surrender themselves, and embark for the colonies. It is said that this plan was proposed by the admiral.* Columbus was, at one time, so discouraged and disgusted with the obstacles which his enemies were so successfully throwing in his way, that he was on the

* Las Casas, "Hist. Ind.," lib. i. cap. 112, MS.

point of abandoning altogether his enterprises of discovery. Gratitude to the queen alone induced him to persevere. The following incident we give, in the language of Washington Irving :

"The insolence which Columbus had suffered from the minions of Fonseca, throughout this long-protracted time of preparation, harassed him to the last moment of his sojourn in Spain, and followed him even to the very water's edge. Among the worthless hirelings who annoyed him, the most noisy and presuming was one Ximeno Breviesca, treasurer or accountant of Fonseca. He had an impudent front, and an unbridled tongue, and, echoing the sentiments of his patron, the bishop, had been loud in abuse of the admiral and his enterprises. The very day when the squadron was on the point of weighing anchor, Columbus was assailed by the impudence of this Ximeno, either on the shore or when about to embark, or on board of his ship which he had just entered. In the hurry of the moment he forgot his usual self-command ; his indignation, hitherto repressed, suddenly burst forth : he struck the despicable minion to the ground, and kicked him repeatedly, venting, in this unguarded paroxysm, the accumulated griefs and vexations which had long rankled in his mind." *

* Irving's " Life of Columbus," vol. ii. p. 99. Las Casas gives a

This was a very unfortunate act. It is always a calamity for a man to lose his self-control and give place to anger. Columbus was very much ashamed of it, and, in a subsequent letter to the king and queen, expressed his deep regret. But it left a very unfavorable impression on the minds of the sovereigns, and added intensity to the malignity of his foes.

Columbus set sail from the port of San Lucar de Barrameda, for his third voyage of discovery, on the 13th of May, 1498. Nearly two years had passed wearily away, as he had struggled in Spain against the innumerable obstacles which beset his path. His fleet consisted of six vessels, with two hundred men in addition to the sailors. On the 19th of June, he reached the Canary Islands. Thence he de-spatched three ships of his squadron directly to Hispaniola. With the three remaining vessels the admiral continued his cruise to the Cape de Verde Islands, which he reached on the 29th of June. After a short tarry, the sails were again spread.

Day after day they pressed on, with a fair wind,

---

similar narrative in his "Manuscript History of the Indies," lib. iii. cap. 126. De Lorgues, in his "Christophe Colomb," livre ii. ch. ix., writes, "The patriarch of the ocean made a step toward his insulter, and, with his fist, dealt a blow on his impudent face. The miserable wretch fell down stunned. The admiral limited himself to giving a few kicks to this vile snarler, who fled in the midst of hootings."

12*

until they found themselves beneath a vertical sun.
A dead calm ensued. The sea was as glass; the
ships motionless. The air was like a furnace. The
blazing sun melted the tar, blistered the decks, and
opened the seams of the vessels. Exposure to the
sun on deck could not be endured, and, below the
decks the heat was as suffocating as that of an oven.
All strength seemed to vanish. The superstitious
sailors were appalled by the thought that they were
approaching the fabled regions of volcanic heat,
where there could be no human existence. The
ships leaked so badly that it was deemed necessary
to make some harbor as soon as possible.

At length a gentle breeze sprang up, Columbus
directed his course to the west. Day after day
passed, and no signs of land appeared. Even the
salt meat became putrid. The hoops of the wine
and water casks burst. Distress and anxiety oppressed all minds. But one water cask, on the 31st
of July, remained in each ship, The prospect before
them was dreadful: that all would perish on that
burning sea.

At mid-day, a sailor at one of the mast-heads
gave the joyful shout of land. Three mountain
peaks pierced the clouds. With characteristic de-
votional feeling Columbus named the island La
Trinidad, or The Trinity. As he ran along the

coast, in search of a harbor, he was delighted with the beauty and fertility of the island. Pleasant villages and highly cultivated fields were scattered along the shore. He ran along the western coast of the island, in what is now called the Gulf of Paria; on his left was distinctly seen the low coast of South America, which he supposed to be an island.

This was the first view Columbus had of the continent of America. He called it the island of Zeta, and estimated that it was about sixty miles in extent. Sebastian Cabot, on the 24th of June, 1497, had discovered North America. Occasionally Columbus landed. The natives were very friendly. He encountered essentially the same scenes he had witnessed on the island of Cuba. The country grew more and more populous. A vast number of canoes, crowded with natives, came off to the ships. Various points he named; but those names are now forgotten. His ship-stores were nearly exhausted, and it became necessary for him to hasten to Hispaniola. He was suffering severely from the gout. And the intense heat, with incessant fatigue, sleeplessness, and watchings had almost deprived him of sight. Sailing in a northerly direction, he discovered the two islands, now called Tobago and Grenada. Several other islands he passed, which he could not stop to explore

At one point, where he landed, he found Indians fishing for pearls. He purchased three pounds' weight of them. Some were very large and beautiful. The malady of his eyes became very alarming. He therefore pressed forward, with all sail, and reached Hispaniola on the 19th of August. The meeting of Columbus with his brothers was very affectionate. But Columbus, exhausted, sick, and careworn, seemed bodily but the wreck of his former self. His indomitable spirit remained unbroken.

Columbus hoped for repose. He found none. During his absence Bartholomew Columbus had remained in command, with the title of Adelantado. Leaving his brother Diego in charge at Isabella, he proceeded, in search of gold, to the south side of the island. He built a fortress, which he called San Christoval, but which others called the Golden Tower. The Indians were hostile. They brought no food. There was no end to trouble. Robberies and massacres ensued. A formidable insurrection of the Spaniards was with difficulty quelled. The once peaceful and happy island had become a Pandemonium.

Bartholomew captured three hundred natives, who were accused of opposing their oppressors. They were all sent, manacled in irons, to Spain, to be sold as slaves. The jurists and theologians had decided that it was just to enslave *prisoners of war*. Fortresses were built. Armed bands of Spaniards, with their accompanying allies, the blood-hounds, scoured the island in all directions, to overawe the natives. No one can deny that, through all these cruel scenes, the Indians manifested far more of the spirit of the Christian religion than did the Spaniards.

There was a very delightful region of Hayti, in a remote part of the island, called Xaraguay. It was far famed for its beauty, its fertility, the loveliness of its females, and the urbanity of all its inhabitants. Bartholomew, while unrelenting in extorting taxes, wished for friendly relations with the oppressed people. With a strong band of steel-clad warriors, he visited the chief Behechio. As the Spaniards approached the beautiful village, which the intolerable taxation had not yet reached, thirty females, of the cacique's household, came to meet them. The only dress of the young girls was a wreath of flowers around the forehead. The matrons wore small aprons of embroidered cotton. All waved branches of the palm tree, and came forward with dances and songs of welcome.

These females were very lovely in person; their forms being as exquisite as a Grecian artist could chisel from the marble. Living mainly on fruit, and without toil, their skin was of velvety softness, and their complexion even more fair than that generally of the Spanish brunette. These innocent daughters of Eve had no more conception of any want of delicacy, in their destitution of costume, than has the European lady, who exposes her face unveiled.

The widow of Caonabo resided there, with her brother Behechio. She was a woman of marvellous beauty. Her name was Anacaona. She was reclining on a palanquin, and was borne by six strong Indians. Her only dress was the embroidered apron, and wreaths of flowers around her forehead, neck, and arms. Bartholomew and six of his principal cavaliers were lodged in the house of Behechio. The rest of the company were entertained by the subordinate chiefs. All were provided with hammocks of matted cotton for beds.

For two days the Spaniards remained in the village, receiving, from this hospitable people, every possible attention. They were abundantly feasted, and various games and festivities were engaged in for their amusement. One of their games was similar to the gladiatorial shows of the ancient Romans. Two squadrons of naked Indians, armed with bows and arrows, approached each other in a real fight. Four were killed. Many were wounded. Shouts of applause arose, as from the lips of Roman senators and matrons, when, in the Coliseum, the arena ran red with blood. The contest would probably have been much more sanguinary had not Bartholomew begged that the game might cease.*

In requital for all this kindness, the Adelantado informed the cacique that he came to take him and his people under the protection of the all-powerful Spanish sovereigns, and to receive from them the tribute which the other chiefs of the island paid. As there was no gold in that region, he imposed a tax, to be paid in cotton, hemp, and cassava bread. There was no excuse whatever for this despotic act. It was as unjustifiable as any deed of robbery perpetrated by a band of buccaneers. The cacique was compelled to submit to the hand of resistless power. He knew the doom which had fallen upon other parts of the island, and hoped, by excessive kindness and hospitality, to avert that doom from his own subjects.†

---

* Las Casas, " Hist. Ind.," tom. i. cap. 113.

† As Mr. Irving recognizes all these facts, it is with surprise that we read the following comments from his pen. " Thus by amicable and sagacious management, one of the most extensive provinces of the island was brought into cheerful subjection ; and had not the wise policy of the Adelantado been defeated by the excesses of worthless and turbulent men, a large revenue might have been collected without any resource to violence or oppression. In all instances, these simple people appear to have been extremely tractable, and meekly, even cheerfully, to have resigned their rights to the white men, when treated with gentleness and humanity."—*Life of Columbus,* vol. ii p. 145.

When the highway robber presents his pistol at your breast, and says, " My dear sir, you will confer a great favor upon me if you will

Misery reigned at Isabella. Sickness prevailed. Provisions and medicines were exhausted. All were quarrelling and murmuring. The Indians had abandoned the region, and were devouring roots and herbs, in rugged mountain retreats, where even the bloodhounds found it difficult to search them out. There were frequent insurrections of the natives. Awful was the cruelty with which the helpless and despairing people were punished. Villages were laid in ashes. Shrieking victims, pursued by mounted and mail-clad warriors, were hewn down by the sabres of the Spaniards. Women and children were torn limb from limb by ferocious dogs. Anarchy reigned. Woe was everywhere. The beautiful island of Hayti had been converted, by man's depravity, in a few short months, into an abode of wretchedness where scarcely a joy was to be found.

be so kind as to deliver to me your purse. I hope you will not impose upon me the disagreeable necessity of shooting you;"—the politeness of his address does not diminish the atrocity of his crime.

CHAPTER XI.

The Return to Spain, and the Fourth Voyage.

A VILE man, by the name of Francis Roldan, had formed a conspiracy against the government of Columbus. With a gang of his followers, he had gone to Xaraguay, where he was plundering the people, trampling upon all their rights, and rioting in every species of excess. While thus engaged, three of the caravels from Spain, whose crews were composed of convicts from the state prisons, driven westward by the currents, cast anchor in those waters. Almost in a body, they deserted the ships to join the congenial villains on the shore. They were lured by the account of the life of abundance and indulgence in which the miscreants were revelling.

These desperate men landed with their swords,

cross-bows, lances, arquebuses, and other military
stores. Columbus, when he learned these facts, was
greatly troubled. Low as was, in some respects, his
sense of justice, he was, in integrity and humanity,
far in advance of most of his associates. This lawless horde was roving at large, and living in the most
revolting profligacy. The authority of Columbus
was set at utter defiance. The rebellion was assuming formidable proportions. Many of the disaffected
joined the rebels. Columbus had not sufficient
strength to give them battle. By some returning
ships he transmitted to the sovereigns an account of
the rebellion. In this letter he begged that more
ecclesiastics might be sent out, for the conversion of
the Indians ; and that, for two years longer, the Spaniards might be permitted to employ the natives as
slaves.*

The ships having sailed, Columbus again turned
his attention to the rebels. He wrote to Roldan in
the most conciliatory terms, and entreated him, for
the sake of his own reputation, and for the common
good, not to persist in his insubordination. A pass-
port was sent, assuring the safety of those who might

---

* ' Six hundred Indians, who had been made prisoners because
their cacique had failed to pay tribute, were at that time confined on
board five ships, to be sent to Spain as slaves ; the ships only waiting
till Columbus should be able to write that affairs in the island were
quiet."—*Life of Columbus*, by Aaron Goodrich, p. 365.

approach the admiral to confer with him. The demands of Roldan and his confederates were arrogant and insolent. At length, after much and intricate diplomacy terms of capitulation were agreed upon. Roldan and his confederates were furnished with two ships, to return to Spain, with certificates of good character. The ships were to sail in October, 1499. The insurgents took many slaves with them. According to Herrera, Columbus was guilty of duplicity, which, however characteristic of the times, merits severe condemnation.

While giving Roldan and his adherents certificates of good character, he wrote privately to the king and queen, saying that these certificates he had been compelled to give, in order to remove the wretches from the island; that they were entirely false; that the men had been guilty of the most atrocious crimes of robbery and murder; he therefore urged that, immediately upon their arrival, they should be arrested, stripped of their ill-gotten treasures, and severely punished.*

The situation of Columbus was indeed pitiable. He was sick and in constant pain. Conspiracies were multiplying against him. The haughtiest grandees

---

* Herrera, "Hist. Ind.," decad. i. lib. iii. cap. 16. Washington Irving, after his careful researches, feels constrained to accept this melancholy statement.—*Life of Columbus*, vol. ii. p. 208.

this world has ever seen, the hidalgos of Spain, were treating him with scorn. He was contemptuously called the "upstart foreigner." His virtues were, in the eyes of the profligate Spaniards, the occasion for envenomed denunciation. There was no treachery of which his foes were not capable. They occupied the most important stations in church and state ; and, with the vilest libels, were endeavoring to alienate the sovereigns from him. He stood alone, almost without a friend. In all Spain, scarcely a man could be found whose condition was more to be commiserated.

In fact, Roldan, having extorted from Columbus about what terms he pleased, decided to remain on the island, while most of his accomplices returned to Spain. He was invested with high authority, took possession of a large extent of territory, which he cultivated by slaves, and, regardless of God or judgment, said to his soul, " Eat, drink, and be merry."

The chivalric, reckless Ojeda had gone back to Spain. Aided by several wealthy speculators, he had succeeded in fitting out four ships, at Seville, for a private enterprise of exploration. A Florentine merchant, Amerigo Vespucci, whose name was subsequently attached to the whole New World, accompanied the expedition. The little fleet sailed in May, 1499. They touched at the Caribbee Islands.

After a fierce battle with the natives, they made many captives, whom they carried away to be sold as slaves. Thence, being in need of supplies, they sailed to Hispaniola. They anchored, at the western extremity of the island, on the 5th of September.

Columbus was much disturbed by this invasion of what he considered as his exclusive realms. He sent Roldan and some of his desperadoes on an expedition to thwart the plans of Ojeda, and arrest him if possible. The two young cavaliers were equally unprincipled, crafty, and reckless. Roldan, with two caravels, and twenty-five resolute, well-armed followers, set out in pursuit of the adventurer. The two men met. Ojeda exhibited his license for the voyage, from the king and queen, and that a part of the profits were to accrue to the crown. This silenced opposition. The haughty cavalier also said that Columbus was entirely in disgrace at the Spanish court, and that it was his intention soon to visit the admiral, that he might communicate some intelligence intended for his ear alone.

With this report Roldan returned to Columbus. The admiral was greatly troubled. It was evident that he was losing favor at court, and that the sovereigns were invading his most important prerogatives. He waited some time for the prom'sed visit from Ojeda. But the adventurer had no idea of approaching the admiral. Roldan was again sent to watch the movements of Ojeda. They were both treacherous men, equal in duplicity. Both alike robbed and oppressed the natives. Ojeda cruised along the coast of Hayti, landing at remote points, and kidnapping the people, until he had filled his ships with slaves. He then returned to Cadiz, where they were sold in the slave market.*

The authority of Columbus, on the island, was virtually at an end. Those obeyed him who were disposed to do so. Other bold and reckless spirits wandered here and there at will. It was easy to elude pursuit. Some ingratiated themselves with the natives. Some, organizing themselves in strong bands, robbed and enslaved them. The kind of civilization and Christianity which the Spaniards had brought to Hayti, had sunk the island to the lowest depths of misery. The detail of the scenes which ensued present a disgusting and painful record of treachery, cruelty, and crime. Columbus struggled heroically against these storms of adversity. Above all others with the exception perhaps of Las Casas, he advocated principles of justice and humanity, and was the friend of the native. And yet it is not to be forgotten that the good Las Casas said, ' We

* Las Casas, lib. i. cap. 109.

ought not to enslave these poor Haytiens. Let us go and kidnap the Africans." Neither is it to be forgotten, in our denunciation of these men, how recently men, women, and children were bought and sold in the slave marts of America, and how many professed teachers of Christianity proclaimed that this was right in the sight of God.

Columbus was at Fort Concepcion. His spirit was harassed and exasperated by the atrocities which everywhere met his eye, and which he had no power to prevent. A wretch, by the name of Mexica, organized a conspiracy to assassinate the admiral. Traversing the island, he engaged in his service a large number of vagabond Spaniards, who were eager to embark in any desperate deeds. Adrian de Mexica had been one of the ringleaders of Roldan's party. His conduct had been so outrageous, that Columbus did not admit him to the general amnesty, but banished him from the island. Roldan had allowed him to return.

A deserter brought Columbus news of the conspiracy, upon the eve of its execution. Not a moment was to be lost. Taking with him a party of ten trusty and resolute men, he captured Mexica by surprise. He was tried, and condemned to be hung. Mr. Irving writes, giving Herrera as his authority:

" He ordered Mexica to be hanged on the top of
the fortress. The latter entreated to be allowed to
confess himself previous to execution. A priest was
summoned. The miserable Mexica, who had been
so arrogant in rebellion, lost all courage at the
approach of death. He delayed to confess, beginning and pausing, and recommencing and again
hesitating, as if he hoped, by whiling away time, to
give a chance for rescue. Instead of confessing his
own sins he accused others of criminality, who were
known to be innocent; until Columbus, incensed at
this falsehood and treachery, and losing all patience,
in his mingled indignation and scorn, ordered the
dastard wretch to be swung off from the battlements." *

The remaining conspirators were pursued, with
great vigor, and several others were captured and
hung.

There were now six quite important fortresses

* Irving's " Life of Columbus," vol. ii. p. 235.

Mr. Goodrich relates this incident in the following language, which
we do not find sustained by any authority. " Adrian de Mexica was
in his power. He determined to put him to death, and thus intimi-
date all who should dare to oppose his wishes, or remonstrate against
his tyranny. Without legal authority, and with scarcely the form of
a trial, Mexica was condemned to instant death.

" Some writers represent Mexica as delaying death as long as
possible, by prolonging his confession, at which Columbus, becoming
indignant, ordered him to be thrown from the battlements. But,
from all we can learn, he met his fate fearlessly, and, in that last

upon the island, forming a chain of military posts, which held the natives in abject servitude. Twenty-seven miles from Isabella was the fortress of Esperanza ; eighteen leagues beyond was Santa Catalina ; about twelve miles farther the gloomy walls of Magdalena frowned. Here the town of Santiago was subsequently founded. About fifteen miles farther, in the midst of the fertile and populous plains of the Vega, Fort Concepcion was reared. It was within a mile and a half of a large Indian town, over which an illustrious cacique, called Guarionex, reigned. Isabella was left with only a sufficient garrison to hold the place. Columbus moved from point to point, making the fortress of San Domingo, on the south of the island, his principal residence.

In the year 1849, T. S. Hennekin, Esq., visited this region. We quote the following from his exceedingly interesting descriptive letter :

solemn moment accused Columbus of the crimes which had brought misery upon the island. The latter, furious at being unable to conquer the spirit of his victim, even in death, in an outburst of passion similar to that he gave vent to in Cadiz, toward Fonseca's treasurer, kicked the manacled prisoner from the high walls of the fortress into the fosse below."—*Life of Columbus*, by Aaron Goodrich, p. 270.

Washington Irving wrote, in his edition of 1829, " Columbus ordered the dastardly wretch to be flung headlong from the battlements." Judge Goodrich correctly quotes this. But Irving, in a subsequent edition, changed this to, ordered the wretch to be "swung off." As I had access to this edition, I suggested that Judge Goodrich, though doubtless unintentionally, had not correctly quoted Irving.

" Fort Concepcion is situated at the foot of a hill now called Santo Cerro. It is constructed of bricks, and is almost as entire at the present day as when just finished. It stands in the gloom of an exuberant forest, which has invaded the scene of former bustle and activity; a spot once considered of great importance, and surrounded by swarms of intelligent beings.

" What has become of the countless multitudes this fortress was intended to awe? Not a trace of them remains, excepting in the records of history. The silence of the tomb prevails where their habitations responded to their songs and dances. A few indigent Spaniards, living in miserable hovels, scattered widely apart in the bosom of the forest, are now the sole occupants of this once fruitful and beautiful region."

Thus far Ferdinand had found his possessions in the New World a bill of expense and not a source of income. This greatly disappointed him. His court was besieged by disappointed and repining men, who were bitter in their denunciations of Columbus, and who were clamoring for large sums of money, which they averred that Columbus owed them. These universal and incessant complaints began to produce an impression even upon the mind of Isabella. The letters of Columbus showed too plainly that the island was in a state of lamentable disorder. This seemed to indicate that whatever might be the purity of the motives of the admiral, he was deficient in administrative ability.

Ferdinand was a cautious and jealous Spaniard. It had ever been some annoyance to him to submit Spanish colonies to the government of Geneose adventurers. The lines of nationality were then very distinctly drawn. The epithet of *foreigner* was generally a title of reproach. The pro-slavery tendencies of Columbus were very annoying to the queen. When the ships with the Roldan insurgents returned to Spain, they brought six or seven hundred slaves. Many of these Columbus had granted to these men by capitulation ; others they had stolen on their own account. Among these captives there were a number of beautiful young females, daughters of chiefs, whom the profligates had torn from their homes. For all these wrongs, Isabella, not unjustly, deemed Columbus in a great degree responsible. He was viceroy of all these realms, and was virtually invested with absolute power.

The queen's sympathies were outraged. She regarded the simple-hearted natives of these wide realms as placed peculiarly under her protection. Indignantly she exclaimed, " What power had the admiral to give away my vassals ? " *

* Las Casas, lib. i

She manifested her extreme displeasure, not only
by ordering all these Indians to be sent back to their
friends, but also directed that those who had previously been transmitted to Spain by the admiral should
be sought out and returned.   Columbus felt this reproof very keenly.   It was decisive evidence that his
popularity at the court was on the wane.   Unfortunately, just at this time, before Columbus had been
informed of the strong feelings of Isabella, a letter
came from him urging the continuance of Indian slavery, as an important source of revenue to the crown.

New troubles had sprung up between Columbus
and Roldan.   The bold Spanish cavalier, who rallied
around him the haughty hidalgos and the lowest
desperadoes, was a formidable opponent.   Columbus
requested that some one might be sent out as an
umpire to decide between them.   This afforded Ferdinand the pretext to act, which he had for some
time sought.

One of the highest military and religious officers
in the royal household, Don Francisco de Bobadilla,
was appointed on this momentous mission.   It is,
however, evident that the mission was intended
against those who were in rebellion.   We read, in the
instructions :

" We order you to ascertain who and what persons they were who rose against the said admiral

and our magistracy, and for what cause; and what robberies and other injuries they have committed; and furthermore, to extend your inquiries to all other matters relating to the premises. And the information obtained, and the truth known, whomsoever you find culpable, arrest their persons and sequestrate their effects. And thus taken, proceed against them and the absent, both civilly and criminally, and impose and inflict such fines and punishments as you may think fit."

These powers were manifestly given to punish those who were in rebellion against the authority of Columbus. It was stated in the preamble, that an alcalde,* and certain other persons, were resisting the authority of the admiral, and therefore the commission was intrusted with special powers to restore order. The royal letter giving these instructions was dated March 21, 1499. Two months afterward, on the 21st of May, a letter was sent to the hidalgos and public functionaries on the island, informing them of the authority thus conferred on Bobadilla. Enlarging upon the absolute power with which he was invested to quell the disturbances, it was written:

"It is our will that if the said Commander Francisco de Bobadilla should think it necessary for our service, and the purpose of justice, that any cavaliers, or

---

* Alcalde; a magistrate, a judge among the Spaniards.

other persons, who are at present in these islands, or
may arrive there, should leave them, and not return
and reside in them, and that they should come and
present themselves before us, he may command it in
our name and compel them to depart.   And whomsoever he thus commands, we hereby order, that immediately, without waiting to inquire or consult us,
or to receive from us any other letter or command,
and without interposing appeal or supplication, they
obey whatever he shall say and order, under the
penalties he shall impose on our part." *

On the 23d of August, 1500, Bobadilla landed at
the port of San Domingo.   Columbus was then at

* Mr. Irving states that there was another order of the same date,
addressed to Columbus, as " Admiral of the Ocean Sea," directing
him and his brothers to surrender the fortress, ships, houses, arms,
ammunition, cattle, and all other royal property, into the hands of Bobadilla, as governor, under the penalty of the punishment to which
those subject themselves, who refuse to surrender fortresses and other
trusts, when commanded by their sovereigns."

There must be some mistake here.   This is an unconditional de-
position of Columbus without trial.   Mr. Irving does not quote the
order, neither does he state where it may be found.   I find, in the
letters of Columbus, no allusion to so cruel and extraordinary an expulsion of the admiral from his high offices.   Mr. Goodrich, who is
very thorough in his researches, alludes to some order about sur-
rendering the fortresses, found in Navarette, " Colec. Dip." v. ii. p.
266, but he does not quote the order, neither does he state under
what conditions the surrender was to be made.   If such order were
given, it can scarcely be doubted that the surrender was to be made,
only in case, after careful investigation, it should be found that the
disorders in the island rendered this absolutely necessary.

Fort Concepcion. His brother Diego was at the sea-port, San Domingo. Bobadilla immediately assumed that he had superseded Columbus in the government of the island, and that his authority was supreme. All the disaffected hilariously rallied around him. With the armed force he brought with him, and the cordial sympathy of all the disaffected, he easily took possession of the place.

Columbus was deposed, untried, and without even a charge being brought against him. It seemed to be the special desire of Bobadilla to degrade the admiral. He took up his residence at the house of Columbus, and seized his arms, gold, plate, horses, and all his letters and manuscripts, both public and private. To win popular applause, he issued a decree, authorizing, for a period of twenty years, any one to search for gold on his own account, paying one-eleventh to the government, instead of one-third, as heretofore.

Instead of summoning Roldan, and those who were in rebellion against Columbus, to appear before him, he treated them with the utmost civility, that he might secure their aid in his usurpation. While Columbus was in this state of great perplexity and distress, the following laconic and somewhat obscure letter from the sovereigns was presented him:

"Don Christopher Columbus, our Admiral of the

Ocean. We have commanded Comendador Francis
de Bobadilla, the bearer of this, that he speak to you,
on our part, some things which he will tell you. We
pray you give him faith and credence, and act accord-
ingly.

· "I THE KING; I THE QUEEN."

The admiral at once decided to yield promptly to
all the requirements of Bobadilla, until he could
accurately ascertain the decisions of the sovereigns.
Bobadilla seized Diego Columbus, and confined him
in chains on board one of the caravels. He then
sent officers to seize Columbus, put him in irons, and
imprison him in one of the cells of the fortress of San
Domingo. The dignity with which Columbus conducted himself in these emergencies has won the
admiration generally, even of his enemies.*

A vast amount of testimony against Columbus
was gathered from the rebels, to be forwarded to
the Spanish court. The settlement at San Domingo
swarmed with these miscreants.†

---

* Las Casas writes, " Hist. Ind." lib. i. cap. 180. " A graceless
and shameless cook riveted the fetters." Upon this statement Mr.
Goodrich comments. " When we find his own domestics, who owed
place and living to him, and who would naturally be supposed to
regret his downfall, rejoicing instead, we cannot but believe the man
to have been thoroughly contemptible. The ' graceless cook,' riveting
the fetters, militates far more, we take it, against the personal character of Columbus, than of his culinary menial."—Goodrich's *Life of
Columbus*, p. 283.

† " It was a perfect jubilee of triumphant villainy and dastard

Early in October, Columbus, manacled like the vilest culprit, was led through the streets to the ship. The jeers of the rabble pursued him. Alonzo de Villejo, a man alike noble in rank and character, was intrusted with the charge of the prisoners. Both he and the captain of the ship, Andreas Martin, treated the admiral, on the voyage, with the most profound respect. Gladly would they have struck off his fetters. But the admiral would not consent. He proudly said:

"No; their majesties commanded me, by letter, to submit to whatever Bobadilla should order in their name. By their authority he has put upon me these chains. I will wear them until they shall order them to be taken off; and I will preserve them afterward as relics and memorials of the reward of my services." *

On the voyage he wrote an admirable letter, to be exhibited to the sovereigns, which he addressed to Dona Juana de la Torres, a member of the royal household, and a special favorite of the queen. Upon the arrival of the ship at Cadiz, this letter was immediately forwarded, and was presented to Isa-

malice. Every base spirit, which had been awed into obsequiousness by Columbus and his brothers, when in power, now started up to revenge itself upon them when in chains."—Irving's *Life of Columbus*, vol. ii. p. 266.

* He did so. His son Fernando writes, "I saw them always hanging in his cabinet; and he requested that when he died, they might be buried with him."—*Hist. del Almirante*, cap. 86.

13*

bella. She read it with the deepest emotion and sympathy. The king and queen were alike indignant in view of the treatment Columbus had received. They sent orders that he and his brothers should immediately be set at liberty, and treated with all distinction. They unitedly wrote to Columbus, expressing their grief in view of his sufferings, assuring him of their gratitude and affection, inviting him to court, and sending him two thousand ducats to meet his expenses.*

On the 17th of December, Columbus, richly dressed and attended by a suitable retinue, presented himself before their majesties at Grenada. The queen, as she greeted him, burst into tears. This touched the heart of the heroic old man, as no severity could have moved him. He fell upon his knees, and for a few moments was entirely overcome, weeping and sobbing convulsively. Columbus was assured of their utter condemnation of the course pursued by Bobadilla, and that he should be immediately dismissed from command. They did not condescend to pay the slightest regard to the accusations which Bobadilla had sent home against him. They took every opportunity publicly to manifest their favor, and assured him also that his grievances should be

* Mr. Irving says that this sum was equivalent to eight thousand five hundred and thirty-eight dollars of the present day.

redressed, his property restored, and that he should
be reinstated in all his former authority.

Under the sway of Bobadilla, every man did what
seemed right in his own eyes. Las Casas gives an
appalling account of the wrongs inflicted upon the
Indians. The vilest wretches assumed the air of
nobles, robbed the chiefs of their daughters, surrounded themselves with retainers like Oriental
princes, and compelled the natives to carry them in
palanquins. They thought no more of killing a
native than of killing a bird.

As soon as possible, Don Nicholas de Ovando
was sent out to supersede Bobadilla. But he had no
power to control the fierce spirits who were rioting
there. Under his administration there was no im-
provement in the state of affairs. He was especially
directed to make amendment to Columbus and his
brothers for all their losses.

In the meantime preparations were being made
for another voyage of Columbus. Expeditions fitted
out from other courts, and private enterprises, had
greatly extended discoveries in the New World.
Vasca de Gama had doubled the Cape of Good Hope,
and was enriching Portugal with the products of the
east. It was thought that there must be a strait
somewhere near the Isthmus of Darien, which connected the Altantic with the Pacific ocean. Colum-

bus was to sail in search of this strait. After many of those delays, for which courts are proverbial, the fleet of four small vessels was ready to sail. The larbest of the caravels was of but seventy tons; the smallest of fifty. The whole company amounted to one hundred and fifty men.*

Columbus was now an aged man. It is supposed that he had attained his sixty-sixth year. His mind was exhausted with anxiety and care, and many bodily infirmities bent his once powerful frame. But his intellectual forces seemed tireless. Columbus was accompanied on this voyage by his brother Bartholomew, and his younger son, Fernando.

On the 9th of May, 1502, the fleet sailed from Cadiz. Touching on the coast of Morocco, and at the Grand Canary, the little squadron reached one of the Caribbee Islands, probably Martinica,† on the 15th of June. Thence a sail of thirty miles brought

* The weary heart of Columbus was much cheered by receiving the following letter from Ferdinand:

"You ought to be convinced of our displeasure at your captivity; for we lost not a moment in setting you free. Your innocence is well known. You are aware of the consideration and friendship with which we have treated you. The favors you have received from us, shall not be the last that you will receive. We assure to you your privileges, and are desirous that you and your children may enjoy them. We offer to confirm them to you again, and to put your eldest son in possession of all your offices whenever you wish.—Las Casas, *Hist. Ind.* lib. ii. cap. 4.

† Navarette supposes it to have been the island now called Santa Lucia.

them to Dominica. Passing Santa Cruz, and the south side of Porto Rico, he was constrained, contrary to his original intention and the instructions he had received, to make a harbor at the port of San Domingo. He explained this necessity in a letter to the sovereigns.

Don Ovando, who had succeeded Bobadilla, was then in command. For some reason not fully explained, Ovando refused to allow the admiral to take refuge in that harbor. Las Casas intimates that the town was crowded with the foes of Columbus, and he feared that he might meet with violence from those vile and desperate men. A fleet was just ready to put to sea, for Spain, when Columbus arrived. It contained a very large quantity of gold, which, by measures of extreme cruelty, had been wrested from the natives. Bobadilla had hoped thus to purchase the favor of the sovereigns. It was the richest fleet, in cargo, which had ever left the islands. There was one immense nugget, which an Indian woman had found, which was said to be the largest piece of virgin gold which had ever been discovered. Its estimated value was over two thousand dollars.

The morning when the fleet was about to sail was one of extraordinary serenity. Not a breath of air moved the leaves of the trees, and the ocean was like a mirror   But the experienced eye of Columbus

foresaw the approach of one of those terrible torna-
does which often wreck the tropical seas.   He therefore entreated the governor to delay the sailing of
the fleet for a few days.   His warning was scornfully
rejected.   A gentle breeze sprung up.   All sails were
spread, and the squadron entered upon its voyage.

Columbus, confident that a storm was brewing,
and grieved at being thus driven, in distress, from
the harbor he had discovered, promptly sought
secure anchorage where he could safely ride out the
approaching storm.   The fleet, returning to Spain,
had been but a few hours at sea, when the tornado
burst upon it with unexampled fury.   The ship
which conveyed Bobadilla and Roldan, with a large
amount of gold, including the celebrated nugget,
was engulfed in the waves, and every soul on board
perished.   Many other ships foundered, and were
heard of no more.   A few succeeded, in a shattered
condition, in returning to San Domingo.   Only one
reached Spain.   And it is remarkable that that one
was the weakest of all the fleet, and that it contained
the property of the admiral.

Columbus, having anchored in a wild and unfrequented bay, witnessed the rush and roar of the
tornado, as maddened clouds swept the skies, almost
midnight darkness enveloped the earth, and gigantic
forest trees fell before the terrific gale.   But he saved

his ships, though with much difficulty. Having re-
fitted in the little port of Azua, a few leagues west
from San Domingo, he continued his voyage. After
passing Jamaica he encountered calms and head-
winds, and the far less endurable trials of mutinous
and fault-finding men. Nine troublous weeks passed
slowly away, when they approached a small island
near Truxillo, on the coast of Honduras.

A canoe came out to the ship, manned by twenty-
five Indians. They had attained a somewhat higher
civilization than the other natives who had been met
with. They had iron-wood swords, copper axe-heads
and hatchets, and flint knives. They also had copper bells, and crucibles in which they could melt
metals. They had sheets and mantles ingeniously
woven of cotton brilliantly colored, of various hues.
But most important of all, they had large quantities
of cacao-nuts; from which chocolate is made. The
Spaniards had never seen this nut before. It soon
became one of the most extensive articles of
commerce.

The canoe was formed of the trunk of a single
tree, and was very large, being eight feet wide and
forty or fifty feet long. Columbus purchased their
whole stock in trade, paying with European trinkets.
The natives seemed neither astonished nor alarmed.

Men and women were modestly clothed with cotton garments.

The mountains of the main land were distinctly seen in the south. One of the Indians readily consented to serve as pilot. Leaving the island, which still retains its Indian name of Guanaja, he stood southerly, until he reached Cape Honduras, which he called Caxinas. It was Sunday morning, August 4th. The admiral, with a large number of the crew, landed, and in a beautiful grove on the sea-shore, attended mass. Two days after, he landed at another point, unfurled the banners of Castile, and took possession of the country in the name of Spain. About one hundred Indians gathered around, gazing respectfully upon the ceremony.

Continuing his voyage along the coast of Honduras toward the east, he struggled, for sixty days, against tempests and heavy rains, with such thunder and lightning as he had never encountered before. Much of the time, Columbus was confined to his bed, suffering extremely from gout. It often appeared, both to himself and his friends, that the end of his stormy life was approaching. At length he reached a point where the line of the coast turned almost at a right angle toward the south. He called this cape, Gracias a Dios, or Thanks to God.

As they sailed along the coast, the country

seemed very thickly inhabited, and presented a charming aspect, with its hills and vales, its groves and meadows. The remarkable fact is stated, that the natives, though very friendly, persistently refused to accept any gifts from the Spaniards, unless the Spaniards would receive native articles in return. This seems extraordinary indeed, when we reflect upon the inestimable value which the European cutlery and trinkets must have possessed in their eyes.

The voyage was continued along the picturesque shores of Costa Rica. Here they found natives with ornaments of pure gold. But the energies of Columbus were, at this time, all absorbed in the endeavor to find the imaginary strait. In his search, he explored several bays on the Isthmus of Panama. He sailed along the coast of Veragua for about forty miles. Several plates of pure gold were obtained. Here the Spaniards discovered, for the first time, edifices of solid architecture, built of stone and lime.

On the 2d of November the squadron anchored in a spacious harbor, to which Columbus gave the name, which it still retains, of Puerto Bello. Natives crowded to the place, by land, and in their canoes. A storm detained the ships here seven days. On the 9th, they sailed about twenty-four miles to Nombre de Dios. The fields were richly cultivated with fruits, Indian corn, and other vegetables. Their vessels were in a deplorable condition, from the piercing of a tropical worm. So long as the natives were treated with civility they were as friendly as one could desire. But Columbus could not always restrain the depraved and brutal sailors. The wretches would swim ashore, at night, and insult the natives in the most intolerable way.

There were not infrequent brawls. The natives increased in numbers, and there was a fight. The ships were near the shore. Columbus feared that the exasperated natives might rush upon him by thousands. He discharged two or three heavy cannon, throwing the shot over their heads. The thunder and lightning terrified them, and they fled in a panic.*

Suffering excruciatingly from sickness, and battered by storms, Columbus set out on his return to Hispaniola. He found very rich indications of gold, but the leaky condition of his ships rendered any further explorations impossible. He attempted to establish a settlement on the river Belen, where he intended to leave his brother in command, while he returned to Spain for supplies. Eighty men were selected to remain. They commenced erecting houses on the banks of the river. It was a fruitful region, abounding with bananas, plantains, pine-

* Las Casas, lib. ii. cap. 23 ; " Hist. del Almirante," cap. 92.

apples, cocoanuts, maize, and many esculent roots.
A great variety of fishes were found in the river, and
on the sea-coast. There could be no fear of suffering for want of food. And Columbus did all in his
power to conciliate the friendship of the natives.

But the chief of that region, a warlike man, by
the name of Quibian, was troubled in seeing the
strangers erecting houses, to establish themselves
permanently in his territories. He was suspected
of organizing a force for the destruction of the colony.
An armed band of seventy-four men was sent secretly
to seize the chief and all his household, and hold
them as hostages. Unfortunately, we have but one
side of this story. The natives had no historians.

The boats, unseen, landed near the large edifice,
or palace of the chieftain. He was captured, with
his whole household, his wives, his children, and his
attendants. In all, they numbered fifty persons. The
chief was bound hand and foot, the boats descended
the river, to convey the captives to the caravel of the
admiral, which was anchored just outside of the bar.
It was the cruel intention of Columbus to convey
them all to Spain, and hold them as hostages for the
good behavior of the natives, until his return.

Quibian, manacled as he was, succeeded in the
night in leaping from the boat, and reaching the
shore. The remaining captives were taken to the

caravel, and shut up in the forecastle. The hatchway was secured by a strong chain and padlock.
At night several of the most powerful warriors constructed a sort of platform beneath the hatch, and
mounting upon it, brought their bent shoulders beneath! and, by a simultaneous effort, forced it up.
In an instant they sprang forth, and plunged into the
sea. The sailors rushed forward, with their drawn
sabres, and, preventing several from escaping, again
chained down the hatchway.

"In the morning," writes Mr. Irving, "when the
Spaniards went to examine the captives, they were
all found dead. Some had hanged themselves with
the ends of ropes, their knees touching the floor,
Others had strangled themselves by straining the
cords tight with their feet. Such was the fierce, un-
conquerable spirit of this people, and their horror of
the white men." *

And now the exasperated natives made the most
fierce attacks upon the settlement. Many of the
Spaniards, and many of the natives, were killed.
Tempestuous weather roughened the ocean. Those
on shore had no means of escaping. Columbus
could send them no aid. Demoniac war was raging,
with its usual concomitants of blood and misery.
After many days of incessant conflict, and many

* Irving's " Life of Columbus," vol. ii. p. 364.

wild adventures, the settlement was abandoned, and with great difficulty, the intended colonists, tossed by boisterous winds and waves, embarked in three shattered caravels, which were hourly in danger of foundering.

Columbus was truly woe-stricken. Aged, sick, disappointed, in constant peril of death, with all his crew, and surrounded with discontent and murmurs, life had become a burden to him. In a feverish dream he was comforted by what seemed to him a vision from God. He gave an account of this to the king and queen.

"Wearied and sighing," he wrote, "I fell into a slumber. I heard a piteous voice saying to me, 'O fool and slow to believe and serve thy God, who is God of all. What did He more for Moses than He has done for thee? From the time of thy birth He has ever had thee under his peculiar care.'"

In this strain the supposed angel visitant cheered his desponding mind. The water in the river was so low that one of the caravels which had passed over the bar could not be removed; and it was left behind. It was the latter part of April, 1503, when Columbus sailed from the scenes of these disasters on the coast of Veragua. Running along the coast, he was compelled to abandon another worm-eaten caravel at Puerto Bello. All were now crowded into two caravels. These could only be kept afloat by incessant labor at the pumps.

On the 30th of May, he reached the cluster of islands on the south side of Cuba, to which he had given the name of the Queen's Gardens. Just then one of the most terrible tempests he had ever encountered struck him suddenly at midnight. Driven to and fro by tempests, in constant anxiety and suffering, with the leaks rapidly increasing, the storm-worn admiral at length succeeded in running into a harbor, which he previously visited, on the coast of Jamaica; and to which he had given the name of Port Santa Gloria.

He could go no farther. His caravels would soon sink, even in port. He ordered them both to be run aground, side by side, within a few yards of the shore. There they were fastened together into a fortress, with thatched cabins at the bows and the stern. Conscious that he could not protect himself against the Indians, should they prove hostile, he allowed no one to go on shore without permission. In the meantime he did everything in his power to secure the friendship of the Indians. The harbor soon swarmed with them. They brought provisions, which they were eager to barter with the Spaniards. It is evident there need have been no trouble with the natives, had not wrong and outrage goaded them to hostility.

CHAPTER XII.

The Shipwreck at Jamaica.

THE Island of Jamaica was, at that time, very
populous and fertile. Columbus prudently appointed
two persons, who alone were authorized to make
purchases of the natives. It was thought expedient
to send off an expedition to explore the interior of
the island. Diego Mendez, with a well-armed party,
traversed the whole island to its eastern extremity.
Everywhere he was received with truly fraternal
hospitality. He passed through the territories of
several chiefs. All were alike eager to exchange
their products for articles of European manufacture.

At the end of the island there was a powerful
chief, by the name of Ameyro. He was a very
intelligent and attractive man, and became very
warmly the friend of Mendez. In token of brother-

hood they exchanged names. Mendez purchased
of him one of those large canoes, of which we have
spoken. He paid for it, a brass basin, a frock, and
a shirt His whole company, and six Indians,
embarked in this canoe with an abundant store of
provisions, and coasted along the shore, stopping at
various points, back to the place of shipwreck.

The traffic thus opened with the natives removed
all fears of famine. But Columbus was oppressed
with the deepest anxiety. He was wrecked on an
almost unknown island, in an unfrequented sea. It
was impossible to repair either of his ships, or to
build a new one. There was not the remotest
chance that any strange vessel could happen along
to his relief. The distance to Hispaniola, from the
eastern end of the island, was over one hundred and
twenty miles; and this was across a gulf swept by
strong currents, and often agitated by terrific storms.
There seemed, therefore, no probability but that the
shipwrecked mariners must remain upon the island
until, one after another, all should die.

The idea occurred to Columbus that the heroic
Mendez might be induced to undertake the perilous
voyage to Hispaniola, in the canoe which he had
purchased. Mendez has given an artless and very
interesting account of the conversation which took

place between them. The admiral summoned the young man into his presence, and said :

"Diego Mendez, my son, none of those here understand our peril except you and myself. We are few in number. The Indians are many, and of irritable and fickle natures. On the least provocation they can throw firebrands on our straw-thatched cabins, and consume us. I have thought of an escape, if it meets your views. In this canoe, which you have purchased, some one can pass over to Hispaniola, and procure a ship by which we all may be rescued.

Mendez replied, "Senor, our danger, I know, is greater than can well be imagined. But I consider it not merely difficult, but impossible, to pass to Hispaniola in so small a vessel as a canoe. It is necessary to traverse a gulf of forty leagues, where the sea is extremely impetuous and seldom in repose. I know not who would be willing to adventure on so extreme a peril."

After a moment's pause, and perceiving that he himself was the person whom Columbus had in view to undertake the enterprise, Mendez added :

"Senor, I have many times put my life in peril of death, to save you and all those who are here ; and God has hitherto preserved me in a miraculous manner. There are, nevertheless, those who say that

14

your excellency intrusts to me all affairs where honor
is to be gained, while there are others who would
execute them as well as I do. I therefore beg that
you would summon all the people and propose this
enterprise to them. If all decline it, I will then come
forward and risk my life in your service."

The next morning the crews of both vessels were
assembled. No one was found to volunteer for so
hazardous an undertaking. Mendez then stepped
forward and said:

" Senor, I have but one life to lose. I am willing to venture it for your service, and for the good of
all here present. My trust is in the protection of
God, which I have so often before experienced." *

The canoe was drawn ashore, and furnished with
a false keel. Weather-boards were nailed from the
bow to the stern, to prevent the sea from breaking
over. A mast was supplied, and a sail. A good
store of provisions was laid in ; and Mendez, with but
one Spanish companion, and six Indians, commenced
his adventurous tour.

It was over a hundred miles from Santa Gloria to
Point Morant, at the eastern end of the island.
Struggling against adverse currents, they slowly
made their way to the eastward. Having arrived at
Point Morant, they were detained a few days by tem-

* " Relacion por Diego Mendez," Navarette, Colec. tom. I.

pestuous weather. A band of hostile Indians attacked them, and without difficulty captured the
boat, with all its freight. As the Indians were dis-
puting in the division of the spoil, Mendez escaped ;
and, entirely alone, put out to sea in his canoe.
Aided by both wind and current he reached Santa
Gloria safely. What became of his Spanish companion is not known.

The chivalric Mendez, undaunted, was ready to
renew the enterprise. Instructed by experience, he
took two canoes. Each conveyed six Spaniards and
ten Indians. Bartholomew Fiesco, a Genoese of
great excellence of character, commanded the second
canoe. An armed band on the shore accompanied
the boats to the end of the island. Here, after a
delay of four days, they launched forth on their bold
voyage, on a serene morning and on a smooth sea

Columbus was left for many weary months in entire uncertainty as to their fate. The state of his
mind may be inferred from the following almost in-
coherent extract found in his diary :

" Hitherto I have wept for others. But now
have pity upon me, heaven, and weep for me, O
earth ! In my temporal concerns without a farthing
to offer for a mass ; cast away here in the Indies ;
surrounded by cruel and hostile savages ; isolated,
infirm, expecting each day will be my last ; in spirit-

ual concerns separated from the holy sacraments of
the Church, so that my soul, if parted here from my
body, must be forever lost!

"Weep for me, whoever has charity, truth, and
justice! I came not on this voyage to gain honor
or estate. That is most certain. All hope of the
kind was already dead within me. I came to serve
your majesties, with a sound intention and an honest
zeal. I speak no falsehood. If it should please God
to deliver me hence, I humbly supplicate your majesties to permit me to repair to Rome, and perform
other pilgrimages." *

Mr. Goodrich writes: "It is even said, though in such miserable
plight, he insisted upon the observance of all the etiquette which he
considered due to the rank of viceroy ; that he caused himself to be
ushered into the thatched sheds, to his frugal meals of Indian fare, by
gentlemen esquires bearing *flabella*, while all rose at his approach.
The Franciscan garb which, in mock humility, he had assumed, must
have accorded well with this ridiculous vanity. Such absurdities are
characteristic of Columbus, who was as tenacious of fictitious, as he
was incapable of inspiring real, respect."—*Life of Columbus*, p. 335.

One is astonished to find that Mr. Goodrich quotes, in support of
this statement, a passage which has no reference to Santa Gloria whatever, but which describes the honors which the sovereigns conferred
upon Columbus, at the seat of the court at Barcelona, upon the first
return of the admiral from the discovery of the New World. Mr.
Helps writes, describing *this reception* :

"Other marks of approbation for Columbus were not wanting.
An appropriate coat-of-arms, then a thing of much significance, was
granted him in augmentation of his own. In the shield are conspicuously emblazoned the royal arms of Castile and Leon. Nothing can
better serve to show the immense favor which Columbus had attained
at court, by his discovery, than such a grant ; and it is but a trifling

Soon after the departure of Mendez and Fiesco, severe sickness broke out among the men in the wreck. Days, weeks, months, passed slowly away. All were sunk in the deepest despondency. They had nothing to occupy their minds. Murmurs arose, and many ungratefully reviled the admiral as the cause of all their calamities.

There were, in the company, two brothers, men of gentlemanly birth and considerable note, Francisco and Diego de Porras. These men, who are represented as vain, insolent, and unprincipled, excited a mutiny against the authority of Columbus, who was confined to his bed, with a severe attack of the gout. Weary of waiting, and having no hopes of hearing from Mendez, they, a rioting, lawless band, took ten canoes, and set out for Hispaniola. They were forty-eight in number. It does not appear that the admiral attempted any violent opposition to their reckless measures.* He was, however, exceedingly annoyed by the insulting spirit of mutiny and defiance with which he was assailed.

But few remained with the admiral, excepting the

addition to make, in recounting his new honors, that the title of Don was given to him, and also to his brothers. He rode at the king's side, was served at the table as a grandee ; ' All hail ' was said to him on state occasions, and the men of his age, happy in that, had found out another great man to honor."—See Goodrich, p. 335, and Helps, p. 124.

* " Historia del Almirante," ch. cii.

sick. The mutineers, breaking loose from all laws, robbed and maltreated the Indians mercilessly. With sneers they told the natives to look to Columbus for their pay, and, if he refused, to kill him. Columbus was left in his bed, in the endurance of as poignant bodily and mental sufferings as can well be imagined. The desperadoes coasted along the island toward the east, like a band of fiends, plundering the natives as they landed at various points. Apparently they wished to excite the hostility of the Indians, that they might be provoked to rise and kill the admiral, and all who were left with him. Thus the knowledge of their mutiny, which would expose them to severe punishment, would never be proclaimed in Spain.

Having reached the end of the island, they procured several Indians, probably by compulsion, to aid them in crossing the gulf. The canoes were small, without keels, and unless carefully balanced were easily overturned. The sea rose. The waves dashed over the gunwales. Death seemed inevitable. To lighten the canoes they threw the Indians overboard, as if they had been sheep or swine. The poor creatures, struggling in the waves, occasionally grasped the side of the canoe, to rest and recover breath. These demoniac men, apparently without the slightest repugnance, lopped off their hands with the sword. The poor creatures, holding up the bleeding stumps, would shriek and sink. Thus eighteen perished.

With difficulty the Spaniards worked their way back to the island. In the storm, they had been compelled to throw overboard almost everything of value. Disputes arose as to the best course to pursue. Some proposed sailing for Cuba, as the wind was favorable. ' Others advised abandoning the rash enterprise and returning penitentially to the admiral. Others were for repairing to Santa Gloria, and seizing a fresh supply of stores. The majority were in favor of waiting for the first fair wind, and then to make another bold push for Hispaniola. After the delay of four weeks, during which time they treated the natives with the utmost oppression, the weather became serene, and they made another attempt.

The tempests again drove them back. Thus disheartened, they abandoned the enterprise, and slowly commenced their return, by land, through the heart of the island. They were strong men, thoroughly depraved, and well armed. Las Casas says that their march was like the passing of a pestilence. In the meantime Columbus, sick and world-weary, was waiting at Santa Gloria, almost without hope, for some tidings from Mendez. There can be no reasonable question of the truthfulness of the following beautiful tribute which Mr. Irving pays to his memory at this time.

" While Porras and his crew were raging about, with that desperate and joyless licentiousness which attends the abandonment of principle, Columbus presented the opposite picture of a man true to others and to himself, and supported amid hardships and difficulties by conscious rectitude. Deserted by the healthful and vigorous portion of his garrison, he exerted himself to soothe and encourage the infirm and desponding remnant which remained. Regardless of his own painful maladies, he was only attentive to relieve their sufferings. The few who were fit for service were required to mount guard on the wreck, or attend upon the sick ; there were none to forage for provisions. The scrupulous good faith and amicable conduct maintained by Columbus toward the natives had now their effect. Considerable supplies of provisions were brought to them, from time to time, which he purchased at a reasonable rate.

" The most palatable and nourishing of these, together with the small stock of European biscuit that remained, he ordered to be appropriated to the infirm. Knowing how much the body is affected by the operations of the mind, he endeavored to rouse the spirits and animate the hopes of the drooping sufferers. Concealing his own anxiety, he maintained a

serene and even cheerful countenance, encouraging
his men by words, and holding forth confident anticipations of speedy relief. By his friendly and careful
treatment, he soon recruited both the health and
spirits of his people, and brought them into a condition to contribute to the common safety. Judicious regulations, calmly but firmly enforced, maintained everything in order. The men became sensible of the advantages of wholesome discipline, and
perceived that the restraints imposed upon them by
their commander, were for their own good, and ulti-
mately productive of their own comfort." *

But provisions grew scarce. The Indians were
unaccustomed to harvest anything. They plucked
the fruit as it grew spontaneously ; and, for their
frugal wants, there was an ample supply. Trinkets
lost their novelty and value. The indolent Indians
would bring in no food from a distance. The Spaniards were threatened with absolute starvation.
Under these circumstances it is said that Columbus
resorted to the following extraordinary expedient to
obtain supplies.

Availing himself of his knowledge of astronomy,
he summoned the caciques to a grand council, on a
day preceding a total eclipse of the moon. He informed them that God, who was the especial pro-

* Irving's " Life of Columbus," vol ii. p. 399.

14*

tector of the Spaniards, was displeased with them for their neglect to bring in a sufficient supply of food. In proof of his displeasure, and of the punishment which awaited them, God would, that night, blot out the moon. Some were frightened, some derided.

Night came. The moon began to disappear. All alike were terror-stricken. The caciques threw themselves at the feet of Columbus, and implored him to intercede with God on their behalf; promising that henceforth they would be entirely obedient to his will. Columbus, after much persuasion, consented. As the eclipse was about to diminish, he retired to his cabin, as if to commune with his Maker. The moon soon shone forth in all its accustomed splendor, and there was no longer any want of provisions.*

Eight months had passed since Mendez and Fiesco commenced their perilous voyage. The rebels, under Francisco Porras, who seems to have been their recognized leader, were rioting here and there at will. One evening, just as the sun was disappearing, a sail was seen approaching the harbor.

* This narrative seems to be accepted by all the historians of Columbus. It is certainly characteristic of the man and of his times. We find it first in an " Account given by Diego Mendez, in his will, of some events that occurred in the last voyage of the Admiral Don Christopher Columbus," as published by the Hakluyt Society, in the "Select Letters of Christopher Columbus," p. 205.

The excitement was intense. The vessel cast anchor, and sent a boat to the wrecked caravels. The unfriendly Ovando, who would gladly have heard that Columbus had perished, learning his situation from Mendez, did not dare to neglect all attempts to rescue him. After many useless delays, he sent an old conspirator against Columbus, apparently to spy out his condition. This man, Diego de Escobar, had been one of the confederates of Roldan. Columbus had condemned him to death, but Bobadilla had pardoned him.

This man came alongside the caravels in his boat. He did not even go on board. He, however, presented the admiral with a letter from Ovando, a cask of wine, and a side of bacon. Then, pushing off a few yards, he informed Columbus that Ovando was grieved to learn of his misfortune, that he regretted that the vessel in the harbor was not sufficiently large to remove him and his companions; and that another would be sent as soon as possible. He requested the admiral, if he wished to send a letter to Ovando, to write it immediately, as he desired to depart without delay.*

---

* " Standing at a distance from Columbus, as if the admiral had been in quarantine, he shouted, at the top of his voice, a message from Ovando, to the effect that he, the governor, regretted the admiral's misfortunes keenly ; and that he hoped, before long, to send a ship of sufficient size to take him off."—Helps' *Life of Columbus*, p. 250.

Columbus wrote a courteous and conciliatory letter, describing their sad condition, and imploring
prompt relief. Escobar spread his sails, and disappeared. The Spaniards knew not what to make of
this strange visit, and were plunged anew in despair.
Columbus tried to cheer them with assurances that
vessels would soon arrive to take them all away.
He said that he had no desire to depart with Escobar, as the vessel was too small to remove all, and
that he preferred to remain, and share their lot.*

Columbus was probably correct in the impression,
which Las Casas also entertained, that Ovando, fear-
ing that the admiral might be reinstated in the government of Hispaniola, hoped that he would perish
on the island of Jamaica.†

We must now turn to the adventures of Mendez
and Fiesco. They paddled along the southern
shore of the island, over a sea as of glass, till they
reached the end. They then pushed boldly out into
the apparently limitless gulf before them. There

---

* " In secret, however, Columbus was exceedingly indignant at the
conduct of Ovando. He had left him for many months in a state of
the utmost danger and most distressing uncertainty, exposed to the
hostility of the natives, the seditions of his men, and the suggestions
of his own despair. He had, at length, sent a mere tantalizing message, by a man known to be one of his bitterest enemies, with a present of food, which from its scantiness, seemed intended to mock their
necessities."—Irving's *Life of Columbus*, vol. ii. p. 404.

† Las Casas, " Hist. Ind..," lib. ii. cap. 33.

was not a cloud in the sky, or a breath of wind to ripple the ocean. The heat of the meridian sun was terrible. The natives often leaped into the water to refresh themselves, when they would again resume their labors at the paddle. The voyage was continued by night and by day. The Indians, who performed all the work, took turns, one half rowing, while the other half slept. The Spaniards also, with their arms in their hands, kept guard, by turns, one part sleeping while the others watched. They feared that the Indians, whom they had undoubtedly enslaved, might rise against them.

No land was to be seen. The frail canoes rose and fell on the majestic undulations of the ocean, giving fearful admonition of the destruction which was their inevitable doom, should the freshening winds dash the angry surges against them. The heat created thirst so intolerable that the small quantity of water they were able to take with them was soon nearly all consumed. The little that remained was administered by spoonfuls to the fainting men. Progress, through the burning calm, could only be made by laborious toil with the paddle.

The third day came and went. The nights were as sultry as the day. There were no signs of land. Nothing was to be seen but sea and sky. One of the Indians, in utter exhaustion fell from his seat and died. His body was thrown into the sea. The suffering from thirst became so great that none could sleep. The last drop of water had been dealt out. The Indians could scarcely move their paddles. One after another, many of them sank down in helplessness.

Mendez sat at the stern of his boat, in despair. It seemed that all must perish upon that silent sea. The moon began to rise, when he thought he dimly discerned, in the distance, some dark mass, slightly elevated above the surrounding surface. Soon he became convinced that it was land, and gave the joyful cry. This infused new life into their paralyzed energies. Still the morning dawned before the enfeebled rowers reached the shore.

It proved to be the small island of Navasa, for which they had been looking. It was a mere mass of barren rock, about a mile and a half in circuit, emerging from the sea at the distance of twenty-four miles from the extreme western cape of Hayti. Though there was not a tree, a shrub, a stream, or a spring, still they found in the hollow of the rocks a sufficient supply of water. Notwithstanding the cautions of the officers, several drank so inordinately that some died in torture, while others were long and dangerously sick. A few shell-fish were found.

Kindling a fire, with drift-wood, they were boiled,
affording a delicious repast.

They spent the day upon the island, reposing
beneath the shadows of the rocks, and gazing wist-
fully upon the grand mountains of Hayti, which rose
above the horizon far away in the east.   As the sun
went down they re-embarked, and the next day
reached Cape Tiburon, the extreme south-western
cape of the island.   In the brief account, which
Mendez gave of the voyage, alluding first to his
departure from Jamaica, where he left the guard
which Columbus had furnished to accompany him to
the end of the island, he writes:

" Finding the sea become calm, I parted from the
rest of the men with much mutual sorrow.   I then
commended myself to God and our Lady of Antigua,
and was at sea five days and four nights, without
laying down the oar from my hand ; but continued
steering the canoe, while my companions rowed.   It
pleased God that, at the end of five days, I reached
the island of Hispaniola, at Cape San Miguel,* having been two days without eating or drinking, for our
provisions were exhausted.

" I brought my canoe up to a very beautiful part
of the coast, to which many of the natives soon
came, and brought with them many articles of food,

* San Miguel has since been called Cape Tiburon.

so that I remained there two days to take rest. I took six Indians from this place; and, leaving those that I had brought with me, I put off to sea again, moving along the coast of Hispaniola, for it was three hundred and ninety miles from the spot where I landed to the city of St. Domingo, where the governor dwelt. When I had proceeded two hundred and forty miles along the coast of the island, not without great toil and danger, for that part of the island was not yet brought into subjugation, I reached the province of Azoa, which is seventy-two miles from St. Domingo. There I learned that the governor had gone to subdue the province of Xuragoa,* which was at one hundred and fifty miles distance. When I heard this, I left my canoe, and took the road for Xuragoa. There I found the governor, who kept me with him seven months, until he had burned and hanged eighty-four caciques, lords of vassals, and with them, Nacaona, the sovereign mistress of the island, to whom all rendered service and obedience."†

"*Until he had burned and hanged eighty-four caciques!*" What an insight does this short sentence give us of the atrocities perpetrated upon the

---

* Xuragoa: so Mendez spells the word. It is now spelt Xaragua.

† An account given by Diego Mendez, in his will, of some events that occurred in the last voyage of the Admiral Don Christopher Columbus, p. 224.

natives by these demoniac adventurers. Ovando made various excuses for not sending aid to Columbus. Neither would he allow Mendez to go to San Domingo, doubtless from fear that he might awaken solicitude for the admiral; and cause some measures to be instituted for his relief. At length, by constant importunity, he obtained permission to go to San Domingo, there to await the arrival of some ships which were expected from Spain.

He immediately set out, on foot, to traverse a distance through the wilderness of over two hundred miles. As soon as he was gone, Ovando despatched the caravel, under the pardoned rebel Escobar, on his inexplicable expedition to the shipwrecked admiral.

Lawlessness and crime always bring misery. The mutineers at Jamaica, quarrelling among themselves and hated by the natives, were in a state of utter wretchedness. Columbus had no doubt, now that his shipwreck was known, that ships must soon be sent for his rescue. Though Ovando might find excuses for delay, he would not dare to leave the admiral and so many Spaniards to perish unheeded. Columbus, learning the state of feeling among the mutineers, humanely sent two of his people to them, to inform them of the visit of Escobar; and of his full expectation that vessels would soon arrive for their rescue. He offered, to all who would return to obedience, pardon, and a free passage to Hispaniola in the expected ships. The ringleaders of the revolt endeavored to conceal these offers from their deluded confederates. They sent back word to Columbus that they had no wish to return to Hispaniola, but that they preferred to live at large on the island.

With the intention of committing the men to acts of violence which would render their pardon impossible, they set out on the march to plunder the wrecks, and make the admiral a prisoner.* Columbus was informed of their approach. Bartholomew Columbus, who had the title of adelantado, took fifty men, well-armed, and set out to meet the foe.† He was instructed to do all in his power, by conciliatory words, to influence them to a peaceful return, and not to resort to violence unless it were absolutely necessary.

But Francisco de Porras refused to listen to any terms of peace. He ordered his men to charge, with loud yells and the utmost fury. He himself led six of the stoutest to attack the adelantado, thinking that if he were killed, the rest would be easily dispersed. A furious battle ensued. Porras,

---

* "Hist. del Almirante," cap. 106.

† "It would appear, from this number, that either there had been some defection from the ranks of the mutineers, or that more than half the Spaniards had remained faithful to the admiral."—Helps' *Life of Columbus*, p. 252.

with a blow of his sword cut through the buckler of the adelantado, and wounded his hand. The sword was thus so wedged in the shield that he could not draw it out. Several men grappled him, and he was taken prisoner. The rest fled in confusion.

A large number of Indians had gathered around the battle-field, gazing in astonishment upon the spectacle of the Spaniards destroying each other. Bartholomew, with Porras and several prisoners; returned to the ships. Several of the mutineers had been killed. Of his own party but two were wounded. The next day, which was the 20th of May, the fugitives sent a petition for pardon to the admiral, signed by all their names. The intensity of their desire to return to their allegiance may be inferred from the peculiarity of the oath which they proposed to take upon the cross and the mass-book. It was as follows :

"Should we ever break our oath we hope that no priest or other Christian may ever confess us ; that repentance may be of no avail; that we may be deprived of the holy sacraments of the church ; that, at our death, we may receive no benefit from bulls or indulgences; that our bodies may be cast out into the fields, like those of heretics or renegadoes, instead of being buried in holy ground; and that we may not receive absolution from the pope, nor from

cardinals, nor archbishops, nor bishops, nor any other
Christian priest." *

Commenting upon these awful imprecations, by
which these guilty and wretched men endeavored to
add validity to an oath, Mr. Irving well remarks,
" The worthlessness of a man's word may always be
known by the extravagant means he uses to enforce
it. †

---

* Las Casas, " Hist. Ind.," lib. ii. cap. 32.
† " Life of Columbus," vol. ii. p. 419.

CHAPTER XIII.

The Closing Scenes of Life.

DURING the absence of Columbus, crimes were
perpetrated upon the islanders, under the administration of Ovando, too horrible to be recorded.
Demons from the realms of despair could have done
nothing worse. I have no heart to describe these
atrocities. It seems one of the greatest of mysteries
that God could have permitted them. These demons of the human race subjected virtuous matrons
and tender girls, young boys and aged men, to every
indignity and cruelty which a depraved imagination
could suggest.

Bands were roving in all directions in search of
gold. The little property the adventurers brought
with them was soon exhausted. They were plunged
into the extreme of poverty and misery. Many

died, cursing the day when they left Spain. In the course of a few months, more than a thousand Spaniards passed away to that tribunal where an account is to be rendered for all the deeds done in the body. A regular system of slavery was organized, to compel the natives, all unused to toil as they were, to the exhausting labor of working the mines. To each Spaniard a certain number of slaves was assigned. They were torn from their wives and children, and subjected to the cruel infliction of the lash. If a slave fled from this barbarity, he was hunted down and torn to pieces by blood-hounds, as a warning to others. Gangs were often driven two or three hundred miles. Many died by the way. Las Casas writes:

"I have found many dead in the road, others gasping under the trees, and others in the pangs of death, faintly crying, 'hunger! hunger!'" *

Mr. Irving, recoiling from these dreadful scenes, writes: " It is impossible to pursue any further the picture, drawn by the venerable Las Casas, not of what he had heard, but of what he had seen. Nature and humanity revolt at the details. Suffice it to say that so intolerable were the toils and sufferings inflicted upon this weak and unoffending race, that they sank under them, dissolving, as it were,

* Las Casas, " Hist. Ind.," lib. ii. cap. 14, MS.

from the face of the earth. Many killed themselves
in despair; and even mothers overcame the powerful instinct of nature, and destroyed the infants at
their breasts, to spare them a life of wretchedness.
Twelve years had not elapsed since the discovery
of the island, and several hundred thousand of its
native inhabitants had perished, miserable victims to
the grasping avarice of the white men." *

The administration of Columbus, compared with
that of Bobadilla and Ovando, was just and humane.
He inflicted no wanton massacres. He allowed no
barbarous punishment. It was his earnest desire to
civilize and Christianize the Indians. Though he
sent many natives to Spain to be sold as slaves, it
was under the influence of that fanaticism, which
was almost universally prevalent in those days, and
which, we blush to record, has been defended and
advocated, within half a century, in the pulpits of
both England and America. For this Columbus
merits severe censure. But a candid mind will make
due allowance for the age in which he lived. The
Bible recognizes sins of ignorance.

A year of anxiety and sorrow had passed away,
since the shipwreck, when, on the morning of the
28th of June, 1504, two caravels were seen approaching the harbor. Despair gave place to almost a de-

* Irving's "Life of Columbus," vol. ii. p. 428.

lirium of joy. The pardoned conspirators were encamped by themselves on the shore. Porras, the ringleader, was held a prisoner. The rest were treated as though they had been guilty of no offence. Still they trembled, in view of their crimes, and were very obsequious in their servility. Columbus appointed over them a trusty lieutenant, and thus the two bands had been for a long time, one on the ships and one on the shore, awaiting the arrival of succor.

Public indignation, at San Domingo, had compelled Ovando to send, though thus tardily, this aid. No time was lost in the embarkation. Columbus raised his admiral's flag on one of the ships, and, magnanimously forgetting the wrongs he had endured, treated all with the utmost kindness. It was quite a long voyage from Santa Gloria, along the southern coast of Jamaica, thence across the gulf to the western end of Hayti, and then along the southern shore of the island to San Domingo.

Tempests, adverse winds, and strong opposing currents delayed the passage, and it was not until the 13th of August, that the caravels cast anchor in the harbor. Columbus had many friends there ; and his misfortunes had caused a reaction to take place in the feelings of many who had joined in the clamor against him. Even the governor, conscience-smit-

ten, was alarmed lest he might be called to account
for his cruel delay. Columbus was, consequently,
much to his surprise, received by all with great courtesy and attention. But neither he nor his son
Fernando was deceived by the hypocritical protesta-
tions of the governor.

Very soon there was a clashing of their not clearly
defined powers. Questions of the right of jurisdic-
tion rose between them. Columbus was deeply
grieved in view of the treatment the natives had
received, and of the desolation which overspread the
island. He had hoped to train the natives to industrious habits, and thus to promote their own welfare
and the revenues of the crown. He wrote to the
king and queen:

"The Indians of Hispaniola were, and are, the
richest of the island. It is they who cultivate and
make the bread and the provisions for the Chris-
tians; who dig the gold from the mines, and perform
all the offices and labors both of men and beasts. I
am informed that, since I left this island, six parts
out of seven of the natives are dead; all through ill-
treatment and inhumanity: some by the sword,
others by blows and cruel usage, others through
hunger. The greater part have perished in the
mountains and glens, whither they had fled, from

15

not being able to support the labor imposed upon them." *

Columbus was powerless to redress any grievances. He could obtain from Ovando no settlement of accounts; and with all his dues unpaid found himself in poverty. He therefore prepared, with his brother, to return to Spain. Two vessels were fitted out. Columbus took charge of one, and the adelantado of the other. Very generously Columbus, from his slender means, provided for the wants of the destitute sailors left behind, even though many of these had been the most violent of the rebels. Scarcely had they left the harbor when a gust of wind carried away the mast of the admiral's ship. The disabled vessel was sent back. Columbus, with his son and attendants, went on board his brother's ship, and continued the voyage.

A succession of storms was encountered. Columbus was confined to his cot, suffering excruciatingly from the gout. On the 12th of November, 1504, the vessels sailed from San Domingo. On the 7th of November, his storm-shattered bark cast anchor in the harbor of San Lucar. He immediately proceeded to Seville. Infirmities, pain, care, and sorrow, followed him. His private affairs were in utter confusion, and he found himself in the depths of poverty.

* Las Casas, "Hist. Ind.," lib. ii. cap. 36.

Queen Isabella was on a sick and dying bed, crushed
with such a load of domestic griefs as few have ever
been called to bear. Ferdinand was a cold-hearted
man, incapable of being influenced by motives of
generosity.

Columbus wrote to his son, urging the necessity
of practising the most rigid economy. " I receive,"
he says, " nothing of the revenue due to me. I live
by borrowing. Little have I profited by twenty
years' service, with such toils and perils ; since, at
present, I do not own a roof in Spain. If I desire to
eat or sleep, I have no resort but an inn. And, for
the most time, I have not wherewithal to pay my
bill."

Isabella, world-weary, heart-broken, whose path-
way through life was illumined by but few rays of
enjoyment, died at Medina del Campo, on the 26th
of November, 1504. Seeing her friends bathed in
tears around her bed, she said to them :

" Do not weep for me, nor waste your time in
fruitless prayers for my recovery ; but pray, rather,
for the salvation of my soul."

She was in the 54th year of her age, and the 30th
of her reign. A terrible tempest of wind and rain
wrecked earth and sky, as her body was borne on
its long journey to the grave. The rain fell in floods,
and one of the most dismal of wintry storms howled

around the towers of the Alhambra, as the remains of Isabella were consigned to their final resting-place in its gloomy vaults.

When informed of this sad event, Columbus wrote to his son Diego, "The principal thing is to commend affectionately, and with great devotion, the soul of the queen, our sovereign, to God. Her life was always catholic and holy, and prompt to all things in His holy service. For this reason we may rest assured that she is received into His glory, and beyond the cares of this rough and weary world. The next thing is to watch and labor, in all matters, for the service of our sovereign the king, and to endeavor to alleviate his grief."

The death of Isabella was one of the greatest calamities which could have befallen Columbus. He spent the remainder of the winter and spring at Seville. Most of the time he was confined to his bed, in severe suffering. Columbus was exceedingly attached to his two brothers, and was very fond of his sons, Ferdinand and Diego. To the eldest he wrote :

"Conduct thyself toward thy brother as the elder brother should to the younger. Thou hast no otner. And I bless God that he is such a one as you need. Ten brothers would not be too many for

thee. Never have I found better friends to right or
left, than my brothers."

Columbus still had many enemies at court, who
successfully intrigued to prevent any attention from
being paid to his wants. He was extremely unhappy, and felt it to be an imperative necessity that
he should visit the court in person. But his infirmities were so great that it was some time before he
could venture upon the journey.

After the blasts of winter were over, availing
himself of the genial weather of May, he set out,
with his brother, the adelantado, to visit the king
at Segovia. A weary, melancholy, neglected man,
bowed down with sorrows more than years, the discoverer of a new world entered the gates of the imperial city.

"The selfish Ferdinand," writes Mr. Irving,
"had lost sight of his past services in what appeared
to him the inconvenience of his present demands.
He received him with many professions of kindness,
but with those cold, ineffectual smiles, which pass
like wintry sunshine over the countenance, and convey no warmth to the heart." *

Columbus gave the king a minute account of his
last voyage. But no smile of kindness or tear of sympathy cheered him in his narrative. The king was

* "Life of Columbus," vol. ii. p. 471.

rot sparing of complimentary expressions, but was cruelly deficient in any practical recognition of the merits or the necessities of the world-weary admiral.*

Melancholy months passed away of deferred hopes and bitter disappointments. From life's hour-glass the last sands were falling. Mental suffering, combined with a torturing attack of the gout, again confined the admiral to his bed. For the sake of his family he was intensely anxious that his dignities should be recognized, and that his property might be protected, so that those he loved might be shielded from want. Still he was far more solici-tous to leave his children the inheritance of an hon-ored name than to recover his pecuniary losses. From his couch of agony he wrote to the king, en-treating that his son Diego might be appointed to the viceroyalty, of which he had been so unjustly deprived.

"This," he wrote, "is a matter which concerns my honor. As to all the rest, do as your majesty may think proper. Give or withhold, as may be most for your interest, and I shall be content. I

* "I know not," writes the venerable Las Casas, "what could cause this dislike, and this want of princely countenance, in the king, toward one who had rendered him such preëminent benefits, unless it were that his mind was swayed by the false testimonies which had been brought against the admiral ; of which I have been able to learn something from persons much in favor with the sovereigns."—Las Casas, *Hist. Ind.*, lib. ii cap. 37.

believe the anxiety created by the delay of this
affair is the principal cause of my sickness."

He at length became convinced that there was
no hope of redress from Ferdinand. Upon his bed
of suffering he wrote the following despairing letter
to his firm friend, Diego de Deza:

"It appears that his majesty does not think fit
to fulfil that which he, with the queen, who is now
in glory, promised me by word and seal. For me to
contend to the contrary would be to contend with
the wind. I have done all that I could do. I leave
the rest with God, whom I have ever found propitious to me in my necessities." *

There is something inexpressibly sad in the death
of this infirm but heroic man, wrecked in body and
mind by the storms of one of the most tempestuous
of earthly lives. It had, for some time, been manifest
to his friends that his end was drawing nigh. He
soon became convinced himself that his earthly voyage must soon terminate, and that he was approaching that final harbor where the weary are at rest.
The elevated character of Columbus shines forth
conspicuously in the will which he executed in the
solemn hours.

His son Diego, in accordance with the law of
primogeniture, was his principal heir. He enjoined

* Navarette, Colec., tom. i.

that the estate should never be alienated or diminished.   He urged that his heirs should be always
faithful to their sovereign, and should do all in their
power for the promotion of the Christian faith.   One-
tenth of the income was to be devoted to the aid of
poor relatives and other persons in want.   He requested that a chapel should be raised at the town
of Concepcion, in Hispaniola, where masses should be
daily performed for the repose of the souls of himself, his father, his mother, his wife, and all who had
died in the faith.*

At length the dying hour came.   Columbus was
fully conscious that the time for his departure had
arrived.   He welcomed the approach of death, as a
friendly messenger to remove him from care and
pain.   His last act was to partake of the holy sacrament.   His last words were : *In manus tuas, Domine,
commendo spiritum meum.*   Into thy hands, O Lord,
I commend my spirit.   It was the 20th of May, 1506.
Columbus was then, it is supposed, about seventy
years of age.   His funeral was attended, in Valladolid,

---

* " Another clause recommends to the care of Don Diego, Beatrix
Enriquez, the mother of his natural son Fernando.   His connection
with her had never been sanctioned by matrimony ; and either this
circumstance, or some neglect of her, seems to have awakened deep
compunction in his dying moments.   He orders Don Diego to provide for her respectable maintenance.   ' And let this be done,' he
adds, ' for the discharge of my conscience ; for it weighs heavy on my
soul.' "—Irving's *Columbus*, vol. ii. p. 481.

with regal pomp. His remains were first deposited in the church of Santa Maria de la Antigua. After seven years, in 1513, they were removed to the Carthusian monastery of Las Cuevas of Seville. Twenty-three years afterward they were transferred, with those of his son, Don Diego, to the cathedral of the city of San Domingo. But even here they were not allowed to find their final resting place. Upon the cession of the island to the French in the year 1797, they were again removed by the Spanish authorities to the cathedral of Havana, in Cuba. There they now remain, awaiting the summons of the archangel's trumpet, at whose call all that are in their graves shall come forth.

Each reader, from the perusal of the above narrative, will form his own estimate of the character of Columbus, and will award the meed of praise or blame, as in his opinion may be just. His eventful life was, on the whole, one of the most joyless and full of trouble of which we have any record. That he had his faults all will admit. That those blemishes of character were redeemed by many and exalted virtues, few candid minds will deny. And Christian faith rejoices in the belief that, life's tempestuous voyage being over, he has gone to that blissful world, where the weary are at rest.

THE END.